A DARK DEMON ROMANCE

DRAG HER DOWN

OTHER WORKS BY ARIEL RAE

The Blood Hunted Series
Blood Hunted #1
Blood Trail #2
Mister Nightmare #2.5
Blood Queen #3

A DARK DEMON ROMANCE

DRAG HER DOWN

ARIEL RAE

SPACE FOX BOOKS LLC

This book is a work of fiction.

Cover design by Rachel A. Desilets

ISBN-13: 979-8-9888483-9-4

Space Fox Books, LLC
First Edition
Paperback Edition: 2025
spacefoxbooks.com

To all the romance readers who thought,
"Yeah, I'd go to the fires for him."

To Samantha,
because I'm starting a fan club.

To allyourpagearebelongtous,
because delulu goals should be fulfilled by chaos and madness.

This book may contain circumstances not suitable for younger readers and is recommended for adult audiences.

If you'd like to read about the **content** in this book, please visit the publisher's website spacefoxbooks.com for additional descriptions for **any sensitive topics**. Your mental health matters, and this is a dark book with dark themes.

Haden

Someone needed to kill the man sitting across from me since I couldn't. I needed his death more than I needed to breathe. Being on Earth had become mundane, made worse by the man hunched over his laptop. I sighed. Even coffee had lost its appeal. When I first ascended, caffeine had jolted my system, zipped through me like an electric charge. Now, it went down as tepid as the human in front of me. Even the dark earthy aromatics of the roast failed to ignite me.

My claws threatened to come out and tear the coffee shop to shreds. I would have too, if it hadn't been for the protective spells Thomas had cast upon me.

After his senior year of high school, Thomas—the lukewarm man sitting across from me—wanted to improve his chances with members of the opposite sex. So, he did what he did best and *studied*. He dove into books about the occult, demons, the king, and the souls of the fires.

Then he set a summoning portal.

And I—being bored in the fires and foolish enough to believe I could counter any curse from the circle—took the bait. Being on Earth intrigued me. A new adventure. Space away from expectations.

At the time, I believed the lure would be weaker than me. Of course, the summoning circle was a trap to bind any demon to the conjurer, but I had heard the stories from other demons who traveled to Earth. Most humans didn't know how to summon properly. Most circles were broken, allowing us freedom to roam until someone sent us back to the depths or we so chose to descend. Surely, whatever was on the other side of the portal would be better than the eternally hot pressure wrapped around me. And yeah, I had grown weary. Everyone and everything burned with fire, and I craved something different. The coolness of an open breeze, the potential for corruption. Something new.

Unfortunately, Thomas's circle had been well-researched. A perfect trap. As far as I knew, I was the first demon to be confined in well over a century. Talk about an embarrassment which wouldn't easily be overlooked. Especially once I got back to the fires.

For now, however, I listened to the endless drone of extroverts in the coffee shop. Their giddy laughter, large hand motions, and sharp chatter roiled around as I watched his fingers click away on a keyboard. I sipped my room temperature coffee, and it tasted as bland as his soul.

I remembered the moment I stepped through the portal. It felt powerful, a way to get out from under my father's thumb. The idea of creating chaos and havoc on Earth? Corrupting souls and dragging them to the fiery depths for an eternity in disgrace? It sounded like divinity on my tongue. It made me hard.

The lure had been so obviously set. The king hated it when we stepped through overt traps. Only a stupid, useless demon would get caught in something so conspicuous. But something so poorly camouflaged had to be broken on the other end, right? If the human linked to the circle was woefully underprepared, they would never control me. Plus, my best friend had assured me it was likely flawed. Silas and I had observed it for hours. The lure was too sophomoric. The other side had to be weak. What could possibly go wrong?

Thomas. He was the problem. Smart on paper, studious, the type of person mothers would love their daughter to date, but so forgettable that his face became a blur to most who met him. This was the fourth time this week we were here, and the same girl barely recognized him when he ordered his coffee. She was more likely to remember his drink than him.

While astute, Thomas had no idea how to take advantage of the power he now wielded. He was too unimaginative and proper to fully utilize a demon's magic. The only thing he had done correctly? Tied me to him, while making me unable to kill him. Attached to death do us part—his death, not mine.

Now, if I could get someone *else* to kill him? The binding spell would transfer to them. And if I convinced them to give me their soul? Well, the possibilities were endless. I could force the person to release me, else I could destroy their soul. Whoever took over needed to be someone better. Someone with an inkling of danger. Someone *worthy*.

Thomas, however, never hung around anyone who would *murder* him.

Over the last three monotonous years, I attempted to give Thomas everything he desired—popularity, sex, adoration—but he met my suggestions with bitter resistance.

I leaned forward and shoved the screen of his laptop down a few inches so he would look at me. "I know how to fix your romantic life."

"I'm not stalking her," he growled, even as his eyes settled on the pretty blond who served him earlier.

"Trust me. She'll *love* it."

"I won't trust you so long as you keep giving idiotic advice."

"I give fantastic advice. You just never heed it."

"You told me to kill my mother and frame my father!" He blew on his latte. Thomas drank his coffee like someone who couldn't handle anything sour in his life—with four pumps of hazelnut and whipped cream on top. It was no wonder he never listened to me. The sweetness of it lingered in the air between us. "How was that going to make me popular?"

"Sympathy." Letting go of the coffee cup, I grabbed a switchblade from my pocket. It took too much power to bring out my claws, but having something sharp made my human facade feel homier. Blade in hand, I twisted it, drilling a small hole in the table. Thomas glared at me, frowning at the destruction I created.

As long as Thomas was alive, I couldn't transform into my true self. Part of his fail safes. So many fucking safeguards. This guy was a walking encyclopedia of demon lore, and most of it had been annoyingly accurate. I would find someone to kill him. I just needed a plan.

His gaze landed on my fingers as I bored the sharp point into the table. He glanced around the cafe. There were plenty of people who *could* see us, but none of them paid attention to me. His protective circles made sure of that. To most people, I might as well not exist. It would take someone who had fire in their soul to see me, based on the limited knowledge I had about the spells he cast. I needed an innocent who was capable of being fully corrupted. Ice cold turned to liquid fire.

Such a person didn't exist in Thomas's life.

To be honest, Thomas had outperformed me. While I had to

admit I was impressed, it also made me hate him more. I tried to kill him and his family once, but my knives missed their marks. Attacking anyone he loved was like trying to slice through water. The molecules parted around me, reassembling on the other side, no worse for wear.

I was stuck—and right now, Earth was becoming inferior to the burning tar pits. It had been a few years since I had pissed the king of the fires off enough to be placed on pit duty, but once I got back? There would be consequences. Dire consequences.

While Thomas slept every night, I did my homework. I studied his spell, every piece he wove together. I needed him to die, but I needed the right person to replace him. If the binding spell was shoved onto someone as plain as he was, I would find myself back in the same position. What I needed was someone I could drag down to the fires with me. Rule their soul instead of the other way around.

Thomas continued protesting our history together. "Then you told me to get with Angie that night at the Halloween party."

"Yes, because she was going to have a great night and then continue seeing you for the next year. You missed an opportunity."

"You told me she'd only get with me if I pushed Bill Parkston into the pool."

"That's correct."

"Bill doesn't know how to swim, and he was so drunk he would have died."

"Your point?"

"He would have *died.*"

"And Angie would have been overwhelmed with emotion. She would have slept with you and continued sleeping with you for the next year. Since the whole thing was going to be a tragic accident, you would have been fine. Not a single stain on your perfect record."

"But Bill would be dead!"

"Bill was an asshole." I glared at him. "It was the perfect situation for you. Get rid of the guy who bullied you your entire childhood *and* get the girl."

"Why does it always involve me killing someone?"

"Thomas," I pronounced his name carefully and pointed to myself with the blade. "I am a demon."

"Yeah, but there has to be another way."

"You should have summoned an angel if you wanted advice that didn't risk your eternal soul."

"I could have done that?" He pressed his lips together in a thin line, staring at me with glossy hope.

"No." I sighed, wrapping my hands around my coffee and bringing the black liquid to my lips. It was brackish and didn't nearly hit the spot it used to. If nothing changed, I would shrivel into a husk from boredom.

His gaze trailed over me before opening his laptop once more. He typed out a few lines on his engineering thesis. I snapped my fingers, and the completed document appeared on his computer.

His lips curled with disgust. "Did you copy this from other people again?"

"Yes, but that's not the point. My point is—you won't get caught because *I* did this for you. My advice would give you what you want. You could be famous, living with notoriety, but instead, you have chosen a life of monotony. When you summoned a demon, Thomas, what did you really want?" After flicking my blade closed, I kicked my feet up on the table and rocked my chair onto two legs, leaning farther back with my arms crossed.

His brown eyes flicked to me. His nondescript features were impossible to describe because he became another faceless random human to almost everyone he interacted with. Brown eyes with no particularly stunning features—not the deep rich that sometimes looks like staring into freshly polished wood or the dark charcoal that made someone jarring to look at, but *brown*. Plain brown. Soil brown. His straight nose, thin lips, and round cheeks did nothing to make him stand out from a crowd. Thomas simply *was*.

Which was why he needed to go to such extremes to make himself into what he wanted to be. Popular with women, famous, and someone history would remember. Except he was too damn *good natured* to listen to any advice I gave him.

It threatened to drive a demon mad, especially since he summoned me for my help to begin with.

"I didn't want to hurt anyone when I summoned you."

"What did you think would happen?"

"That I would make a deal to trade you my soul or something."

I snorted. "Why would I ever want *your* soul?"

A blush crept across his cheeks. Lips parted in a frown. "You don't have to be so horrible."

I pointed to myself. "Demon."

He narrowed his eyes and opened his mouth to say something else, but stopped the moment the bell chimed above the front door. His gaze shifted, and he visibly swallowed.

If this was another bully from his high school years, I would convince Thomas to kill the man, because I was sick of his sad puppy look. The moment I turned around, however, the world ceased existing.

Every living person's soul on Earth had an aura in varying degrees of warmth, most of them tepid. Some were warmer than others, others cooler. These temperatures surrounded their souls, indicating how likely they were to end up in one place or the other. Thomas's was always room temperature, blending into the space around him. Summoning me had been the most corrupt thing Thomas had ever done. And since he never *used* me, the stain on his soul had been minimal.

The woman who just walked in, however, had the coldest soul I had ever felt. It swept over me in a wave, and I fought back a shiver. Her elbow was locked around another woman's—the latter had the fieriest soul I had come across. Interesting pair.

Saliva coated my mouth. The girl with the glowing, delicious innocence had a flicker of heat right over her heart. She could be corrupted. She could become something dangerous. Her soul practically screamed for me to crack her open, give her a reason to embrace her darkest self.

Oh, *this* I could work with.

"Who is that?" I asked Thomas, gauging his reaction.

"Zoe and Mercedes."

"And which one has your jaw unhinged?"

Thomas snapped his mouth shut with an audible click. The two women walked up to the counter and placed their order. The one with the fiery soul had platinum hair and creamy skin, while the other had a tanner complexion with chestnut brown hair and light hazel eyes. They were too wrapped up in each other to notice the hungry gaze of the man across from me.

Well, Thomas got more interesting.

"Mercedes. She was kind of like … the unobtainable girl in high school, and I am pretty sure she's still dating someone now."

"The blond. You want to get with her?" I leaned forward, sliding my blade back into my jeans.

"I did, desperately."

"And now?"

"I don't want to ruin her relationship."

"What if I told you she was already thinking about breaking it off?" Truly, I didn't know who she was with, nor did I care. I simply needed him to listen to me for *once*. Because I needed *her*. Or more specifically, her friend. The brunette. The one that felt like an ocean breeze rolling over me.

His eyebrow arched. "I'm listening."

There was no other way to remove the man sitting across from me. I couldn't kill him. My claws had tried, my knives had attempted, and flames help me, I wanted to pull a trigger on a gun. Something stopped me every time I tried. When he slept, I reached into his back and tore his spine straight out—except it had only been his blanket in my fist when I finished.

It was decidedly annoying not being able to murder him.

While I was bound to him, if someone *else* were to kill Thomas, my binds would be transferred. Sadly, the man never went out past dark, and I encountered no one who had a soul I wanted to be attached to. If the binding didn't break, I would be right back where I started if I chose an incorrect partner. Stay with the devil you know, which was ironic, seeing as how I had been so ready to escape the confines of fires in the first place.

But now … My gaze sharpened on the spark around Zoe's chest. It wasn't a flame like I previously thought, but potential. It was a single ember, coiled and hot like the tar pits, but surrounded by a swamp of cold.

It was waiting for someone to let it out, let it breathe, stoke it into being.

"Throw a party at your lake house." I turned my attention back to Thomas and kept my gaze steady on him. "Invite her. She'll say yes. She'll bring her boyfriend, but I promise you, they will not be walking out of there together." That was the truth. Neither would leave if I had anything to do about it.

"My parents would be furious if anything broke at the—"

I reached over the table, latching onto the collar of the man. Getting up in his face, I snarled, "Do you want to please your parents, or do you want to get your dick wet for once in your pathetic life?"

He blinked at me. "You can't hurt me."

"No, but I can shake some sense into you." I shoved him back into his chair, where he grunted. "You want this girl; you are going to take this girl. Throw a house party. Invite everyone from high school. You are back in town for the summer. Isn't that what people do when they are on summer break?"

Thomas shrugged his slender shoulders. "I can't say. I've never done it before."

"It's a party, Thomas. I didn't ask you to kill or stalk anyone. Take the win."

His jaw clenched. "And I'm just supposed to ask her to come?"

I waved my hand and presented him with a piece of paper. "Give this to her."

"A paper invitation?"

15 Lakeview Lane
Friday at 9:00pm
A Bloody Good Time

"What's wrong with paper?"

"No one has used paper since phones became a thing."

I flicked my hand at his phone. Ten phones in the cafe pinged. I glanced around. "This many people were from your graduating class?"

"I didn't consent to this."

"Demon." I pointed to myself again but kept my gaze on those picking up their phones and staring into the glowing screens. "Seriously? This many people come back to this tiny coffee shop *every* summer? What are they doing? I know what *you* are doing—

working on your precious thesis—but what are the rest doing?" Taking in our surroundings, I realized it was a bunch of people who looked relatively the same. Humans tried so desperately to fit into the masses when all they really wanted was someone to recognize them as unique, special. Unwilling to stand out, yet desperate to be seen. Curious.

Thomas shrugged. "It's one of the few places you can get a decent cup of coffee in town."

"Hey, Thomas, since when do you throw parties?"

His jaw unhinged again. I rolled my eyes. Mercedes and Zoe had approached our table after the text went out. I moved my chair over next to Thomas and pressed his jaw shut for him. "Maybe you should say something instead of staring at the poor girl?"

He swallowed. "I thought I would try something new. It's senior year next year, and who knows where we will go after that?"

"Ain't that the truth." Mercedes tossed her hair over her shoulder and took a sip from her latte. Pink lipstick coated the plastic lid. "I am glad to hear someone is going to throw something. And wow, at Lakeview Lane? I didn't realize you were rich." A coy smile curved her lips.

Thomas shrugged. "My parents did okay."

"Okay is an understatement." Mercedes nodded, more to herself than him. "Well, I guess I'll see you then. It's better than spending another weekend at the drive-in." She turned away.

Zoe stayed glued to the spot. "Hi," she said. One hand held her coffee, the other trailed over the hem of her shirt, fiddling.

Mercedes stopped and turned around on the edge of her heels.

"Are you a friend from college? I haven't seen you before."

It took me a moment to realize Zoe was looking *at* me. Everyone else on this forsaken planet tended to ignore me, rarely seeing my presence because of whatever protections Thomas had cast. Not being noticed was my personal fire, something I carried with me at all times. Deserved, as Father would put it once I was back in the depths.

Except *her* eyes were on *me*.

I smirked. "You could say that."

"Are you going to be at the party?" Zoe asked. Her voice trailed along my skin, caressing it with a cool softness that went straight to my head.

Mercedes finally shifted her gaze to me. She blinked several times as if she couldn't figure out how I miraculously appeared in the chair.

"I wouldn't miss it." I looped my arm over Thomas's shoulder. He winced at the contact. "Where this kid goes, I go. You know?"

She smiled. It was bright and innocent, but her eyes pierced through me. "I know the feeling." Her fingers tightened around her coffee like it would save her from the outside world. That small gesture made me want to *bite*.

"Come on, Zoe. We have to meet the others." Mercedes hiked up her purse. "See you both Friday."

"You're coming then?" I asked.

Zoe's gaze stayed steady on me. Rich hazel with rings of gold, brown, yellow, and green. Flecks of color that lingered. "If you want me to."

"Oh, I want."

She bit her lower lip and nodded, spinning to catch up with her friend. Her wild, brown hair bounced behind her as she swept out of the coffee shop.

I would have to play my cards right to make this house party go the way I needed, but if everything went as planned, I would be free of Thomas and attached to a much more interesting soul by the end of the night. If I had any say in the matter, I knew exactly whose fiery heart I wanted to be wrapped around, and the bell had just signaled her exit.

"You don't have to be so creepy."

I turned to Thomas. "You know nothing about women."

"I know enough not to stalk them!"

Standing up, I stretched my arms over my head. I needed a second cup of coffee. "I stand by it." My thumb hiked toward the barista. "She is an exhibitionist with a consensual non-consent fantasy, and she likes generic men like you. All you would have needed to do was stalk her, give her a safe word, and then take her. She would have *never* used the safe word, and she would have *loved* the fact that you gave her one."

His brows flattened over his eyes. "Maybe I *don't* have a consensual non-consent fantasy."

I snatched my mug. "So be it. But this party is another chance for you, and let's not ruin it. Yeah?"

2 Zoe

I gritted my teeth together as I waited on the end of Mercedes's bed. It wasn't that I was dreading the party; it was … that I was dreading the party. Ridley and the others were already in the van, hanging around for us, but Merce was determined to make us late, as usual. It was encroaching on eight thirty, and my anxiety was already getting the better of me. I didn't want to be social tonight. I hated bar scenes, restaurants, and even found it hard to venture out for my once-a-month mandatory club meeting.

Never mind a party full of people I knew back in high school.

High school had been the worst time of my life. I had been awkward, depressed, and hated myself. I hadn't dealt with a lot of the emotional baggage I carried. My breasts hadn't filled in—too many guys turned me down for my non-existent curves. I had been too skinny, too delicate, and too untouchable. No one gave me a second glance.

And if someone did? It was a practical joke or as a dare.

Whereas Merce could bat her eyelashes and have a guy tripping over themselves to get with her. I was the maladroit sidekick—the person guys used to get to the girl they really wanted. At one point, I had debated bleaching my hair, wondering if it was the brown that turned people away.

At least now I didn't carry around my virginity like some weird scarlet fucking letter. The irony of *that* was not lost on me. I had removed that title during a bungling two-month fling at the beginning of college. Mostly, I hooked up with the guy so I could wrench the bandage off and toss it in the trash. I found men reacted one of two ways when they discovered my virginity—they craved it or were repulsed by it.

So, I never told the guy I slept with that I was one, and that was that.

Merce walked out of the bathroom, pulling down the skirt that hugged her like a second skin. Each of her hands grasped a set of earrings as she lifted them, presenting each to me. "Which one?"

I had to unlock my jaw. It felt like hours of my sitting here, perched like a caged bird, waiting for her so we could leave. This was how it had been in high school, and I found myself wrapped back up in Mercedes's orbit. Doing what she wanted, letting her set the timeline, drifting in her shadow.

She, of course, had no idea I felt this way. Could I hold it against her if I never *told* her how much it frustrated me? I might as well have been a third pair of earrings, another accessory to her outfit.

"The green. It works with your ensemble and brings out the flecks in your eyes."

She tossed me a kiss and threw the other set on the dresser. It took her seconds to loop them through her ears. "I want to make Alec jealous."

My brows lowered. "Please tell me you are not still thinking about him. It's been three years."

Scowling, she went to her closet and threw the doors open, flipping through until she found a light jacket. Despite it being the middle of the summer, the air held an odd coolness to it. It was the chill that came with potential change. I needed things to shift, to be different than they were now. Things in my life had … fallen apart, and I still wasn't sure how to put the pieces back together.

My lackluster major wasn't helping.

"I am not *still* thinking about him. I have Ridley." She paused. A brief frown crested her pink lips, but she shook her head and plowed on. "But I want Alec to realize the mistake he made by dumping my ass at senior prom." She shrugged on her jacket and tossed her hair behind her shoulders. As far as I knew, every guy who wasn't with Mercedes regretted not being with her. She was *that* kind of girl. "Ready?"

"I've been waiting for you."

She put her hands on her hips and considered me. "That's what you are wearing?" A perfectly plucked eyebrow rose.

I held up my hands. "Nope, I am not here for a makeover sequence. I like my jeans and t-shirt, and I have my bikini underneath in case there is a hot tub. That's all I need. Besides, if I have to carry your drunk ass around, I need sneakers."

Merce sighed. "That's what Ridley is for."

"Ridley will get just as drunk as everyone else, and you know it."

"Why don't you drink?" Mercedes turned to her floor-length mirror and grabbed lip gloss from her dresser. She pursed her lips and applied a thick layer. "I thought going to college would have changed that about you, but no, you still don't. So, what gives?" Rolling the gloss over her lips, she shoved the tube closed.

I drank; I just didn't get drunk. Big difference in my book, but Mercedes never saw it that way.

In high school, I had to take care of my alcoholic grandmother. None of my friends knew about that. In fact, no one did. After having to deal with her, I decided to never lose control like she did. I had an occasional glass of wine or a singular beer, but there were plenty of other things to do that had nothing to do with drinking. Plus, who would take care of my friends and kick the balls of any man who tried to take advantage if we were all sloshed?

No, it was better if one of us stayed sober.

Truthfully, I hated being home for the summer, and I missed college. I had chosen a tiny private school several states away in order to escape everyone who once knew me—or thought they knew me. As much as I loved Mercedes and the rest of my friends for making high school tolerable, they hadn't changed much since leaving town. This was partly due to them being confident about who they were back then.

I was still finding myself. I spent high school hiding how horrible things were at home while navigating my group of friends. While I still didn't know who I wanted to be, I had changed more than they had. I had become more ... *me*. Instead of focusing on making my friends happy, I took time for myself. I explored what I wanted to do. I dabbled in numerous arts and crafts, waiting for something to stick.

But this party? This party I could tolerate for one night, but it was certainly not something I would fasten to my future.

I had to admit there was a small part of me which was excited about seeing the mysterious guy again. His dark eyes had connected to mine first—raked along my skin like I wanted to do with my fingernails to his bare back. He started when I spoke to him. And that expression on his face? One of pure reverence ... it did something to my soul. *He* was the big reason I let Merce drag me out tonight.

The smaller reason was because this was the last summer before college was over. After that, I planned to move away and never look back, so perhaps Merce was right. We needed to live it up, enjoy ourselves, and say fuck it.

Though, I'd rather be saying fuck it with a bottomless bucket of popcorn while watching another movie at the drive-in, but no one seemed interested in that idea. Extroverts comprised my group, and I was their adopted introvert.

"Come on." Mercedes weaved her way to the door, down the stairs, and out of the house. Her hair bounced in waves, done to perfection. It kissed her shoulders with each step. Her skirt hugged every curve—if Alec was at the party tonight, he would be jealous.

I drifted two feet behind her. Envy reared inside me, but I stuffed it down. Merce made everything look effortless but knowing how much time she spent preparing for the party eased some of my insecurities. I looked fine. Not picture perfect, but fine.

Besides, if someone needed me to be flawless to be interested, then they weren't worth my time. No one was flawless. No one.

We slipped into the van, and judging by the obnoxious booming voices around me, our friends had been pre-gaming. At least Ridley seemed okay, and he was driving, so I let it go. Mercedes rode shotgun, whereas I had to climb over Everett and Corbin to get to my seat in the back. This was a normal summer procedure, where we all stuffed ourselves into Ridley's mother's minivan.

"Hey, Zoe," Everett mumbled as I maneuvered around him. As usual, Everett and Corbin had their hands roaming over each other's legs when they thought no one was looking. Every year, they broke up. They were in separate colleges, but each summer, they came crashing back together like two asteroids. I hoped they figured it out long term. They had been through a lot over the years, and I respected their decision to separate during school.

While the guys at least acknowledged my existence, my other two friends were so into each other that they barely noticed me. Tate's hand rested far up on Sasha's inner thigh. They had gone to state school together, somehow making their tenuous high school relationship work despite the odds. Sasha's fiercely cut bob was already mussed.

Meanwhile, Ridley and Merce had made a two-hour distance work, proving all of us wrong. They had only gotten together after that fateful senior prom night, when Ridley comforted Mercedes after her horrific breakup with Alec.

Despite each couple having their hiccups and numerous pints of ice cream split with me in the middle of the night during several summers, my friends had stayed in their pairs. High schoolers weren't supposed to be together for the rest of their lives—at least, that was my humble opinion. We were supposed to grow up, change, take new shapes. While it seemed like they had grown together, I was left with the question: how?

Corbin and Everett had dated other people, having taken the time to learn about themselves while they were at different schools. But every summer, it was the same old thing.

Perhaps this was jealousy talking, because I never *had* the passion my friends seemed to have. I was the odd one out. Never dated anyone after Kent—my few month fling. Never had a genuine relationship. I hated feigning interest in something I had none in, which seemed to be what every guy wanted. Small talk was abhorrent, but I was still as horny as everyone else. I didn't want to spend time at clubs or bars to find a one-night stand, because I hated the noise. I wanted that spark, that tension with someone. But getting there meant all the above. My worst nightmare.

As we drove toward the party, I contemplated how people held each other's interest. My friends had made their relationships work, but how did they *stay* together? How do you keep someone enraptured? How do you not get bored?

One night, I had tried doing a sexy dance for Kent. Instead of being into it, he did an actual spit-take on the soda he had been drinking. The whole mess was so unflattering, I ended up feeling more inadequate by the end of the night.

Dating seemed like a recipe for catastrophe. I'd rather be at home, watch movies, play video games, and read the occasional book. Why be social myself when I was perfectly content not talking at all?

"Hey, Zoe!" Corbin's lips were swollen as he gazed at me through hooded lids. His grip roamed until he found Everett's fingers. They interlocked together. "It's been a hot second."

"Sure has."

"How's school going?" Corbin had a kind of movie star face. Clear cut jaw, dark stubble that stretched across his white skin, curved cheekbones that were perfectly defined. His eyes were viciously light. Next to Everett's dark features, they were a striking pair.

Everett had a face that put everyone at ease. Light, bright smile and dancing liquid brown eyes. His cheekbones made his easy grin seem bigger. His dark brown fingers trailed lightly over Corbin's knuckles, and there was a gentle, urgent fire in his eyes whenever he looked at his boyfriend.

They were stinking adorable.

But we had been back from school for a month, and despite Corbin and Everett being two of my best friends in high school, this was the first time they chose to grace us with their presence since the summer began. They didn't want to go to movie nights—not sure why; though I suspected it had something to do with the asteroid effect—but Corbin's question made my gut twinge. It

sounded more like something a distant aunt would ask instead of an
old best friend.

"It's great. And you?"

"I'm thinking about dropping out."

Everett knocked him on the cheek lightly. "But he won't. He's
going to law school, after all. He hates studying."

"It's the worst." Corbin gave me a tight-lipped smile. It didn't
meet his blue eyes. "I am tired all the time."

"Merce?" I asked. She had struck up a conversation with Sasha,
not caring about how Tate was getting dangerously close to giving
us all a show in the van. The star? Sasha.

I hated when my friends drank. Why couldn't they wait until the
party? At least then I could have ducked into a dark corner and
stayed there until the night was over.

"Do you know where we are going?"

"On it." She typed the directions onto her phone and connected
it to the center console. "You're still going to law school, Corbin?"

"Maybe," he grumbled.

"Zoe is going to switch majors," Mercedes added.

I glared at her. She winked at me.

"To what?" Everett asked, his gaze steady on me. Something
about him always made me feel at ease—like he actually cared, even
if we hadn't talked in a long time.

"I don't know, but I hate math and cannot imagine doing it for
the rest of my life." I let out a breath. "It seemed practical at the
time, because so many people need accountants, but now ..."

"You should switch to marketing, like me." Merce's grin
widened, blazing white next to her pink lips. "We could go to New
York together. It'd be incredible! You and me taking the city by
storm." She waved her hand in front of her, as if imagining our
names on some marquee.

"And where am I in this scenario?" Ridley asked, eyebrow arched.

"Still going to school to become the hot veterinarian you'll be in another four years." She placed a quick kiss on his cheek. "And once you've graduated and have a ton of student debt, I will have worked my way up the ladder and will help you open your practice. I can manage your social media for you." Merce wiggled her fingers, as if that were magical enough to make their dreams come true.

Though, sometimes it felt like her personality was infectious enough to conjure her dreams with little to no effort.

Ridley grunted, keeping his eyes steady on the road.

"I am not switching to marketing," I grumbled.

Merce's green eyes shot to mine. "Suit yourself, but you need to figure it out. Senior year and all that."

Accounting would be the path of least resistance, seeing as how any major changes would result in my going to school for another year or two. And the leftover money from my grandmother's dwindling accounts was running out. There was no family left to help me—and the one family member I had *wouldn't* help me. Once the funds hit zero, I was on my own. My mind spun whenever I thought about the paperwork to apply for loans and financial aid. After dealing with attorneys, my estranged cousin, and probate, I didn't want to fill out any additional forms if I could avoid it.

But once the money ran out ... The thought tormented me. What would it be like to have nothing? Perhaps that's when my real life would start. Maybe then I'd feel some kind of passion instead of idling. I had paused while the rest of the world carried on, and I wasn't sure how to jump start anything.

And not a single person in this car knew *why* I was thinking about switching majors. No one asked. They just accepted it.

My grandmother had died last January, and the financial garbage thereafter had been a nightmare. My friends liked to pretend I was normal. They liked to believe I still had parents around, a home here, a reason to cling to this place like they did. Instead, I was holed up in my dead grandmother's single bedroom condo that smelled like mothballs without her spoiled wine seeping into every crack and crevice.

The only reason I hadn't sold the place and moved was because my cousin had a stake in the home too. The courts decided we had to split ownership. My cousin didn't know what she wanted to do with it, but she was fine with me living there during the summer, so long as I maintained it. The complicated relationship between her and me only got more strained as we navigated the rest of the paperwork. Dealing with the money in the aftermath of my grandmother's death was another reason I didn't want to major in accounting anymore.

Maybe if my grandmother hadn't drunk so much, perhaps I wouldn't be alone. If my mother hadn't gotten into a kayaking accident with her boyfriend, maybe I'd have more stability. If my dad hadn't disappeared when I was five, maybe I'd be less … lackluster. If anyone in my family had put me first, perhaps I would have found something to be excited about, like the rest of my friends. Have hope for the future. A sense of pride and wonderment in my life.

Instead, I had … me.

"Math sucks," Tate said, voice coming out muffled by having their face pressed against the crook of Sasha's neck. Their dark brown, almost black, hair swooped over their eyes. They never grew out of the scene kid phase. They had tawny, golden-brown skin.

Sasha's cheeks flushed bright red. Tate's hand had disappeared underneath her skirt.

This was not the first time I had been close to them when Tate got physical. I had heard Sasha orgasm more times than I cared to admit, and they had given me first-hand knowledge that I lacked a voyeur kink. Sasha, however, was an exhibitionist, which spurred Tate on. They were obsessed with her and everything she liked.

"No one would blame you for wanting to ditch it. Isn't that right, Sash?" Tate's voice dipped low.

"Of course." Sasha turned in her seat to look at me. Her lips screwed up at the edges, but she kept the emotions out of her blue eyes. "You only get one life, so do what makes you happy." She smoothed her hands over her auburn hair, cut short around her chin. The locks framed her face perfectly.

"And what makes you happy?" Tate whispered, dropping their voice. It had been a question only for her, but we were so cramped in the van, I heard everything.

Including the sound of their fingers pumping into her.

I sighed as Sasha turned back toward Tate. Her eyes widened as a giggle spilled from her lips.

Honestly, I wasn't bothered by the act itself, but more from the envy that clawed up my stomach. While I didn't want to have such a public display, I wanted *something*. Jealousy was an ugly feeling, something I couldn't help having around them. What would it feel like to be so captivated by that much yearning? To find someone who understood you and embraced what you loved?

Hearing Sasha's moans made me want someone—almost as much as I wanted out of this vehicle.

Thankfully, it didn't take long to arrive at the lake house. The thumping bass trudged over the lawn, reaching us from across the overflowing driveway. People parked on the street and meandered toward the house. Arms slung over each other as the ambling drunks made their way inside. Apparently, my friends weren't the only ones who settled on pre-gaming.

The bright cabin surrounded by dark night reminded me of how moths were drawn toward a flame. Ready to burn ourselves alive.

Letting out another breath, I resigned myself to *try* to have a decent time. Nothing about a party appealed to me—other than the possibility of seeing that guy again. But beyond that, this had been the last thing I wanted to do. Everyone in high school had treated me like I had been lesser, never looking my way for more than a second, and now I was willingly walking back into that beast's belly.

I heard what they said about me. Strange, weird, *other*. More than once, "Why does Mercedes hang out with her?" Back when I was trapped in a stall, carving my initials into the wall just below the toilet paper dispenser. Small enough so only I knew they existed, but big enough to prove that I was real. A piece of myself left behind.

As my friends stumbled out of the van, Merce threw her arm over my shoulder. Ridley flanked her side. "Come on, Zoe! We'll spend some time in Thomas's hot tub—I mean, he *has* to have one, right? Look at the size of this place! We'll have a few drinks and head out. Might as well take advantage of the lake house, right?"

I didn't point out how it was too brisk to enjoy the lake, but whatever.

"And at the very least, we can watch these idiots get drunk off their asses and make fools of themselves. Bet you more than one stupid girl tries to table dance tonight." Ridley belly laughed, as if he had told the funniest joke in the world.

Merce rolled her eyes, meeting my gaze. She mouthed, "Boys."

Screw it. I stared at Ridley. "You might also get drunk enough to table dance, Ridley. So, include yourself in the stupid equation."

Ridley crossed his arms over his chest. "Your math is impeccable, Zoe. Maybe you should go into accounting." His hand went through his shaggy, black hair. "Whatever. We'll have fun tonight." Rolling his shoulders, he shook himself off and grinned. The smile cut through the freckles dotting his face.

"Seriously, why are you two still dating?" I aimed my question at Merce. It hadn't meant to come out as rude, but there it was.

Ridley played it off, putting a hand to his chest. "Ouch, Zoe."

Merce laughed. "Because he has a really, really great cock."

"And that's why I have an ego, folks," Ridley said to no one in particular, throwing his hands out wide.

"Things I didn't need to know." Shrugging her off, I hustled a few feet in front of our group.

"Come on. I was kidding!" Merce chased after me.

"Nope, we're sticking with your first answer!" Ridley yelled.

I kept running ahead.

"That's no fair! I have heels!" We broke out into laughter as she tried to catch up to me but stumbled instead. When I reached the front door, I waited for my friends before ushering everyone inside.

A wave of sound hit me immediately, choking all thoughts from my head. Pounding echoed throughout my brain, reverberating into my marrow. Drenched me with the need to run. Too loud. Too many people. Lots of noise from all angles.

"I'm going to find something not alcoholic," I said. A drink would make this better. Any kind of drink to keep my mind busy on something other than the volume. Seriously, how did people exist in places like this?

"Live a little!" Merce shouted after me as I ducked under a few outstretched arms and couples already forming inside the entrance. Bodies jostled me, and I knew without a shadow of a doubt, this was going to be one of the longest nights of my life.

Haden

The third beer dangled from my fingertips as I watched the humans file into the party. Thomas greeted everyone with a wicked grin, like he had been the one to plan this event. A few people forgot his name, which gave me the deepest pleasure of watching him fumble over their faux pas. He had never been filled with grace, even when it would serve him well.

I offered to give him grace once. Told him all he had to do was read a book. His eyes had narrowed with suspicion. He didn't trust me when I told him it would change his entire life. It was a self-help book by some douche, but Thomas would have fallen for it—hook, line, and sinker. Then, he would have applied those concepts to his vanilla life and lived a much more interesting existence.

Instead, he decided I was tricking him, and he ignored me. Again. If there was one way to piss off your summoned demon, it was to ignore them. Repeatedly. I had a thing about getting attention, and he never gave me enough.

I took another swig as several couples funneled into the room, rotating around each other and swiping drink after drink. Thomas hadn't believed me when I told him we needed at least four hundred dollars' worth of alcohol, but with how quickly it was going, I was second guessing myself. Maybe we needed more.

But my estimates were rarely wrong.

My third beer was empty by the time I brought it up to my lips again. Tilting my head to the side, I realized I never factored my drinking into this party. Ah well, if things progressed as they should, then the six-pack I was pounding back would hardly matter.

Sighing, I hopped off the counter and pushed through the crowd. No one looked at me, which was going to make tonight's announcement harder than expected, but I could use some magic to counteract Thomas's temporarily. It'd be a limited amount of time, but I only needed long enough to get my point across.

This evening would have a few unknowns, since I had never tried this particular demonic curse before. But my plans were already underway. There was no turning back now.

As soon as the last guests crossed the threshold, the magic would seal behind them. With each human walking through those doors, the thrum of power edged throughout the lake house. The more people, the more the spell fed. It was the only way to cast the curse, since my power was mostly bound. Mostly. But the humans? Well, they all had a little magic in them—none of them knew how to use it. And *that* I used to my advantage. After several more people arrived, the walls threatened to explode with power, and I was determined to make it mine.

Thomas would never know what hit him.

He laughed at something some pretty blond said, likely a replacement for the one who got away. Good for him. Maybe he'd have fun before it was too late.

I reached into the fridge and pulled out another beer, twisting off the top like it was nothing more than a soda. I slipped the door shut, and the girl from the cafe was on the other side. Her brunette hair was smoothed down, unlike the wilds from earlier in the week. Her hazel eyes blazed, and this close, I noticed the flecks of green and golden hues.

Stunning.

"Oh, hey," she said, voice coming out soft in the surrounding swell of noise.

I blinked, offering her the drink after a moment's hesitation. She gazed at me like no one else in this forsaken place did. I wondered why that was. Was it the spark marring her soul, singing to the siren within her as it waited to drag her down? Or was it because of her innocence, as cool as a night's breeze?

I hoped for the first part, because I *would* drag her down. Happily.

"Uh, thanks, but I don't—" She stared at the beer and frowned. Her lips parted, lower lip jutting out in a pout. The look stirred something dark inside me. A want. Determination flitted across her face, and her shoulders rose in a shrug. "You know what? Fuck it. Thank you."

"Please don't fuck the beer." I opened the fridge again and grabbed another one for myself, twisting the top off and tossing the cap onto the counter.

"That's not ..." Her cheeks flamed red, and the muddled confusion on her face sent shivers down to my dick. If that's how she reacted to a simple innuendo, I'd love to witness what happened when I actually tried. Her eyes met mine. Her pupils were wide, expanding into the gold flecks of her hazel gaze. "You were joking."

"Of course. Who fucks beer bottles?"

"I think I saw it in a porn once."

I arched an eyebrow. "Admitting you watch porn in the second conversation with someone. I'm impressed."

Her teeth sank into her lower lip. "I didn't … Listen, thanks for this, but I should probably find my friends. I'll see you around?" Her eyes swept over me. So fast, most people wouldn't have noticed. She swallowed.

"Sure."

She turned and practically fled the room, which strengthened my instinct to chase. Oh, this was going to be a fun night if that's how she ran. I drifted through the throng of people, using enough of my will to bend them out of the way as my sights stayed on her retreating ass. It swayed in her jeans. She wore a simple t-shirt and running shoes. A girl after my heart, and the perfect attire to survive the night.

Because I would make sure she outlasted, especially after I made her scream my name in one of the many bedrooms. I wondered if her airy voice would turn husky when full of need. I wondered how many ways I could make her fall apart.

Zoe's eyes scanned her surroundings until her gaze landed on that blond girl again. The blond was hanging out with a full group, all paired into couples except for the one I had handed a beer to. Good. That meant I had no competition, not that it would matter. Since Zoe could see me, unlike the rest of the people at this bloody party, I wouldn't have to manipulate her … much.

In fact, I might not have to manipulate her at all. Not with the promise of fire inside her. I only needed to draw it out, give it a way to burn.

The blond grinned at Zoe as her eyes swept over the beer in her hands. The group had found the punch station, piling tons of the pungent alcoholic liquid into their cups and passing filled ones around. Zoe caved in on herself, hugging one of her arms across her stomach and occasionally scratching the inside of her elbow. The beer dangled, practically forgotten, from her delicate fingers.

She should have been larger than life, but whatever jokes lit up the faces of the others made her shrink inward. She became small. Her soul should have commanded space, captured attention, turned heads. Instead, her innocence made everyone slide away from her, using her internal beauty against her.

This wouldn't do. Not at all.

Plans formulated in my head, changing to accommodate these new feelings. I needed to get her underneath me before the curse became known to the rest of the party. To jump start the death game, I needed a violent act—one so violent that no one could ignore the true consequences of the curse.

If she witnessed that before she got to know me, it'd be harder to convince her to embrace my darkness—*her* fire.

Since Thomas's physical protections only extended to his biological family, there were plenty of inconsequential people to choose from tonight. One of their souls would be used to announce the curse and commence the game. Then I'd watch the chaos. It would be the perfect opportunity for Zoe to embrace everything she was and ever will be. Power, hunger, vengeance. There was so much potential locked inside her soul. Tonight, it would burst open.

As Zoe melded into the background, I forced myself to wait. There would be a time for me to move, a way to irrefutably tie her to me. I had to play it right.

Because if I corrupted at least one soul, Father couldn't claim this was a wasted trip.

And if things went my way, Zoe's soul would be mine before morning—and mine for every morning after that for the rest of eternity. That was something to look forward to.

4 Zoe

Alcohol had never been my thing, but when the dark-eyed blond handed it to me, I said fuck it.

Please don't fuck the beer. The way his lips quirked up his angular jaw unraveled something inside me, made me want to become something more. Maybe I was finally ready to try this whole relationship thing out.

I chuckled, shaking my head.

"What's so funny, Zoe?" Mercedes bumped into my hips with her own. Despite her thin frame and being on heels, I was still somehow the one knocked off-center. "And what made you change your mind?" She leaned in conspiratorially. "Don't tell me, a guy?"

"Nothing, and no. I just … He handed me a beer, and I took it." I shrugged, remembering how it dangled from his fingers. It was a middle of the shelf brand with a white and blue label. I forced myself to take a sip. I had never drunk this variety before, but it went down easily enough—which was part of why drinking in excess scared me.

It ran in my blood, my history, my family.

Oh well, this would be my one and only drink.

I took another sip as my friends tossed back more of the mystery juice. While my grandmother's struggle with alcohol had made me cautious, there was something else too. The couple of times I got drunk in college, I felt like I stood at the edge of a precipice. Something inside me welled up, trying to break free from my skin. With inhibitions gone, I panicked over what might happen next.

If I allowed myself to stand on the cliff's edge too many times, would I leap off? And how terrible would the fall be? Who would catch me at the bottom? And how different would I be because of it?

A single beer, however, was not getting drunk. Besides, Merce was right. The guy who handed me the drink snagged my attention in the cafe a few days ago. He was Thomas's friend, but there was a peculiar energy around him. A quiet intensity I wanted to crack open, sink my fingers into, see what my nails pulled back as I dragged them along his skin.

I had never felt that kind of … fervor before. A want deep in my core. It was new, heady, and I liked it.

Mercedes promised the party would be good for me, and perhaps she was right. Maybe there was something I was missing. Then again, maybe I wasn't missing *anything*, because an arm slipped around my shoulder, and it was not attached to the guy from earlier.

"Yo, Zoe!" I blinked at Dan, not sure where he had manifested himself from. He elongated my name, adding a sing-song to the e as it spilled from his lips. "I haven't seen you since, like, forever."

"Hi, Dan."

We shared a few classes together in high school. He still had the same boyish face from then, but with slightly more charm. Unfortunately for him, he was one of those middle of the road guys.

There was no pining or desperation, and he was certainly not someone you would brag about. But he was safe, polite, and kind. He'd probably end up marrying some model someday, because he would make her feel emotionally strong. He was a hype guy. That, however, wasn't my type.

I wasn't sure who was. Except my brain focused on the dark-eyed man who handed me the beer, and I found myself glancing toward the kitchen. Should I have stayed with him longer? Asked him out? Pressed my lips to his? Inhaled his breath into my lungs?

"It's been a year at least, right?" Dan pulled on my shoulder, bringing my attention back to him.

"Two and a half." We had run into each other after freshman year of college at the town beach. After a few laps, we ended up making out in the shade of a tree. It lasted about twenty minutes, and after, he announced he had to leave. Said he would call me.

Once he was in the parking lot, I realized we had never exchanged numbers. Probably for the best, seeing as how the make-out session felt more like a chore than effervescence. Plus, his stubble had scratched away the skin around my mouth.

Now he was here, throwing himself at me like nothing ever happened. Must be nice living in a fantasy world.

"Single again, Dan?"

"How did you know?"

"Well, I know you're a good guy." I kept my voice steady and neutral, but I placed my fingers on his chest and turned slightly toward him. "So, I know you wouldn't do this if you had someone in your life."

He gave me a wide smile, like I'd said the most wonderful thing in the world.

Mercedes peered over her shoulder. Her eyes searched both of us, finally tossing a wink at me before she sidled up to Ridley. The fact that my supposed best friend believed this guy was *the* guy, well … It made a part of me coil tighter. How well did any of them know me anymore?

Dan leaned toward my ear. "We could do a little more exploring, if you want." His fingers trailed along my shoulder. My skin prickled, but not from Dan's touch. I glanced across the party, and I swore for a moment I saw a flash of dark eyes.

"Why don't we play a game of pool? Winner gets to choose our … activity for the night?" I stepped back from him, and his arm dropped to his side.

The dopey look stayed on his face.

Dan was *too* nice for me. Except the matter of ghosting. That was decidedly rude.

"Sure. Sounds like fun, Zoe."

I beamed at him, hoping to mask any discomfort. This party was uncomfortable; what was one more thing on top of that? He headed toward the billiards. The table was nestled in the middle of the grand living room with vaulted ceilings. Long wooden beams stretched across the space. This place was sprawling. And as if Dan had been worried we would get separated, his cool fingers found my wrist. He led me the rest of the way as if I were a child.

When we reached the table, I kicked at the boots of two people making out and told them to get a room. They scurried away, giggling. Faces red and flushed. I would never get that from anyone here. Except …

My eyes shot toward the kitchen. The huge, open arches gave some sight in between the bodies moving around. I caught a glimpse of blond hair. His gaze raked over my skin from the shadows. I narrowed my eyes in his direction. If he wasn't going to come here and claim me, maybe I needed to make him. It would be fun to oblige, and while I didn't consider myself an exhibitionist, *kissing* was fine.

"One kiss every time one of us sinks a ball. The person who made the shot chooses where to kiss on the other person's body. If it becomes too much, we say *pool table* to get out of it. Okay?" I placed my hands on my hips and looked Dan up and down. Would he do this with me?

His eyebrows arched. "Get a little kinky while you were away, Zoe?"

Not as much as he wished. I tossed him a noncommittal shrug, but he accepted my terms as he racked the balls. I broke. White ball hit straight on, sending two stripes and a solid spiraling into pockets.

"Stripes," I announced.

"And where do you want to kiss me?" His lips stretched up on his face.

I glanced around the room. It roared with noise. Between the music, the conversations, people dancing and sloshing drinks, I could barely hear Dan. I didn't *want* to kiss him, but I had a feeling someone else would venture out of the shadows if I became a little reckless. While a part of me felt guilty over taking advantage of Dan, I reasoned that a truly good guy wouldn't have left me hanging after a twenty-minute make-out session.

Picking up his hands, I placed a chaste kiss on the top of his knuckles, then rotated his arm so it was palm up. I kissed the inside of his wrist. My eyes stayed steady on his. I willed myself not to look for the guy.

"Interesting choice, but I appreciate a slow burn."

"Do you?" I dropped his fingers from mine.

"Adds to the tension, don't you think?"

It depended on my mood, to be honest. Right now, I was *not* up for a slow burn. I had one night to be with this guy, and I was ready. My body was practically begging me to open my legs for the first person who showed me any attention.

The problem wasn't my body, but my mind. She was the real venomous creature who wasn't satisfied by just anyone. I had no interest in one-night stands or small talk or any of it. But I wanted *him*, emotionally and physically. I didn't know his name, but I still desired him.

"Sure." I plastered on a smile. Turned my attention back to the game. "Well, let's see how quickly this will be over." I leaned on the table and sank another ball into the pocket.

Dan's eyes twinkled. "If I didn't know any better, I'd say you hustled me."

"Would you be angry if I did?"

"Not with these terms." He took a step closer to me. We were about the same height. His cologne smelled nice, but generic. Forgettable. "Show me where, Zoe."

Haden

She had leaned over the table with expertise, readying the cue in steady fingers. When she lifted her gaze again, her eyes met his. He walked over to her, trying hard to take up space. Puffing his chest out like he had a presence. There was nothing about him that made him stand out. If anything, he was quite … ordinary. Brown hair, fairly light skin, blue eyes. Perhaps to other people, he might have been special. But to me, he was room temperature. Tepid. Safe.

Her eyes slid through the crowd again. Not finding what she wanted, she chugged down the beer and slammed it on the felt pool table. She licked a rogue droplet off her lips. Her hands came up and wrapped around his nape. Zoe leaned in and placed a kiss on his neck, letting her tongue slide up his skin.

I glowered, taking a step forward as my jaw clenched.

Her eyes snapped open, still holding onto him like a vise. The hazel irises gazed right at me. Her teeth sank into his neck as she caught my eyes. She sucked his skin in between her teeth, lids lowering as she kept her gaze steady on me.

Oh. This wasn't about him at all. She wanted to play games. I arched an eyebrow and tilted my beer toward her, as if giving her cheers or my blessing—what a hilarious notion that would be. A demon blessing a mortal.

Though, this defiant act made me wonder if she would be open to sharing—after I had her for myself, of course. We could have a lot of interesting games in the fires if that were the case. Silas would certainly love her, but he loved almost anyone.

Zoe scowled and pulled away from the guy, turning back toward the table. Pink covered his cheeks, but she seemed unamused by what had just occurred. Her interest was trained on me, despite the game unfolding in front of her. She might be playing with him, but it was me who would become her prize.

Couldn't say I minded. Certainly would make my plans to seduce her easier.

I turned my back and walked into the other room with Thomas. His arm was slung over the blond. I marched up to her and whispered in her ear—something that would make him finally get one good night in his stupid insignificant life.

I was nothing if not generous. Besides, tonight was going to give me everything I ever wanted. He should have a taste of freedom— of everything he *could* have become if he had listened to me. Sure, most of my advice would have come with the corruption of his soul, but it was a small price to pay for infamy.

As soon as I finished speaking, the girl's teeth dragged along her lower lip as she tugged on his hand. He arched a brow at me but followed her obediently as she towed him upstairs. Good. He was out of the picture, which meant it was only me and Zoe. Since no one else paid attention to me, I could do *whatever* I wanted.

A smirk spread across my lips as I swiped two more drinks from the fridge. We had about two hours until midnight, which meant my alcohol would run out early. No matter. The beer was more a prop than anything—it wasn't like my metabolism would let me get *drunk*, just heady.

I missed demon mead.

Being without the comforts of home was getting annoying. Everything on earth was so … smooth and fluffy. Where was the bite? The danger?

The crowd parted around me as I approached the pool table. Zoe sank another shot. Dan opened his arms wide, and she slunk toward him until she caught my eye. Her steps halted. I was only two feet away.

"You really going to keep kissing him?" I arched a brow.

Dan glanced in my direction, but his eyes glazed over as he looked through me. "Everything okay? Did you see Alec or something?" I had no idea who Alec was, or why he would be the one to make Zoe hesitate.

She narrowed her gaze at me, suspicion creeping into her expression. "Uh, no. I mean, everything's fine. Just … getting a little thirsty." Zoe plucked the extra beer from my fingers. Her lips wrapped around the top of it. Her eyes never strayed from mine as she tossed back a sip.

My cock gave a jolt. It had been too long since I'd had a good fuck.

Her lips were slow to release the bottle, her tongue lingering on the drop that caught on the rim of the glass. She brought it back into her mouth with nothing but pure sex.

"If that's practice for later, I can give you some pointers," I drawled.

Choking, she wrenched the drink away from her lips. My gaze

stayed on her, even while Dan cooed over her. Once she caught her breath, she glanced between both of us. "Do you … not see him?"

"No one sees me," I said, shrugging. I pulled myself over the edge of the pool table and sat back, leaning on my palms and watching the exchange.

"See who?" Dan glanced around, alarm crossing his features as his brows furrowed. "Are you all right, Zoe? We can go sit down. Somewhere quiet?" The hope in his voice made me snicker.

Her eyes narrowed briefly at him before she focused again on me. "Why doesn't he see you?" she hissed under her breath.

I leaned forward, placing my hand underneath her chin. "Because people are oblivious. Not you, though." I ran my thumb along the lower part of her jaw. Soft. So fucking soft.

"How could I miss you?" Her eyes sparkled. Red crept into her cheeks. Her wild, brown hair would look fantastic wrapped around my fist. That blush would look perfect surrounded by the color signaling a lack of oxygen.

A smirk sliced through my face.

"Zoe, are you okay? Maybe you should cool it on the—"

"I'm fine, Dan." She straightened, and my hand fell away. Her head tilted as she considered me. She had to wrench her attention away to glance back at the human. "But I think … maybe I'm not feeling the game so much anymore."

Dan shrugged. His smile faded to disappointment, but he kept his head up. "Let me know if you change your mind. I'm going to get another beer. Do you want—" He noticed she was staring back in my direction. Dan took the hint, shook his head, and trudged out of the room.

"Not feeling the game or not feeling him?"

"Why do I get the feeling that sleeping with you would be the worst and best decision of my life?"

"Who says you're going to get the opportunity?"

"You're saying I'm not?"

I hopped off the table, spinning us so I was in front of her. Her ass backed up against the edge, pressing against the frame. Placing my hands on either side of her, I enjoyed caging her in. "You're not wrong. But you're also not right. Sleeping with me would be the *best* decision of your life. Not the worst."

"I will definitely regret it."

Reaching up, I tucked her hair behind her ear. My fingers lingered on her cheek, feeling the warmth flaming under her skin. The flicker in her chest danced at my touch. It was fucking stunning to watch her soul, so desperate for warmth, drawn to me without knowing why. Her breath came hot and heavy, brushing my lips.

This was only from touching her cheek.

Fuck, I was going to enjoy the fires out of this.

"What if I told you … you would never regret it? Not for one second. Though you might have a brief moment of shame over wanting it again. You might realize something new about yourself, and that's where the mortification will come in. But no regrets. Never." My fingers trailed down her shoulder to her arm, settling just beside her hips.

Her hand gripped the side of the pool table, seemingly for dear life. But she had no idea what it was like to hang onto something so precious, not yet. She would, though. Soon. Everyone would realize how treasured life should be. They only needed the prospect of death to get there.

"Seems like you're pretty full of yourself, if you ask me."

"Says the girl who cannot stop staring at me, searching me out. Playing games with other guys to catch my attention?" I quirked an eyebrow, opening space for her to deny it.

She swallowed, blinked. Her eyes cleared for a moment, and she stared at the beer in her other hand like it had personally offended her. I plucked it from her fingers and placed both drinks on the table.

I tipped my head to the side, waiting for her response to my accusation.

She didn't rebut, but changed the subject instead. Her body curved toward me, but we still weren't touching. "Why couldn't Dan see you?"

"Would you believe me if I told you I'm cursed, and part of that curse is to make most people ignore me? Most people, except you?"

"No."

I shrugged. "Then there's nothing to tell—if you don't believe in magic, curses, or supernatural powers."

She snorted, and the laugh curled straight into my bones and knotted my veins. "So, what? Am I the princess who will break the curse by kissing the charming prince?"

A smile crested my lips this time, and her eyes drunk me in. "I'm not the prince of anything charming, I'm afraid. So no, you will not break this curse so easily, but I do think it will be you who creates something bearable."

She arched an eyebrow. "Has that line ever worked on girls? Telling them to turn your curse into something ... bearable?"

"Never. As I said, they can't see me, so I've never had the opportunity. Good line, though, isn't it?" I winked, allowing the joke to settle between us.

"Zoe!" Mercedes bounced over. Her hands were occupied by two different drinks. Platinum hair hung loosely over her shoulders, brushing Zoe's t-shirt when she leaned in close. "I've been looking everywhere for you."

"I've been here the whole time. Mercedes, you remember ... uh ... What is your name?"

"Haden."

"Haden. From the coffee shop?" Zoe gestured to me, staring at Mercedes.

The blond watched me. And as if Zoe's attention could make her finally see me, her eyes widened slightly. "Of course. Haden. From the coffee shop. Is this the guy?" she whisper-yelled the last words, not meant for me, but I heard them easily.

Zoe's cheeks flamed red, and if that wasn't the sexiest thing at this party. "Merce, how much have you had to drink?" Her voice sloped low.

"Does it matter? We found the hot tub. It's *inside*. Like … there's an indoor pool and hot tub and patio area. Isn't that crazy?" She leaned on Zoe, nuzzling her shoulder.

Zoe patted her friend. "Why don't you get everyone else, and I might meet you there?"

Merce nodded. Her eyes glossed over me once again. "Huh. Guess your guy left." She stood up straight and skipped into the throng of people.

Zoe glanced at me, mouth askew. "Cursed." Her arms crossed over her chest. "Cursed?!" She shook her head, but the simple declaration indicated she was handling this better than expected.

"Cursed. You saw."

"Okay, so let's say I do kiss you. That won't break the curse?"

I shook my head. "Though I wouldn't deny that particular request."

She snaked her fingers through my belt loops. "So, if I kissed you, what would everyone else see?"

"Probably you making out with air. I don't know how it works." I leaned over her, using my fingers to ease her face toward mine. "Do you want to test the theory?"

"I don't know if I want people to think I'm weirder than they already do."

"Who the fuck cares what they think? They will all be dead someday. What do *you* want?"

She blinked at me, huge hazel eyes widening as she swept over my features. "I think I want to do something I'm going to regret tomorrow."

"I told you, you won't regret it."

"Then something I might feel shame about later," she corrected.

I smirked, brushing my lips against the corner of hers. "I promise it will be the most luxurious shame you've ever felt."

She shuddered, placing her hands on my arms. Fingertips grazed my skin. I wanted to consume her, press my lips to hers and devour her soul, and make the spark inside her flicker to life. But instead, one of her friends came up and threw his arms around her. His face reddened from the alcohol, and a goofy look plastered on his lips. He sang her name out, and I wanted so badly to tear him from her and toss him across the room for daring to touch what I wanted.

But not yet.

It wasn't time.

But soon.

6 Zoe

"**Z**oeeee!" The sing-song way Ridley said my name made me cringe. He swooped his arms around me. "Come to the hot tub with us." He yanked me away from Haden, but not before I caught the murderous look dancing across Haden's face.

That should have terrified me—the darkening glower. But instead, it made me want to stay with him, curl inside the depths of his soul, and see how far the bottomless pit went.

I practically tripped over my feet as Ridley dragged me through the crowd. "I was in the middle of a conversation." His arm wrapped tighter around my shoulder as I tried to shrug him off.

"You looked pretty lonely to me, but don't worry, Merce and I got you."

I rolled my eyes. They never *had* me. I was the accessory, an addition—often forgotten about. But that's how they convinced me to join them on dates and outings. Mercedes was my best friend, had been for all our lives, and once Ridley joined us in middle school, we were a core group. But then they became more on prom night, and I still … was.

"Help me," I mouthed over my shoulder to Haden.

His lips twitched, amusement crinkling the corners of his eyes. The look was innocent, but the way he prowled after us was not. Everyone seemed to bend out of his way as he walked through the party. Meanwhile, Ridley bounced off every person in front of him, making me stagger with him. Brett—total asshole—screamed at Ridley, shouting for him to watch where he was going.

I would accidentally spill a drink on him later. Maybe some red wine.

Ridley snickered. "Don't mind them. We're going to where the cool kids hang out." He gave my shoulder what should have been a reassuring squeeze but ended up annoying me. I wasn't a child, and I didn't need whatever babysitting Mercedes and Ridley thought I did.

"Does anyone really say *cool kids* anymore?"

He shrugged. "Obviously, the cool kids do. Don't be such a bitch, Zoe."

My jaw clenched. He said it with a lightness that insinuated a joke, but I knew how these jokes worked—it was a thinly veiled attempt to hide his true thoughts. I thought about shrugging him off, kicking him in the nuts, and going back to Haden.

Haden. I glanced behind us. His presence was thick, expanding throughout the crowd and blanketing everyone. Whatever *curse* he claimed to have, I didn't believe it. How could I? But I had seen it. Maybe it should petrify me, but watching his dark eyes on me, tracking me … I felt strangely comforted, especially knowing I wouldn't have to brave the hot tub with my drunk friends alone.

Sure, I wouldn't have been *alone* with them either, but sometimes,

I felt surrounded by them while remaining unseen. At least Haden would give me something to focus on, even if he was cursed. What a strange concept, if it were true.

My mind raced. Did I believe in the paranormal? Not really. But how could I explain my luck if not for some sort of destiny being at play? I wasn't out of college yet, and I had no family left except for my spiteful cousin. Barely any friends. A few folks in college understood me, but not really. No one knew who I was. I had self-isolated. And in an ironic twist of fate, being surrounded by people only made that separation more pronounced.

Which was why I hated summer.

Hated parties.

These people reminded me of how nonexistent I truly was.

Except … the way Haden studied me stripped me down to my soul and breathed knowledge of what lurked underneath. I had just met the guy, but maybe he was right. Maybe I would do something shameful.

Mercedes's laugh squealed above the others as she splashed Corbin right in the face. The grin melted off his mouth as he cussed her out, asking if she knew just how long it took him to look that good.

"No time," Everett said, pulling his boyfriend close and nuzzling his neck. "Because everyone knows you're perfect."

"Cringe," Tate said. Their swooped hair had miraculously remained dry.

"As cringe as you groping Sasha while we were in the van? It's poor form." Corbin tossed a wave at the other two.

Tate grinned wickedly as they shook their hair out, meeting Sasha's eyes with a threat that they'd do it again.

"Look who I found!" Ridley sang over the others. He tore off his shirt in a fluid motion and jumped into the hot tub. Shorts and all.

I was fairly certain he still had his car keys and phone in his pockets, but I wasn't about to point that out.

"Zoe!" Mercedes yelled, pulling Ridley into her and making space on this side of the hot tub. Some of the water trickled over the edge.

It felt strange standing there fully clothed watching them. This was how horror movies started. A group of long-term friends trying to have a fun night before they headed back for their senior year of college. And it was always because of some—

"You look like you're thinking too much." Haden's hand landed on my shoulder, and I sucked in a breath.

Heat crept along my skin, the same feeling I had earlier when I was pressed against the pool table. Ignited from the inside out.

"You shouldn't grab random girls at parties," I lowered my voice.

"Oh?"

"You never know if any of them are armed."

"Armed with what, I wonder?" Haden's breath brushed against my neck.

"Who is this?" Mercedes asked, glancing up at me.

"The guy from the cafe? The guy you saw earlier?"

"It's a fun party trick, isn't it?" His words licked the shell of my ear, meant only for me. "It's been like burning in the fires, and the irony isn't lost on me."

"Are you coming in?" Mercedes acted like I hadn't spoken, but I shook it off. Bizarre things were happening tonight, and it wasn't just because of seeing every single high school clique hanging out in the same place at the same time.

"Sure." I reached for the hem of my shirt, but Haden's fingers found my wrists.

"Allow me?"

Goosebumps pebbled along my skin. Nothing could have prepared me for the way his voice dropped low into a growl. The sound cascaded along me like raindrops, reminding me there were other parts of my soul that were alive.

What in the fires was wrong with me?

I stepped back and turned to face him. Roaming his features, I admired the nearly inky black eyes that had electric dark brown edges. A strong jaw with dark hued stubble. Blond hair that lay in heavy, chaotic waves with darker roots. He wore a simple hoodie and jeans. Nothing that should have made me gush.

Except his jeans fell on his hips in a way that promised definition. His broad shoulders filled out the sweatshirt, and I would put money on everything underneath that being very lickable.

Maybe I should run away. Because there was something about this cursed guy that made me forget how I didn't *have* these feelings. Not normally.

"Sure," I said instead, feeling like my tongue was about to plaster itself to the roof of my mouth.

He stepped forward. His fingers grazed my waist as he dipped them underneath my shirt. His eyes stayed on mine as he lifted the fabric up and over my head. As my hair cascaded down along my face and shoulders, he tucked a lock behind my ear. Fingers lingered against my skin. I expected him to look down, ogle me like some kind of prize.

But his gaze stayed firmly on my eyes.

The intensity stripped my soul clean from my body. I stood in the middle of the party, but I might as well have been on the other side of the universe. The tension between us built like a lava flow underneath the surface, ready to erupt.

"Zoe!" Mercedes whined. "Get your ass in here. You're taking forever, and the water is delightful."

I didn't want to jump into the hot tub. I didn't want to climb in with my rowdy friends. I didn't want to watch Tate try to sink Ridley into the bubbles. I didn't want to see Corbin and Everett give each other light, reassuring touches. Nor did I want to hear Mercedes and Sasha talk about how fantastic their junior years in college were.

My breathing picked up, nostrils flaring. "I think ... I'd rather do something shameful."

Haden smirked. An eyebrow lifted in invitation.

"What the heck does that even *mean*?" Mercedes leaned over the side of the hot tub, looking up at me. Her big eyes would bend anyone else to her will, but not me. Not this time. "You should have fun, not do ... whatever you were planning to do."

"Oh, it will be a lot of fun." Haden took a step closer to me. The smoldering look in his eyes held promise, made the air spark with it. I wanted to strip him down right there, have him take me however he wanted.

On an exhale, I forced myself to calm down and broke our eye contact. It was like standing on the edge of a cliff, looking down at the face of it. Watching as the bottom stretched farther and farther away. My toes curled inexplicably over the crumbling dirt. I wanted to fall.

Worse, I believed every word Haden said. His fingers hooked underneath my chin, tilting my face so I would have to look at him again. His lips hovered close to mine, and his breath reminded me of cinnamon—fiery and feral.

"Some might say it could be *sinful*, though I never particularly liked that term."

Our mouths were moments apart from colliding. I forgot how to breathe as I perched on the precipice. My life was about to change forever. We inched closer together. Energy charged between us. Electricity tore across my skin as tingles of anticipation stretched out along my nerves. I wanted this, wanted him. Needed to experience everything this man had to offer.

As soon as our lips nearly brushed, Ridley jerked on my arm, toppling me straight into the hot tub while I still had my pants on with *my* phone inside them.

I jumped up, soaking wet in the middle of the jacuzzi, and whirled on Ridley. "What the fuck?!" Grabbing my phone, I tossed it onto my dry shirt, hoping the new water-resistant feature would actually work. Goodness knew I couldn't afford a new phone on top of everything else. "I was in the middle of something!"

"Yeah, taking your sweet ass time. Chill, Zoe. It's a party."

If this asshole told me to relax one more fucking time.

I glanced up at Haden, pushing my hair out of my eyes. The soaking brown strands spread across my face. I expected him to be annoyed, frustrated, or turned off. Because men hardly ever enjoyed witnessing the rage of women.

Instead, amusement crested his features, eyes hooded as he watched me. He smirked and slowly unzipped his hoodie. Shoulders shrugged out of the material, and it tumbled to the ground. His t-shirt was nothing special. Plain. Black. But the way it stretched across his chest played with every sense in my body. I wanted him more than *anyone*.

Mercedes wrapped her arms around me. "What *are* you staring at?"

"Yeah, Zoe." My name on his tongue spread fire to my core. "What are you staring at?" His fingers trailed along the hem of his shirt. "I'll show you mine if you show me yours."

I contemplated taking off my royal blue bikini. It hugged me like a sports bra. But with his eyes raking along my skin, I crossed my arms over my chest. Never had I felt more exposed than in this moment, and I certainly wasn't going to make matters worse. Heat flooded my cheeks, not just from the spa.

Mercedes, clearly over my long pauses and my inability to speak, drifted back toward Ridley.

The moment hung in the air, me with my arms stubbornly crossed while he stared at me. It was as if everyone in the hot tub had boiled into oblivion, melting into the background.

"Not able to be corrupted?" he asked.

"By you?" My voice gasped out. "Maybe."

"Zoe." This time, my name was like ice water poured over my libido. My friends were calling for me from miles away. I was swept in the tidal wave of lust for Haden. The last thing I wanted was to face them.

"What?" I asked, turning back to the group. Heat rose to my cheeks. Every part of my body wanted to be set alight. "You're a dick, Ridley."

He grinned, ruffling his black matted hair. "Takes one to know one."

"Did you spend all year thinking about that comeback?"

"Obviously." Mercedes wrapped her arms around him, pulling him close. She burrowed her face in his neck, peppering him with kisses.

Before I had another chance to argue, arms enfolded me. Haden dragged me onto his lap. Fingers curled around my hips. He had gotten into the water so fast, and now … my cheeks must have been bright red. He was shirtless. Sculpted. Perfection. A masterpiece. I had to lick my lips to make sure I wasn't drooling. Yeah, everything about him screamed *delicious*.

"Oh, hey, it's the pretty boy from earlier," Merce said.

"How does this curse work if they can see you now?" I kept my voice low, glancing over at Mercedes. She seemed momentarily uninterested in Haden, as if he was sometimes there and sometimes not.

"Sometimes, I can break through it—the barrier that separates me from everyone else."

"But you didn't have to break through it for me to see you," I said as a statement.

"No, I didn't," he agreed. "And it appears your friends can see me when you're close to me or interacting with me, but not all the time." Haden's voice licked the shell of my ear as I nestled back against him. "But otherwise, most people haven't—or don't—see me."

"What about me? Aren't I pretty?" Ridley gave Merce brown puppy dog eyes.

There I went again, forgetting the rest of them existed because my attention had been trained on Haden. Something about him sucked me in, and I liked it. I'd love for the rest of the world to disappear and for it to just be us, get to know him, figure out what made me want to peel back his layers.

"You've always been pretty," Tate said. Sasha had been running her hands through their hair, making it stick up at odd angles. Their normal emo swoop gone in lieu of the wet, mussy, dark brown mop. "You were voted … what was it?"

"Most likely to turn into a pop star?" Everett suggested.

"No, it wasn't that mundane. Our superlatives were unhinged." Tate grinned.

"It was most likely to get held for ransom that someone would pay," I said. Every single person in our graduating class had a superlative. It was a tradition at our high school and was not *officially* school sanctioned. But every senior class did it, and everyone had one.

Except me.

Just like I was readily left behind for events, I was easily forgotten about in the superlatives. Sometimes, I wondered if I even existed. Maybe that was why I saw Haden. In my mind, I gave myself the *most likely to disappear with no one noticing* award. The self-deprecating humor made me feel better, but only just.

Everett and Mercedes were the two who made me feel seen within our group. Sasha and Tate had always been involved with each other—their relationship was akin to something magnetic. Ridley, before he found himself wrapped up in Mercedes, had been a decent friend, but we drifted farther apart the moment he started dating her. It sometimes made me wonder if we had ever been friends at all. And Corbin was fine—nothing against him, but we hadn't clicked.

"Right!" Mercedes clapped her hands together, causing a small spray to cascade over the rest of us. "And I got most likely to become a biker chick. As if. Those things are death traps."

"Bitch, you take selfies next to every bike we go by," Sasha laughed.

"Because it's part of *marketing* myself. Do you know how many followers those get me?" She rolled her eyes. "It's like you don't even know me, Sasha." They erupted in a fit of giggles.

"Forget those. Remember Everett's?" Ridley said.

"Nope!" Everett yelled. "No way."

"What was it?" Haden whispered into my ear. Goosebumps rose where his breath kissed my skin.

"Oh, shit!" Tate yelled, laughing. "I totally forgot."

"Do not, Tate," Everett warned.

Sasha giggled.

Corbin's face grew red as he fought back his own laugh.

"Corbin!" Everett put his palm over his face. "Not you too."

"Most likely to be seduced by a vampire." I turned toward Haden. His fingers roamed around the hem of my jeans, which were now adhered to me like a second skin thanks to Ridley.

"I really liked those movies, okay? I watched them one too many times, and well …"

"You had a thing for—"

Everett must have elbowed Corbin, because there was a grunt, and he abruptly stopped talking. The conversation continued around us, but I was no longer paying attention.

Haden's fingers had curled around the button of my jeans. "Do you want to get rid of these?"

I nodded, sucking in a breath as he unhooked the button. He slipped his thumbs under my pants and tugged down. My heart thudded against my chest. My bikini was still securely on, but that didn't stop his hands from roaming over my skin as he peeled the jeans down my body. His eyes stayed locked on mine. So much eye contact, and yet, it felt like his gaze roamed over the plains of my skin. With the way heat rushed to my cheeks, I was glad none of my friends were paying attention.

"Shit, that's right! They never gave Zoe one, did they?" Tate said, slapping themselves on the forehead.

Pressing my eyes shut, I tried to maintain a sense of calm, of completion, of telling myself I was enough. Just as myself.

"Eyes on me," Haden's husky voice bolted through my skin. My eyes snapped open. His dark ones held my gaze as his hands trailed under my ass, bringing my pants along with them. And fuck if he wasn't doing something to my core. My body sang for him.

"That was bullshit if you ask me," Sasha said, insulted on my behalf.

"We should come up with one for her right now," Corbin said.

Helpful. All of them. So helpful.

"Lift up for me," Haden commanded. His voice kept me grounded, placing me firmly in this moment between us, as much as a part of me wanted to disappear.

I swallowed, doing what he told me to. His palms trailed along my thighs, inching my pants lower in a languorous gesture.

"Good girl." His voice curled into my bones.

I needed him. Screw this hot tub, and screw everyone else. Except … maybe I should wait until my pants weren't tying my ankles together.

"Most likely to major in something she hates?" Ridley suggested.

I fought an eye roll as I settled my head against Haden's shoulder, arching my back to give him better access.

"Most likely to become way more successful than the rest of her friends?" Corbin added. Okay, he officially gained some points.

"Most likely to move to New York with me!" Merce yelled.

"Babe," Ridley whined.

"Most likely to own a bunch of cats?" Everett snorted. "Sorry, Zoe, I had to."

My grip dug into Haden's legs.

Haden's fingers tickled the back of my knees as his chest pushed us forward. He shimmied my pants off the rest of the way.

"Most likely to come around my fingers." His tone was low, directly in my ear. The words seared through my body, piping hot and going straight to my nerves.

Why in the fires was I in the hot tub instead of … Right, Ridley's fault.

My pants came up and out of the pool, slapping against the ground next to my shirt. I'd have to find the washer and put those in later. No one seemed to notice the tension between Haden and me, as they were consumed by their desire to figure out what superlative I should be.

"It's interesting, isn't it?" Haden's arms wrapped around me and pulled me into him. There was no mistaking his hard length. "The world can go on without you. It can go on without me. Oblivion can come and suck us away, and everything would continue. But I promise, if you let me, I will show you a future where you are more than an anecdote." Brushing my hair away from my neck, he kissed my skin.

I clambered out of the hot tub.

"Where are you going?" Merce asked.

"Going to dry my pants." I glared briefly at Ridley to sell the act. I didn't give a *shit* about my pants at the moment.

"Oh, come on, Zoe. I didn't mean anything by it. Don't be like that."

Merce slapped him on the shoulder. "She's not being like anything. You did get her phone wet. Find some rice and dump it in there, babe. We'll see you when you're ready." Mercedes gave me a conspiratorial wink. As Haden climbed out of the water, her eyes glanced at him. A knowing smirk stretched across her lips. "He's hot," she mouthed.

Cursed or not, I would not let tonight go to waste.

Haden

Her friends had made this easier than I had anticipated. The spark inside her soul had grown hotter the longer we were around them, and when they started picking apart the type of person she should have been, it was an inferno threatening to consume her soul. But as soon as we were away from them, her soul's temperature died back to a cool breeze.

Still, the potential was there.

And it made me hungry.

She snatched her clothes and marched away from the pool area. I grabbed mine as well, only in my boxer briefs, but I couldn't give a shit as I followed her while bending others out of her path. The sooner I could fuck her, the better. My cock ached, wanting nothing more than to make her mine. Claim her for all eternity. This was the type of soul we longed for back in the fires.

The not yet corrupted.

Most people were lukewarm. Performing a mixture of selfish and selfless acts in their lives that combined to a mediocre existence. Most of those people would ascend. Most. But these souls, the cool ones, the ones that *should* ascend? If we could debauch them, turn them to depravity, well … that was something worth bragging about, a status symbol in the fires.

But this wasn't about status. No. I wanted her.

Mine. The word echoed inside me, burrowing like a seed into my heart. Wanting to burst forth with something new, blossom into an unadulterated passion stronger than anything known in the fires.

She trailed up the stairs, sauntered down the hallway, opened a bedroom that had double doors, and walked inside like she owned the place. I slammed them shut behind us, but she was already off, opening other closets. This was the en suite, with an attached bathroom and huge vaulted ceilings. I had been to the cabin before—Thomas came here to get away on holiday. Plus, he always felt nervous whenever I was around other people for too long. He thought I would hurt them if given enough access.

Judging by the curse I had settled over the house, he wasn't wrong.

I leaned against the wall, crossed my arms, and watched as she continued to open every single door. "It's on your left."

She slid me a glance but crossed the small hallway that led to the bathroom and slipped open the door. A stacked washer and dryer stood behind them. She let out a breath. "I swear if my phone is dead, I'm going to kill Ridley." Zoe stuffed her pants inside the washer and started a quick cycle. Then she fiddled with the blackened screen in her hands. "Fuck. Maybe I need rice."

As she crossed by me, I plucked the phone from her fingers. The screen flickered on. "It's fine. See?" I dropped it to the ground. It clattered, sounding heavier in the confined space. I stepped toward her.

She retreated a step. "Okay, cool. Uhm …"

I hooked my finger under her chin and forced her to look at me. I loved how tan she looked against my light skin tone, but I craved to see how perfect she'd look against my demonic form. "Where's the confidence from earlier?"

Her hazel eyes blinked up at me, pulling me in. I wanted to bite her neck, fall into her, make her come apart on my tongue. My *real* tongue. "I don't know. It's … a front I get with them. A mask?" She blinked, shaking her head. "Fuck, I don't know why I said that. I don't talk about this shit."

"Talk about it." I took another step forward, closing the gap between us. She was in nothing more than her bathing suit, and I was in my briefs. "Tell me everything."

She shuddered. "Okay, well, I'm pretty sure *that's* the most seductive thing a guy has ever said to me. You actually want me to talk?"

"As long as you are able to, yes." I pressed my lips against her cheek, trailed my tongue along her skin. She tasted sweet, but the hot tub chemicals masked it. That wouldn't do. "I don't know how long you'll be able to talk, but if you can speak, you can tell me."

"What's that supposed to—"

She didn't get to finish, because she yelped as I scooped her into my arms. I brought us to the bathroom, turned the shower on, and placed her down inside. The icy stream quickly warmed, hitting both of us as I backed her up against the slate tile.

"Okay, well—" She gasped as my teeth grazed her neck. "I lost my mom when I was pretty young. My father was long gone before that. It was me and my grandmother. She was kind of a nasty woman and suffered from alcoholism. And my friends, well, they don't really *know* about any of that, because I kept this facade. The quiet girl, the nice girl, but really, being home felt a bit like—ah!"

I exposed her breast, kissing the top of the sphere. My thumb grazed a line over her nipple, marveling as it pebbled underneath my touch. I made circles around the sensitive peak, and she arched into me, pressing herself against my length.

"Okay, this is like … totally not a sexy thing to be talking about right now."

"Mm … Do you want to talk, or do you want my tongue to split you open?"

"The latter one. Please."

I chuckled. "If that's the compliance I get from touching your nipple, I'd hate to see what happens once I get you to orgasm on my face."

"I'll probably do whatever you want," she breathed. Eagerness widened her eyes.

"Whatever I want is a dangerous game." My thumb swiped back over her hardened nub. Her hips thrust forward, but I pressed mine into her, letting her feel just how hard I was. Desire pooled inside me, wanting to be unleashed. My demonic form pressed against my skin, welling with need. I wanted to unchain myself, but the fail safes refused to let me go. "I don't think you should give me that kind of power. Not yet, anyway."

I met her gaze. She sucked her lower lip in between her teeth. With my fingers trailing the delicate swell of her breast, I said, "You never told them any of the shit going on at home. Why?" Tracing my palm up her neck, I cupped both sides of her jaw, angling us so my lips hovered an inch from hers. Her breath hit my skin. I wanted to taste her, but I also wanted to know her. "Why tell me and not them?"

She shrugged. "I don't know. You feel … like you *get* it." She had no idea just how much. The pressure to conform, to be the perfect specimen, to become something greater than yourself. There was constraint in that. "And when my grandmother passed, leaving me and my cousin behind, I don't know … there was this sense of relief. Because I wouldn't have to deal with her anymore, but that makes me feel guilty, you know? Because why should I wish death on anyone?" Zoe shook her head, pressing her hands against my chest. "Okay, can we … refocus, because I distinctly remember a few promises you made?"

"Which one do you want me to fill first?" I ran my tongue along my lips. "The one where you can't breathe anymore, or the one where you stop being a footnote in someone else's story?"

"Both?"

I smirked. "Both it is." I sank to my knees. She sucked in a glorious little breath as she gazed at me with a yearning I hadn't seen in a long time.

"Haden, I—"

"I'm going to take care of you." My hands ran down the length of her body, pausing at the sides of her breasts. I ran my thumbs under the delicate, soft skin as her brown hair fell in wet rivulets, perfectly framing her. I leaned forward, pressing my lips to her mound as she sucked in another breath.

"Do you want to know why I moved us into the shower?" I looked up as I slipped the ties of her bikini off. "Because I want to *taste* you without the chlorine." Pressing my nose into her skin, I inhaled, sucked a breath so deep it threatened to make her part of my bones. "And you smell delicious."

She wiggled under my touch, arching toward me with the slightest undulation. "It's just … it's been a bit for me, so I'm a little nervous," she admitted. Her jaw worked. "I don't know why I'm telling you all this."

Likely because of her pull toward me, the sway in the very fabric of her being. The way the fire clawed inside her to get out, to be near me. "Don't worry. I'll get you ready for me." I gazed up at her. "You good?" Water caught on my eyelashes as the shower ran over our skin, dripping from her onto me.

"Of course." Her pupils dilated.

"Good." My hands found her hips, and I backed her up against the wall. "Hands on my shoulders. Do not move."

Her eyes grew huge and glossy, but she pressed her lips together with a solemn nod.

I leaned forward and placed my lips against her sensitive nerves. Her body jolted, but didn't go anywhere with my grip firm on her. "You smell incredible."

"Come on, I can't—"

I didn't give her a chance to finish, because I gave her a long, languishing lick. My tongue swirled around her as I brought her clit into my mouth and gave a delicate suck. Her breath caught in her throat as her hands found my shoulders. Her fingers dug into my skin as her hips sought more.

I stopped and pulled back abruptly, staring at her from my half-lidded gaze. "What did I say?"

"Don't move?" she squeaked.

"And are you going to listen to me?" I ran my hands down her hips, feeling the smooth skin of her upper thighs as I wrapped my hands around her, edging her apart.

"I don't know," she rasped.

"Honesty. I like it." My thumbs traced her inner thigh. "Every time you move, I'll stop moving. Deal?"

"No deal. That sounds like torture."

"It just might be." My eyes darkened, and I had to rein in the demonic part of me. Because edging was the most wondrous kind of torture. Maybe once she warmed up to the idea of who I was, she'd be more amiable to me having my way with her. But this was a question, seeing how far she was willing to go, to play into everything I fancied.

Were we a good match or had I been deprived from touch long enough that the first person to look my way had sent me spiraling? Father would likely say the latter, due to my internal weaknesses. But he wasn't here, and she was. No one from the fires was here, which meant I had no pressure to be anything more than who I was. My sole focus became giving her pleasure that bordered on pain.

"Slightly different wording then? If you move without my permission, then I'll stop. And I will give you permission to move *sometimes*. Deal?"

She swallowed, gazing down at me. Her lips parted, and as the water traced down her face, catching on the pink swell of her mouth, it made my cock twitch. I would sink in between those perfect lips someday. I would wrap my fist around her hair and watch as she took me down. Force her to swallow as I entered her throat.

I'd love watching her eyes well with tears, all because of me.

"Deal." When she agreed, it felt like a part of my soul was being set free.

I smirked, pressing my tongue against her slit. She sucked in a breath, but her hips stayed still. Her fingertips tightened around my shoulders, but I liked the pressure, so I let that go. Running my tongue along her, I toyed with her clit again. I reached around to her perfect ass, pulling her firmly against my mouth. My other hand found her entrance.

I sank the tip of one of my fingers inside her, testing how wet she was for me. She was soaked, but as soon as I brought my finger out for a taste, the water washed it away. With a growl, I dove between her legs, pushing my tongue into her.

She gasped and bucked against me. I stopped moving, tongue barely inside her. A glorious whimper escaped her lips. She stilled with eyes steady on me as she waited on bated breath. I gave her a wink and slowly thrust my tongue in, wishing I wasn't bound by Thomas's summoning circle. The things I could do with my mouth alone … For one thing, my tongue was longer than a human's, and I ached to fuck her with it, feel her flutter around me as I plunged in and out of her.

I pulled back, circling her nerves again as I shoved two fingers into her. She gasped. Feeling her body clench against me was almost enough to make me stop, but her hips trembled without too much movement. "Now you're going to ride my face until you come. That's the only movement you get. Understood? No hands, and your eyes stay on me."

She almost nodded but caught herself with a confused frown. "Yes."

"Eager to please. I also like that. Very much." My fingers were soaked as I rotated my wrist, curling them. I watched her hooded eyes. Her pupils blew, and as soon as I hit that spot, her hips bucked forward, riding my mouth exactly like I asked. That sensitive place inside her was all I needed. Keeping a steady rhythm, I listened to the beautiful moans escaping her mouth. It was a symphony to my ears. Those delicate gasps followed by desperate panting as she moved her hips, thrusting into my mouth like she was the dominant one.

But she had given me power over her.

She was perfect for what I needed, a treasure, and it excited me to see what we could make together. Of course, she'd be pissed when she discovered the truth. The cold piece of her soul would be indignant, but the spark inside her wanted to flare to life, become a glorious firestorm bigger than anything the world or the skies could handle.

No, she'd be destined for the fires, eventually. I would make sure of that.

Especially now that I had her flavor on my tongue. She was a burst of sunshine, a cloudless summer sky, a promise of light that comes after years of only seeing the dark. As her moans escalated into shrieks, I couldn't help but smile.

"Come with my name on your lips."

"Haden, I—" She sucked in a breath before another wail escaped her mouth. Her body clenched around me, a pulse of wetness surrounded my fingers as she rode out her orgasm. She sucked in several breaths as I continued my gentle ministrations, allowing her to come down to earth slowly. Once the fluttering inside her subsided, I eased out of her.

I slammed the water off, standing up in one swift motion. Picking her up, I walked both of us out of the shower and into the bedroom, tossing her down haphazardly on top of the bed. Her drenched body soaked through the comforter. I enjoyed watching her boneless, sprawled out and ready for me.

She blinked hazily at me. "What are we doing now?"

"We?" I crawled on top of her, cupping her jaw so she'd look at me. "We're not doing anything. I'm fucking you. And if I'm feeling really generous, maybe I'll let you fuck me, too." Pressing my lips to the side of her jaw, I trailed my tongue along her skin, sucking her neck in between my teeth.

I bit hard.

She gasped. Her arms circled around me as if on instinct and pulled me into her. I was determined to get lost in her. I would allow myself this moment of bliss before the chaos began.

Zoe

His teeth sank into the skin on my neck. My arms wrapped around him, pulling him closer instead of wrenching away. I had never felt confident exploring anything with Kent, and I wasn't sure what I liked and what I didn't. But this? I liked *this*. The way he commanded me, the power he held. I wanted to give myself over to him. I trusted him, despite him promising me shame later.

And maybe it was because of his suggestion that I trusted him more.

I appreciated his directing me, because without it, I had no idea what I was doing. Sure, when I had clambered out of the jacuzzi earlier, this had felt like the best decision I had ever made. Forget what the future would bring, because being able to come while riding his mouth? There was no shame in that—only carnal pleasure that grew inside me, threatened to stretch my skin from the inside out.

He had made me feel so good—so *confident*—that I might never be ashamed again. The reverential way he took me in captivated me. His energy sucked me in, making me want to stay forever in his orbit. His eyes hypnotized me and had seemed to darken the moment he tasted me. Being his sole focus had made me come apart. It had been easy to lose myself in that moment.

Plus, he was gorgeous. Every part of him was chiseled edges and honed muscle. Defined, smooth plains I wanted to lick. His grip had been controlling, demanding, and I swore he could break me apart with nothing more than a look.

I wanted him to unravel me.

We hadn't spent a lot of time conversing, but while it had been brief, he already knew more about my life than my friends did. With the way my heart raced inside my chest at the promise of *more*, I was certain this was a terrible thing growing between us, something infectious I wasn't sure I could get rid of.

We were still drenched from the shower, but nothing deterred him. His hands roamed my skin with expertise. He explored me, as if he wanted to know me—*all* of me. Inside and out.

"You're gorgeous." His voice dipped low, as his hand hovered right over my sternum, placed in between my breasts.

"I'm okay."

His eyes flashed black. A frown pulled at his lips. "Don't disparage yourself."

"Until I feel the shame you spoke about earlier?"

Lips quirking, his fingers roved over the soft swell of my skin. "Yes, until then. Right now, you should feel nothing but ... pleasure." He pinched my nipple softly, plucking it between his fingers and setting my body alight. My back arched. He chuckled, low and throaty. "You have stunning curves, soft skin, and your hair."

I rolled my eyes.

He wrapped one of his hands around my chin, forcing my face toward him. His eyes rimmed with brown, rich and deep, but the dark flecks became boundless as he took me in, searching my gaze with his. Almost like our souls were meant to meld.

I had never felt this intensity from anyone else.

"I think you don't believe me." His fingers traced lines down my chin onto my neck, where he settled his grip. He didn't apply pressure, but his hold was firm. "And that won't do. So, tell me. What can I do to convince you of your beauty?"

I wanted to squirm from the question. No one had treated me as anything special. Brown hair. Hazel eyes, which were probably the only unique thing about me. White skin that tanned okay in the sun, so it looked good right now since we were in the middle of summer. But I had been so busy dealing with my personal life that I had neglected a lot—like getting a proper haircut. Sure, I had curves, but I also hadn't been working out recently, so my muscles held a softness.

I couldn't find the motivation to care, not when everything else felt overwhelming and my life kept falling apart. Haden, however, made me care. He made me feel reassured, but that was a stupid thought. I had just met him, and I couldn't allow myself to fall for something like this. He said the right things, but it was to get what he wanted. And right now, I reciprocated that desire. If we were on the same page, I could allow myself an indulgence.

Deep down, I knew what I needed—self-confidence, without some guy boosting it up. For the moment, though, it felt right. I enjoyed being the object of someone's affection; not because he wanted Mercedes, but because he wanted *me*.

I frowned, having thought entirely too hard about his question.

"You don't have to answer." His free hand cupped my breast, bringing my stiff peak toward his lips. His tongue flicked out, and his eyes never left mine, even as he licked. My core clenched as his teeth molded around me, nipping at my nerves as my body ached for more. As his tongue played games, his hand drifted down, wandered over my stomach, brushed against my mound, and spread my thighs.

I sucked in a breath as his fingers found my entrance. He swirled my wetness as his smirk grew. "Ready for me already?" His finger sank into the first knuckle, and my hips rose unbidden off the bed to meet him.

"See, I don't believe it. Someone as stunning as you second guessing yourself? That's not you. That was poison placed there by someone else. Likely a man, likely someone seeking to ruin you. Because I see it." He worked inside me, thrusting in and out as my breath came to me in small gasps. A second finger joined the first, and I rolled my hips against him in response.

I still couldn't take my eyes off him. The intensity of his gaze held me spellbound. Normally, I would feel bashful, shy, but not with him. Not while feeling so exposed and hungry for more.

"I see the confidence ready to break through the surface. It's all yours, but you need to give yourself permission to find it."

How was he splitting apart pieces of my soul while he brought me toward the edge? How could he see inside me and feel the borders of my uncertainties? Was it possible to connect with someone this quickly?

No, I told myself. Because things this easy always had a catch. Every single person had a dark side, even guys who made me feel like I was the meaning of the universe they sought for their entire life. There was always something malicious, a layer underneath. Would it be a wickedness I could handle or something that would tear us apart?

Whatever. Right now, I wanted to take advantage of this moment. I loved the way his eyes drank me in, as if I were an oasis in the desert. I enjoyed how his fingers expertly curled in me. He chased my pleasure like it was the only thing keeping him alive. My body bloomed under his touch, flourished into something new, something I could believe was beautiful.

"I want to feel you fall apart on my fingers one more time. Make sure you're ready for me." He pushed in a third, and I gasped at the invasion. Twisting his hand, he scissored his fingers, and I sucked in a breath. "Fuck, you're tight."

"Haden, please …" I wasn't normally one to talk during sex, let alone beg, but the words slipped out of my mouth.

"I need to get you ready. Can you hold on for me?" he asked, edging on a desperate growl. Perhaps there was a bit of evil in him, but if this was it, it was the most delectable kind.

My teeth plunged into my lower lip as I squirmed. He thrust his fingers in, fluttering them against my nerves, and the precipice drew closer. His teeth clamped around my nipple, and I screamed as I came apart, everything inside me clenching as I shamelessly rode him. He coaxed me through my orgasm, holding me tightly with his other hand as I spun off into space.

A desperate mewl escaped me as he pulled his fingers out. He brought his hand to his mouth. He sucked each finger dry, eyes still on me. I was breathless, and my heart stopped beating.

"You ready?"

"Ready?" What could I possibly be *ready* for when I already felt boneless and spent? Pathetic really, as he was ready to go longer into the night.

"Third time's the charm."

"Haden, I—" I had never come so much during sex, and we hadn't *had* sex yet. I felt like I should stop, like I needed to stop, but I didn't want to. My body screamed to keep going, to see what more he could give me. I deserved a night of fun, a night of attention, a night of passion. "Yeah. Okay." The words came out clipped, chased on the edge of a breath I couldn't gather.

That smile appeared back on his lips as he brushed his knuckles gently over my breast. My body stretched to meet his. "Yeah, you're ready?"

"We need a condom."

He stared at me, blinking long and slow. His brow furrowed, not with annoyance, but with something akin to curiosity. As if the thought of protection had never occurred to him.

"Is that what you want?"

My eyes widened, gearing myself up for an argument. Kent had tried to get me to fuck him without a condom, and that night hadn't ended well for either of us. I swallowed. "Of course. Don't—I mean, I don't really know you."

"You will. This isn't a one-time thing, Zoe. Not at all. But—" His hand ran over my cheek, thumb pressing against my lower lip. The way he searched my expression might as well have been a lightning bolt into my essence. "But whatever you want, I'll respect. If you want me to use one, I will."

My nerves unraveled. I had been expecting him to protest, but no, he accepted my needs without a blink. This was only for one night, I reminded myself, not an eternity. Perhaps he thought we'd have a date or something in the future, but he could also say anything to get me to drop my guard. Either way, I wanted to sleep with him, regardless of what happened tomorrow. But tonight, we'd use protection.

Thankfully, Mercedes hadn't let me come to this party without preparation. She had forced me to take a condom, and while I had protested at the time, I was suddenly grateful for it. I supposed I should also thank her for dragging me out here in the first place, because this man had the fingers of a god.

"There's one in my pants that—" Oh. Went into the pool and then the washer.

Fucking Ridley.

"Relax." Haden ran his fingers down my sternum, over my stomach. He pressed a careful peck to my lips and rolled off the bed, grabbing one from the top drawer. "I've been here before."

Heat rose to my cheeks as I got a good, hard look at him as he took off his boxer briefs. His sculpted muscles pointed in a v-shape directly to his—holy shit. He was *big*. It was no wonder he used three fingers to get me ready, because that hadn't been enough. Four fingers, at least.

"There's lube if we need it too, but—"

I shook my head, because wetness pooled between my legs. He had worked me up enough that I didn't need any. Or at least, I wanted to try to take him without any.

He rolled the condom on, watching me while his fingers expertly ran along his dick. "Look at you, gorgeously presented before me, but still eying me like you're the one in charge."

"I'm not?"

"Not anymore." He smirked. Climbing back on top of me, he pulled my legs open, displaying me before him. His fingers ran along my thighs. "I'll give you whatever you need to make you feel in control, but Zoe, I have to promise you something." He leaned over me, holding himself above me on his muscular arms. His hips pushed forward so the head of his cock rested against my entrance. He looked huge next to me, but I could take him. My core clenched at the anticipation of being full.

"What's that?" I asked, breathless as he ran his length along me. He glided along my nerves, making me drip for him.

"I will be the dominant one in bed, but if you ever want to stop, we stop. I'll try to make you feel so good that you'll want to keep going. You'll be my queen outside of this room, and I'll worship the ground you walk on. But in it? You're my perfect little slut." He sank inside me with those words, and the stretch was unreal.

No one had ever said that to me and meant it with affection, and my mind blanked with bliss. I gasped, latched onto his shoulders, and dug my nails into his skin. *Fuck.*

He grabbed onto my chin, and my eyes blinked open. I hadn't realized I had closed them.

"Watch."

My eyes trailed down his chest, to his hips, to where he spread me wide before him. He was barely inside me, just the head of his cock, but he pulled back and thrust forward again. He slipped farther in. It had been so long, and Haden was right—I was tight. The way he filled me demanded compliance from my soul.

I panted heavily. My breath turned raspy as his fingers tightened their hold. His other hand swept along my skin, down to my core, coming to my bundle of nerves. He pressed down with his thumb, making slow, circular motions as he watched my reaction.

With every thrust, he closed the gap between us. My hips bucked to meet him, desperate to have him all the way inside me. A whimper escaped my lips. As soon as he pushed his hips flush against mine, I cried out. Between his thumb working my clit and how much he stretched me, I was close. Again.

This man might become the death of me.

"Not yet," he said. "I want you to come apart when I command it."

"Then—" I whined as he understood, taking his fingers away.

He smirked. "You good?"

Sucking in a steadying breath, I tore my eyes away from where we were seated together, meeting his dark gaze. "I'm good."

His lips crashed against mine. He fucked into me so hard and fast

I gasped into his mouth. He sucked my breath away, catching my lips with teeth and ferocity. We were fire, coming together as explosions threatened to blot out my vision, but I held back as I found myself again. I grazed my teeth against his lower lip, and he growled into my mouth. The vibration in his chest shot menace through me—this desire to *take* and *consume*, which I had never felt before. Was it from me or him? Did it matter?

His grip on my neck increased. My fingers grasped his shoulders as he rode me, each buck of his hips becoming more desperate. My eyes threatened to roll back in my head as the feeling became too much. Every one of my nerves was fried, sensitive; every part of me ignited.

"Zoe, stay with me." His hand pulsed along my skin, bringing me back into the moment. He was consuming me; I was sure of it. I would gladly hand over everything if it meant falling apart one more time at his hands. I would burn with him, eviscerate this house if it meant getting one more night.

Inky darkness threatened to swallow us whole, but my eyes stayed on his as he carried me through. Dancing along the edge of a knife, feeling the bite of it into my marrow. Fire threatened to overtake me as sweat beaded along my skin. I needed to explode. I needed to—

"Now," he growled, thrusting deeply.

My body splintered apart. I was split open, down to the very fabric of my soul. The skies parted, and several stars died. Haden continued a steady rhythm, rocking into me with a quiet command until my soul spun. He kissed me again. Long and deep, claiming and lingering. In this moment, I realized I was obsessed with this man. I wanted more, wanted his punishment, wanted his praise, wanted everything he deemed to give me.

His eyes searched mine as he pulled back. He combed his fingers through my hair, smoothing my locks away from my face. His cock pulsed inside me, causing a shiver to run down my spine. His smirk curled his lips up. "You good?"

"I'm good." Better than good. The best. Felt like I could conquer the world. Outside these doors, the party waited. The people, the fraternizing, the sham of it. Outside, I had to be someone different. But with him inside me, completely naked before him? I felt powerful. I felt alive. I felt *more*.

"Good." He pressed his lips to my nose, brushing the softest kiss against me. "Because there's something happening soon that you can't miss. A little surprise I put together for Thomas." His fingers trailed along the inside of my thighs. He pulled out of me, and I immediately missed the feeling of him nested inside me.

I had just met this guy, but I felt needy for him.

He rolled the condom off and chucked it into the waste basket without looking away from me. "When we do sleep together again, I'm not wearing a fucking condom. I want your cunt dripping with me. I want you to watch as I shove my cum back inside you." The words coiled around my brain, heady and full of promise. He toyed with my entrance with his finger, miming the gesture. I clenched around nothing, finding myself wanting the exact same thing. It should have scared me, terrified me, but ... "That's another promise."

"And if I say no?"

"You won't. Even with the shame you're about to feel."

I tilted my head at him, narrowing my eyes. "You say that, but I don't feel any different. This was ..." Perfection. Everything I needed. How could I ever feel ashamed of what we had just done? The universe had expanded, taking me with it.

His brow arched, eyes curled, as if he knew he had blown my world apart.

"Okay, sure. I feel *different*, but it's only because I had a mind-blowing orgasm or two."

"Three. I counted." He climbed off the bed and crossed to the laundry closet. I got a glorious view of his ass. It was tight, carved, just like the rest of him. And it looked incredibly edible. He grabbed my clothes. I hadn't remembered putting them into the dryer—only the washer—but when he handed them to me, they were crisp and warm. "When you look at me like that, it makes me want to stay naked with you."

I sucked on my lower lip as I began dressing. "If it were my choice, we would spend the rest of the night in here." I pulled on my shirt, still watching him. "But my friends might ask questions, and you said something important is going to happen. Is it Thomas's birthday?" Frankly, I had no idea when Thomas was born, nor did I care. In high school, he had never thrown a house party, so getting an invitation to one now was out of the ordinary.

Haden shrugged. "Not really, but I do think this party will be a night he remembers for the rest of eternity."

"Ominous." My lips twitched upward.

His laugh coiled around me. "I thought women liked a side of danger with their men."

An amused smile stretched across my face. "Of course. Wouldn't have fucked you otherwise."

"Is that what you did? Wasn't it the other way around?" He tugged on the collar of my t-shirt, pulling me in for a quick kiss. "I look forward to seeing your reaction to the announcement tonight. I cooked up something for this party, a night no one will ever forget. One that will make you more than you ever thought possible." The darkness in his eyes sucked me in like a black hole.

"I thought you already did that."

He nipped my lower lip. I could feel his smile as he thoroughly ravished my mouth. My cheeks hurt, my body ached, but I was elated down to my atoms. Muscles I hadn't used in a long time were coming back to life. Passion was a wick, and Haden the fire.

"Yes, and I'll do it again if you ever doubt yourself. Get your pants on. Find your friends. I need to grab Thomas so the true fun of tonight can begin."

My mouth opened.

He rested his finger on my lips. "And no, it's not to share you with him or anyone. At least, not anyone here. If you do, however, want to explore something like that, we can discuss it later. There are a few … people I'd be fine taking you with, but Thomas is not one of them."

That hadn't been what I was about to ask, but I blinked as heat flooded me. While I had no desire to be with someone like Thomas, was being *shared* something I wanted? I didn't know, but *anything* with Haden sounded like a good idea. I watched as he tugged on his shirt and left the room. Puffing out a breath, I sank back onto the sheets and reached in between my thighs. I was a little sore, but my stupid body desired to have him again. I hadn't had sex in a while, and apparently, my pussy wanted to make up for lost time.

Still, the suggestion of shame needled me. When he had said I'd feel shame, there had been an unbelievable amount of promise behind his words. So far, I hadn't. While I still didn't know his last name, I was confident he wasn't ditching me. This wasn't a make out at the beach and dip situation. The energy we had was cosmic. No, if anything, we'd be escaping here together in the morning.

I smiled at the thought, wondering where my newfound confidence had come from. Maybe it was from the three orgasms. Or maybe it was his promise to fuck me bare. Either way, I pulled on the rest of my clothes and headed into the booming bass and endless chatter. Curiosity struck me. What party trick was up next?

Haden

It tore out a part of my soul to leave her behind. She had been perfect, splayed out underneath me. Willing to do whatever I wanted to chase her own orgasmic high. Zoe was full of surprises, and I couldn't wait to see how she'd take all of me. Being with her had been better than I had imagined.

And the way she tasted.

I couldn't wait to see the flavor we made together, how sweet it would be on my tongue as I shoved my cum back inside her. But for now, I had a game to start, a curse to finish, and her survival to ensure.

Thomas's tepid soul was like a beacon in the sea. He felt a spot of nothing—blending so perfectly into the background he might as well have been wallpaper. Plus, having my time on Earth threaded to him meant our unending and frustrating connection. I couldn't wait for it to be transferred to someone else.

I turned straight for his old room but paused at the threshold.

Listening for a few moments, I sighed. Instead of the throes of passion, I heard crying. For fuck's sake. This was supposed to be a way for him to get something halfway decent before his inevitable demise, but instead, he was in a room with a crying girl.

I burst the door open without knocking.

Thomas had his arms wrapped around the girl. His eyes met mine, and a frown creased his lips.

Her face was buried in his shoulder, crying fervently. "I'm sorry for dumping this on you, but it was all—I don't know. I feel *stupid*." She startled and pulled away from him. Her eyes rose to view the doorway, but she looked past me.

After having someone stare at me with endless desire, having someone look through me was a blow to my ego. I enjoyed being seen, being heard, being acknowledged. Zoe's gaze had pierced through the three years of misery I had on this planet, stripping me down to the barren wasteland that sat in place of my soul. As this random blond woman failed to see me, my hatred for Thomas whirled to the forefront again.

Being invisible was its own kind of torture.

Him and his stupid fail safes.

I would say I was sorry for what was about to happen, but that would be a lie.

"Sorry." She rubbed underneath her eyes, peeling away thick layers of dark eyeliner. She shot up from the bed, smoothing out her shirt. The sheets appeared wrinkled, so maybe something happened before she cried? "I ... maybe we can talk about this some other time? Or like, I don't know grab dinner. I just ... I wasn't prepared for all these *emotions*. Seeing him after three years did something to me I wasn't ready for. You're great, though, you know?" The blond tucked her hair behind her ears and sucked her lip between her teeth. "You okay?"

"Are you?" Thomas asked, his eyes glancing at me. They seemed to ask for help, begged for it. I folded my arms over my chest and leaned against the door frame. Now he wanted my help? Fuck if that was happening.

"I'll be all right. I mean, I have been, right?" A watery film covered her eyes as she shook her head. Her mouth opened and closed a few times before she forced a giggle. "Shit. I said I wasn't going to do this. Let me grab a few more drinks or whatever, and then I promise I'll get you off."

"This isn't an exchange. I was happy to help." Thomas smirked. And there was a shine on his lips.

Well, at least he achieved *something*. Also, there was still time. Sometimes, the prospect of death unraveled the propensity for prim behavior. He might still get fucked before he got *fucked*.

I had to bite back a laugh. If I thought that was funny, I was further gone than I thought. I had been up here too long—too bored.

"Well, we'll see how the night goes. Thanks for doing this. And listening. And, uh, that." A blush crested her cheeks, but she fled the room before Thomas could get another word in. I sidestepped out of the way, watching as she rushed down the hallway, back to the thumping bass of music.

Thomas let out a breath and shook his head. His tone was low when he asked, "What do you want, Haden?"

"Did you have fun?" I raised an eyebrow, leaning against the threshold once more.

"Until she started crying." His nostrils flared. "You seemed to think this was a for sure thing."

"Look, I can give you advice, but you're the one who has to execute it. Seal the deal, as it were. It can't all be up to me. I give you the power, you wield it." I shrugged. A few locks of my hair fell into my eyes, dried despite having been drenched earlier. Part of the demon in me. "Maybe your performance wasn't good enough."

He glowered, and it was likely the most menacing he had looked in his entire existence. Standing up, he wiped his mouth off with the back of his hand. "Maybe you need to give better advice." He marched toward the door, but I stepped in front of him, holding up my hand. We had spent three years together, and despite how much I despised him, I felt like I owed him *something* for getting me to this moment. With her.

"Okay, you want one last piece of advice? How to make this party unforgettable? How to make people keep talking about it for as long as they are alive?" Granted, there only be *one* person talking about it, if I had any control over the way the rest of the night went.

His brown eyes narrowed. "Does it involve me killing anyone?"

I smirked. "No. You don't have to kill anyone. In fact, I would prefer it if you didn't." I pushed away from the threshold and stepped up to his face. Grabbing his chin, I pulled him close. He grimaced. "All you must do is get everyone at this party into the living room. Pack them tight, pack them in. Every last soul needs to be in that room. And then the real fun can begin."

"That's it?" he asked through smashed lips.

"That's it." I patted his cheek and opened the space between us. Glancing at the wall clock in the corner, I announced, "You have fifteen minutes to get it done."

Thomas's eyes widened. "This is the easiest thing you've ever told me to do."

"And yet you still aren't doing it."

He blinked but got his legs under him and moved. Finally. He was fucking listening to me. It only took three years, a house party, and a very elaborate trap to make him become a good boy.

"We could have had so much fun together," I spoke to his

retreating form.

Oh well. Time for me to move on. For me to get her under me again, once she learned the full scope of who I was. I hoped she would embrace the fire burning deep in her soul instead of running from it. Turn toward the light instead of away. Time would tell. Soon.

I had to give him credit. When Thomas wanted something accomplished, he set out to do it with efficient speed. By the time I reached the grand living room—the one with the pool table where I had eye fucked Zoe earlier—there was an odd settling in the air as drunks swayed with no music and the murmur of the party had died down to an obnoxious whisper. So many voices with not much to say. And here everyone was, ripe for the picking, waiting in the biggest room in the cabin for Thomas's announcement. Several brows were folded low over eyes. Restless feet shifted in the crowd. No one was happy to have their night interrupted.

I waited with my hands folded behind my back as several more folks meandered in. Thomas gestured wildly to usher them the rest of the way into the room. I rocked on my heels, trying to hide the amusement stretching across my features. If our relationship had always been this easy, I would never have created a curse to begin with.

Though, perhaps that was correlation and not causation, because Thomas thought he could control me. As the king of the fires would point out, I refused to be controlled. Thomas and I were oil and water, bound to separate eventually.

Zoe's eyes found me, and the moment I felt her gaze, I thought of how tight she was as I pushed into her. How wet she had been, ready for me. I wanted that again, to feel her pulse around my cock as she fell apart.

I needed to focus. While I didn't really *need* everyone to be in this room, as the curse was already underway, the announcement was the best way to get what I wanted—chaos. The more people who witnessed the event, the better. I aimed to break down decorum— widespread and bloody, so I could pay attention to Zoe and keep her alive.

While I might be a demon and about to make everyone fight for their lives, I played fair. If everyone heard the announcement of the game, then it was an even field. Equal grounds, equal chances. That would make it even sweeter when Zoe came out of the inferno surrounded by nothing but flames.

Plus, if I wanted to guarantee Thomas's death tonight, I needed everyone to be peeved. Take him out of the equation first and foremost, as the person who killed him would know little about what Thomas did. They wouldn't know the protections or safeguards. And if they didn't know the power they lorded over me, then I could threaten them. Make them do what I wanted.

It was all in the presentation. The pretty packaging around the death trap inside.

"What the fuck, Thomas?" One of the stocky males checked Thomas with his shoulder. His brown eyes stared at the man I was bound to with disgust. "We were just starting to have fun." Judging by the wafting smell of sex off him and the girl who hung off his side, I could guess what type of fun.

"It will only take a minute," Thomas squeaked in the nasally way he had when he was nervous. "And then I will get out the shots." He blinked at me. "We have shots, right?" He mouthed the words.

I shrugged. Probably.

"I already found them." The guy winked at Thomas and pulled the girl in close, brushing his nose along her cheek. She rolled her eyes but leaned into him as his fingers ran over her shoulder. He toyed with the thin strap there, and she sucked in a breath.

My eyes shot to Zoe. She had been watching my line of sight, and a glorious blush crept over her cheeks. Her hazel eyes absorbed me like a sponge. That pesky soul of hers was a cold spot in the otherwise lukewarm room. Despite how she fucked a literal demon less than thirty minutes ago, her soul still felt like the upper atmosphere settled down to earth. I wondered if she had a guardian angel on the other side protecting her. But more likely, it was about intention. Her spark hadn't grown because she had no idea about the evil running underneath my veins. That's where her shame would come in, and I hoped she would feel it all the way to her core.

I hoped it excited her as much as it disgusted her. I hoped she had to rub her thighs together to get relief. And when I thrust my hand down her panties, I hoped my fingers would come back soaked with the delicious tartness that invaded all my senses and refused to let me go.

She settled onto the bulky arm of the living room couch. I fought a territorial growl at how close she was to a bunch of the guys. She perched, waiting as Mercedes forced a few people to move over for her and Ridley to take up spots next to her. People bent away from the group as soon as Mercedes asked. Fucking blonds.

I was one to talk.

Upon seeing how everyone reacted around her, I recognized how much easier it would have been for me to fall for someone like Mercedes. Her soul already flickered with electricity running through her, screaming to be tipped over the edge. By the end of tonight, she'd likely be off to the fires herself, not because of a deal I made with her, but because of destiny.

But no, a soul like Mercedes's was too easy.

What I needed to impress the likes of the king was a soul full of possibility. Someone cool and breezy, at least for now. If I banished the good inside Zoe, I could drag her down with me. Bring her to the other side of the afterlife. Make her my toy for eternity.

Because her spark drew me in, even when I tried to keep my head clear.

Her eyes stayed focused on me. Hungry.

I was going to love watching the conflict cross her face.

"What gives, Thomas?"

"Yeah, come on, man. We didn't come here to sit around."

"Screw this. Let's get back to it. There are more shots in the kitchen."

Since Thomas's brows were lowered over his eyes and he hadn't left to find anyone else, I had to assume this was everyone. As the protests rose, I enjoyed the single moment of chaos before stepping forward. I clapped my hands together and flinches rippled through the crowd. The side of my lips quirked. "Friends, I promise we can get back to the festivities in a minute, but I needed Thomas to retrieve each and every one of you before anyone thought to leave tonight. For you see, we're in for a very special night."

Eyes snapped to me. I had to use lots of my magic, too much power to drive their attention to me. Part of the reason I never bothered before. His fail safes made it hard for me to interact and fighting them was an uphill battle. If I had ever found anyone worthy, perhaps I would have made myself known. But tonight was the right occasion. Everything was in place, and I only needed enough time to explain the rules of the game.

Thomas floated through the crowd, trying to reach me. I didn't miss how his body kept angling toward Mercedes. He practically drooled over her. Too bad tonight wouldn't be *the* night for him. Poor guy never stood a chance, though I had such high hopes for him when I had first arrived.

"Because tonight, I will no longer be bound to the man standing among you. The owner of this house summoned me, but by this time tomorrow, I will become bound to one of you instead." I grinned.

Thomas halted in his steps. "What?"

Whispers arose from the crowd. Zoe's hazel eyes drifted to Thomas before settling back on me again. With an arched eyebrow, her gaze sharpened.

"I didn't come here for some larping bullshit," some girl snarled and stood up. She turned to the crowd. "Come on. There's still a hot tub and booze."

My smile widened as others shifted in their seats. Murmurs spread, but curiosity got the better of most. "You're in luck, because this is no role-playing game. Well, it could be." My gaze shifted to Zoe. Heat rushed to her cheeks, and it made me want to strip her soul bare. Her teeth worried her lower lip. I would split her lips open the next time we got together, feast on her flesh, and take her into me. And then keep my promise to her.

The girls tittered at the joke, and some guys groaned.

"But here's the problem. I've been joined to Thomas for three years. In those three years, it's been terribly boring. Tiresome. I'm sure you get it."

One guy snorted from the back of the room.

"He understands." I jerked my thumb at the guy. "Anyway, he was gracious enough to throw this party. It's a bit of a going away celebration. A present to me."

"What the fuck, Haden?" Thomas put his beer down on the end table. He took a step toward me, but I ignored him. If it came down to something physical, he had no hope of taking me on. I might not be able to kill him, but I could chain him up for someone *else* to get the job done.

"For three years, I've watched this guy ruin every opportunity he had to become greater, but you wouldn't be like him, would you?" My eyes swept the crowd, but I was only interested in the reaction of those hazel eyes. She watched me steadily, rapt. "You would take the opportunity to become something more, something greater, something infamous."

"Get to the point!"

"My point, friends, is one of you will walk out of here owning your very own spawn of the fires. I'm a demon, and whoever survives tonight will be who I am bound to for the rest of their lives. And you better not disappoint me, because if it's one more day with him—" I hooked my thumb toward Thomas. "—I may take it out on each and every one of your families."

"What the fuck, dude!" Thomas finally found his feet, crossed the room, and grabbed my shoulder. I shoved him back. He stumbled, almost falling over another guy.

"Don't touch me." I took a step forward, towering over him as my shadow stretched out from me. My veins darkened as my demon form threatened to come out. I wanted to play, but the fucking fail safe chained me down.

"Dude," someone said.

A few people sucked in a breath.

I snarled, "I have listened to your pathetic excuse of an existence for three tiring years. And tonight, that changes."

"But you said the binds won't move to someone else unless they kill me." Thomas's chin worked.

"I don't think you're understanding, Thomas."

Fear etched into his eyes. The first I had seen since my summoning.

Fire ran through me, through the shadows that wanted to consume me. My true form threatened to tear out of my skin. "When I say whoever survives, I mean one person. One person gets to walk away from this cabin." I turned to the audience, who was now watching with cautious skepticism. "Everyone else will die tonight. And like I said, I hope one of you takes out this asshole, seeing as how he's the reason you're trapped at a house party with a demon."

A few people exchanged glances.

"This is really fucked up." The muscular guy rose from the couch, approaching Thomas with a pointed finger. "I don't know where you found this guy, but I am—"

I didn't let him finish. Crossing the space between us, I bent his finger so far back it popped in several locations. He shoved me away before the pain registered in his head, and he screamed. He turned back toward the audience. "You see this shit? We knew Thomas was weird, and he hangs out with guys like this. I'm out. And you're sure as shit hearing from my attorney."

"You can't leave," I said plainly.

"The fuck I can't," the man snarled at me. He was still holding his finger like it would fix itself if he applied enough pressure. Pain marred his features, and it felt delicious on my tongue. "I can walk straight out that door, and this entire party will follow me."

"I think you aren't hearing me. You can't leave. The exits are sealed, and there is no way out of this house until only one person is left alive. I cast the curse myself."

Thomas swallowed, approaching me as if I were a feral animal. Good. He should have learned this lesson a long fucking time ago. "Can you stop it?"

"Don't pretend we're friends. You were my captor for years."

"This is bullshit," some girl said in the crowd. "I'm out. We have to take Jet to the hospital, anyway."

"Yeah, let's go."

More echoes came alive in the crowd as people shifted to their feet. No one believed me.

Zoe stayed still. Hazel eyes fixed on me. Her pink tongue flicked out, and there was the glorious first sign of what I told her would happen. Shame crossed her features. If a small thing like breaking a finger got her going, wait until she saw what happened next.

I sighed. "I hate when people don't listen to me. Very well." As Jet turned toward the front door, I punched a hole straight through his back and wrapped my fingers around his spine. My claws extended, shooting straight into his bones, and I wrenched back. His vertebrae popped out one by one. Once his spine was in my hand, his body swayed for a mere second before collapsing in a bloody heap on the floor. Several screams spread throughout the pool hall as people scrambled over each other in a fit to get away.

"The last one standing wins!" I yelled. "And so help me if you all decide to play nice. I will kill every last one of you instead, and Thomas gets to continue having me as his personal pet." At least he would be sent to prison for the events of tonight. I would make sure of it. He had better hope he wasn't left alive, because I could make his life far worse than anything the fires had to offer.

I dropped the bones, and they thudded to the floor with a wet slap. My eyes drifted back to her. Zoe watched me, not with the horror of those screaming around her. Not with the panicked look of Mercedes, who tugged on her arm. No, she watched me with the scrutiny of a person who became aware of the darkness trapped inside themselves. The possibility to embrace the fires, embrace the heat sparking wildly in her soul. Her thighs clenched just a tick. Blood dripped from my fist as she took the image in. What a sight it must have been.

I gave her a wink before her best friend pulled her out of the living room.

10 Zoe

Horror kept me rooted to my spot as my brain tried to register what had occurred. Haden had commanded the room, walked out in the middle of the crowd, and claimed to be a demon. A spawn of the fires. A creature from the depths. And I had seen it, hadn't I? The shadows roaming under his skin. The inky way they seemed to travel inside his veins. How they pressed against him, longing to come out and claim me.

When no one believed him, he reached into Jet's back and plucked out his spine like it was a stubborn apple on a branch.

My gaze had been fixed on him during his speech, not wanting to miss a single thing as I tried to parse the man in front of me with the one from earlier. The cockiness was there, as was the smug expression. The heat I sensed from him prickled along my skin with a knowing; something inside me buried deep down called to him. Along with his self-assurance, there was also a cold calculation that hollowed out his cheekbones, things I didn't notice while wrapped in his embrace earlier.

With his hand curled around the dripping red bones, his focus shifted to me. His eyes seemed like liquid black pits of tar. Except when they trailed along my skin to gauge my reaction, they still held an eerie softness. And perhaps even … doubt? Earlier, there had been a brown edge to his irises, but now … they were pure black, all darkness. A part of me wondered if I had made everything up, because there was no way this had happened. Right?

Except the room erupted into chaos. Everyone was in shambles, becoming a monstrous amalgamation as people tried to run over one another. Screams and cries roared together into a cacophony.

My mouth parted, sucking in a breath as he dropped the bones to the floor with a wet slap. Everyone around me shrieked, panicking in the utmost chaos, but I couldn't bring myself to move. There was something so … terrible about what had unfolded. However, I couldn't put my finger on what was wrong. There was the obvious— the dead body and Thomas screaming at Haden about betrayal and his summoning spell.

But underneath that, there was something else. Lurking.

And that's when I realized it.

Shame. As he had promised. I swept my eyes along Haden—the *demon*—again, and a coy smirk stretched on his lips like he knew. He *knew,* and he winked. Because I wasn't feeling bad about Jet's death or about how everyone else might be doomed to die tonight. I wasn't feeling terrified or scared of him. No, because instead my body *sang* with the need for more. As demented as that sounded, as horrible as it made me, there was something there, building between my legs. A heat I had only felt in bed with him. An explosion crept over my senses as I watched him, his hand coated in red. Droplets plummeting to the floor.

This was worse. Far worse than anything I had envisioned for my future. I was *turned on* by Haden's explicit act of violence. What kind of person did that make me? The way I wanted to throw myself at him, the way I wanted to tell him to tear my clothes off. Beg him to let me come apart again at his hands.

A part of me hated him for it, the other part was desperate to feel him inside me again. Traitorous body.

Merce's fingers hooked around my wrist as she yanked me off the couch. "Zoe, come on!" She pulled me with her into the tide of people running toward the door. Ridley plowed others out of the way as we rushed through the living room. My legs finally found a will to live, and we raced toward the front hallway.

I glanced over my shoulder. Haden observed me with a smirk curling the corner of his lips. Why did I feel *regret* over leaving that room? Over leaving him?

"What the fuck!" Merce yelled over and over again. "We have to find everyone else and stick together. We have to get out of here." Her nails dug into my skin as she tumbled us after Ridley.

Tate and Sasha had been swallowed by the crowd. I didn't remember seeing Corbin and Everett. Everyone had darted out of the living room faster than we had filtered in. There was an exit by the pool, as well as the kitchen—I always looked for egress whenever I came to one of these things—but everyone had bottlenecked in the front entry, trying to shove themselves through the main door. Panic made everyone stupid. Shouting, coughing, swearing, and trampling feet eviscerated any coherent thoughts.

Ridley and Merce pushed their way through the crowd. Merce did what she used to do in high school—acted like everyone should bend to her. She had a presence I never understood. People actually let them through, giving them space at the front. There was no room in the hallway, but still, we edged forward as our former classmates inched away from her. She paved a path all the way to the door.

The main entrance was wide open, showing a quiet, cricket-filled summer night outside. Twinkling stars, a crescent moon, and several low-hanging clouds rolling over the sky. But the people in front of the threshold had halted, unable or possibly refusing to pass through. Was there something outside I couldn't see?

"If you're not leaving, make room." Merce and Ridley forced the last few people out of the way. Some girl's glasses ended up on the floor.

I bent down and scooped them up for her, handing them back.

"Thanks," she breathed, as she took them with shaking fingers and placed them back on her nose. They were skewed from the fall. "We can't leave." Her voice was a squeak. "There's a force field or something. We can't leave."

Merce rolled her eyes. "This isn't some stupid fairytale." She tried to take a step forward. Her foot hovered in the air, right over the threshold of the door. It halted—*she* halted. Her nose wrinkled, lips curling down in a tight-lipped frown. Her hands went up. She thrust them out in front of her, only to be met by an invisible barrier—she looked like a mime as she sprawled her fingers on empty air, flattening them against nothing. "What. The. Fuck."

I turned to the girl. "No one can get out?" I asked her.

She shook her head, a few strands of hair escaping the loose bun she had piled it in. I didn't remember seeing this girl before in high school, but maybe she was a friend of someone else? Who knew? Bet she regretted coming to this party now.

Ridley attempted to punch the thing but shouted a curse as soon as he made contact—his knuckle splitting open with blood.

We were trapped with a demon.

I wanted to regret coming to this party too; I wanted to be scared like everyone else. Needed to feel the terror gripping my veins. Except ... I didn't. Not with the sultry look on Haden's face, the way the blood dripped from his skin.

Nothing I felt was reflected in the roiling crowd.

The roaring shouts grew desperate, hysterical, as more and more people realized we were trapped. Someone knocked into us from behind. I slammed into the wall next to the door, and Mercedes let out a grunt.

Ridley turned his head toward the crowd. "Cut it out!"

"Then exit the fucking house!" An angry voice sprang up.

"We're going to die if you idiots keep standing there!" Another angry guy.

A bunch of feral howls rose from the mob. I grabbed Merce's hand. "We need to get out of here," I urged.

She latched onto Ridley's. Unfortunately, I only got two steps away from the door when the throng surged forward. I toppled into the girl with glasses. She stumbled backward into the open doorway. Her back slammed against the barrier, but people kept writhing. I fought back, ducking under elbows, shouldering people out of my way. Ridley charged forward, and thankfully, he was strong enough to push against the wave.

Shouts rose from behind us. "She can't breathe!"

"Back the fuck up!"

"Fuck you!"

"Leave the fucking house!"

"Let us out!"

"We're all going to die!"

"Someone call the police!"

"My phone isn't dialing."

"Mine either!"

I pulled my phone out, but no reception showed in the upper right corner. We were so royally fucked.

The cacophony grew louder, erupting into a gale. Crazed pleads, prayers to the unknown, and endless begging stretched in all manners of voices. Ridley reached the stairs, charging upward. We climbed above the group, and once we were safely away from the pressing weight of the masses, I could finally see what was happening.

The girl I helped earlier was crushed against the barrier. Wheezing. Her arms flailed, trying to gain purchase underneath herself, get space between her and the invisible wall, but to no avail. Her mouth opened and closed, with no noise coming out to add to the chaos that surrounded her.

I whistled, tried to make it loud enough to catch everyone's attention. If I didn't do something, she was going to die. I took a step down the stairs.

Mercedes latched onto my shoulder. "Don't. I see it too, Zoe, but don't."

"She's going to die." I whirled on her. "If it weren't for Ridley, that'd be us." Rage coiled inside me. I had to do something, didn't I? Weren't we obligated to help other people?

But hadn't I just been turned on by Jet getting his spine torn out of his skin? Hadn't I witnessed one of the most fucked up things in my life, only to feel something deep down in my core? It wasn't because of the death, I reasoned with myself. It was because it had been Haden doing it. The power, the force, the brutality. The wretchedness that came with Haden—that's what made me ignite.

This? This was a senseless act. A horde who acted like rats trying to escape a sinking ship, ready to clamber over each other in an effort to run. But there was no leaving. We were stuck. And watching her, the red spreading across her face, the puckering around her eyes, how her veins popped from her skin as it turned to a purplish hue. It looked painful.

A few people struggled against the trampling herd, but like the ocean, there was an ebb and flow none of them could control. As soon as they gained space, another wave pushed against the door, breaking against the barrier, and the poor girl couldn't catch a breath.

"It's wicked, right?"

I started at the voice from above us. Glancing up, I saw Juniper watching the whole thing unfold with sparkles in their eyes. Juniper hung out with the goths in high school, and they hadn't changed much—traded in their black baggy attire for a more form-fitting black lace with denim. It looked good on them, like they had come into their own, found themselves.

"This whole thing? It's kind of fucked, but I'll be honest, I will happily die if I see a bunch of them go first." They nodded to the sea below us.

Ridley crossed his arms over his chest. "Unreal. Of course someone like *you* would be happy about this."

"What's that supposed to mean?" Both Juniper and I said at the same time. We exchanged a glance, and they gave me a solemn nod.

"Goth. Fuck, I'm not that much of a dick." Ridley scowled. "You're like into death and stuff like that."

Juniper narrowed their eyes.

"Holy crap." Mercedes gasped, her face turning white as a sheet. "We're going to actually have to kill people. Like we will, right? In order to survive, we have to kill people?"

"We don't know that," Ridley said.

Juniper laughed. It was more of a bark than anything. "Of course we know that. You *felt* it. You saw it. That demon has powers, and we're trapped here until only one of us is left alive." They leaned forward on the banister. "Question is, who will it be? Because I sure as shit ain't leaving this thing alive. I don't want to live with all that regret. Fuck that. Oh, and if anyone asks, the gun safe is already empty." They twirled around and marched down the hall.

Ridley's mouth dropped open. "There was a gun safe?"

"Shit," Mercedes said, running her hands through her hair, making the tousled locks into an absolute mess.

Transfixed in horror, I watched as the girl stopped moving. Her body pressed against the threshold, empty and lifeless. The crowd surged again, rocking back away from the barrier. A bit of space opened. Too late.

Her body collapsed.

The screaming started again. It ricocheted off the walls, vibrated off the stairs, and the sound spiraled straight into my bones. Gasps, cries, prayers, everything coiled into chaos.

"She's dead!" someone shrieked.

"What the fuck did you guys do?!"

"Someone had to go first, right?"

"What the fuck!"

"They talk as if they know what the depths of the fires are like."

My heart stuttered in my chest. I sneaked a glance at Ridley and Merce, but as I suspected, neither of them had heard a thing. Turning slowly, as if I were trying not to spook a cornered cat, I faced him. Haden. He stood in the same spot Juniper had been moments earlier. There was not a single drop of blood on him.

Had any of it been real?

"And this doesn't compare?"

"What?" Merce asked.

I didn't look at her—couldn't. Nothing could make me drop my gaze from the blond-haired demon standing two steps above me.

"Not even close. This is one horrible night—and in the grand scheme of things, it will barely mar most of their souls. They should consider themselves so lucky to die young, before years of life lay regret on their shoulders, whispering everything they've ever done wrong whenever their head hits the pillow."

"You speak like you know."

He shrugged. "I've been around." Gesturing to the people below us, he said, "She will be the first of many. She's not someone to mourn, not when your own life is on the line. You don't have time."

"Who in the fires are you talking to?" Mercedes asked. "Is the demon here again?" Her nostrils flared as she took a few steps forward, up toward the landing. "Bitch, when I get my hands on you—"

I barked out a laugh. I couldn't help it. Merce was advancing on a spot on the hallway wall like she was going to murder it. Haden had this amused smirk on his face, and Ridley gaped down the stairs, as if finally realizing the gravity of what was going on. It was so utterly *silly*. And somehow, once I started laughing, I couldn't stop. Hysterics bubbled up as I doubled over, holding onto the hand railing as the horde shifted below us. Their yells turned to anger, to accusation. Their pain to anguish. Soon, it would become something more vicious and viler.

"What is wrong with you?" Ridley screamed. He grabbed onto my shoulders and shook me.

Haden let out a low growl, and my eyes widened as shadows stretched, dancing along his skin. Why in the fires hadn't I seen any of that when he was fucking me? Was I that oblivious? Or just that desperate?

"It's fine," I said to him, grabbing hold of Ridley's hands. "I'm fine." I focused on my friends. "Look, we still need to find the others and stick together. This doesn't change anything." My gaze slid to the body, now visible as everyone flooded out of the room, screaming obscenities and looking for another way out. There wasn't one. From the depths of my soul, I understood this feeling of being trapped. We were stuck here. Haden had been telling the truth. If only one person were to walk away tonight, we needed to make sure it was someone from our group.

At least, I'd prefer that.

My friends might have problems, but in their hearts, they were decent people. I couldn't say the same about many others at the party. So yeah, it should be one of us. Why not? It should be easy enough to do if we worked together.

"Where did you last see the others?" I asked Ridley, because his gaze kept wandering back down to the corpse. I tried not to think about her and swallowed my feelings, because we were in for a long night.

Haden was right—as fucked up as it was, we still needed to survive. Whoever made it out of here, they would be the one to bear the burden of mourning us. We could feel terrible for the rest of our lives, but one of us needed to make it there first.

"I don't know. In the hot tub? Or wait … Sasha said she wanted something from the kitchen, so she might have tried to escape that way. I don't think I saw Everett and Corbin at the … announcement." Ridley's throat bobbed as he swallowed.

I nodded. "Okay, we start there. They are probably in a room, and Thomas didn't want to interrupt."

"Of course he didn't get everyone." Haden let out a breath. He rolled his eyes and folded his arms over his chest. "Knew I shouldn't have trusted Thomas with even something as simple as being an errand boy."

I shot him a glance. He gave me a non-apologetic shrug. To my friends, I said, "We start with Everett and Corbin. We find them, then we'll come up with a plan for Sasha and Tate. We have to stick together."

"If you want my help—" Haden started.

"No," I snapped. "You've done enough."

"Suit yourself." The twitch at the corner of his lips made me want to smack and kiss him at the same time. I didn't have a moment to unpack any of my feelings, so I buried them.

Mercedes threw a punch at the air she thought contained Haden, then let out a growl. "Okay, fine. That does it. If I can't kill that demon, I can sure as shit kill Thomas. Where is that asshole?"

"It is his fault you're in this mess," Haden said.

"Do you really want to be strapped with a demon for the rest of your life?" I asked. A wave of possessive jealousy ran through me. As angry as I was, as frustrated as I was, I didn't want to see anyone else attached to him but me.

"Better me than him. I'll at least know how to have some fun with a demon by my side before I figure out how to shove him back in the pits." Mercedes stalked downstairs, each step clipped and calculated.

"Uh …" Ridley scratched the back of his head. "I think we follow her?"

"You follow her. I'll figure out where Everett and Corbin are. And then I'll come and get you both."

"This sounds a lot like the 'we should split up' trope that gets people killed in horror movies."

"We're not dying yet. Not … first." I paused, my gaze going to the mangled girl on the floor. "Not third," I corrected.

Two people were already dead. And there were too many left to count. My heart thudded in my chest. At least no one had purposefully turned on each other yet, but I had a feeling that it would end soon. There was a strange truce going on during these moments of shock, and we needed to take advantage of any time we got.

Haden

Was it wrong of me to want to fuck her when she was pissed off? Her nose scrunched in this adorable way that made me want to have her submit. Brows deeply furrowed on her forehead. Lips tilted in a pout that would look perfect wrapped around my cock. Her face flushed with a gorgeous crimson. And the heat and fire from her? Exquisite.

"Okay. Okay," Ridley said, nodding to himself. "We got this. I'll keep Mercedes safe and you'll … Fuck, you're going to talk to that demon again, aren't you?"

She shook her head. "No, I'm not."

"Going to ignore me, then?" I folded my arms over my chest and arched a brow.

Her glare turned straight toward me. "I'm not going to *talk* to him, because I'm going to fucking kill him."

My lips quirked. *Adorable and fuckable.* Exactly as I said.

"Okay. Sure. Uh … Be careful, Zoe. I need all the help I can get."

The poor guy hovered his hands over her again, as if to hug her or pat her on the shoulder or something, but he seemed to lose his nerve. He tucked his arms to his sides and marched down the stairs, his movements jerky, as if being controlled by string.

I noticed how he had said *he* needed help, and judging by the cross look on Zoe's face, she hadn't missed the pronoun, either. I opened my mouth to say something more, but before I got a chance, she whirled on me.

Her shoes slammed against the stairs as she got right up in my face. She poked my chest with her finger. "So, what happens now? The whole party kills each other one by one until there is only one person left that … what, is stuck with you, the one who put them through this chaos?"

"Yeah, kind of." I shrugged.

"And you decided not to tell me because …?"

"Is that what you're upset about?" I chuckled, stepping toward her to crowd her space. Her finger drilled against my chest, unwilling to shrink away from me. "Not the fact that many people will die tonight, not how you will potentially become a murderer or get murdered yourself, but you're pissed because I didn't *warn* you ahead of time?"

She jerked back as if I slapped her. That spark in her chest flickered hot, seeking fuel for the ignition. I wondered what she would do if she learned her soul had set this plan in motion. I had waited three *long* years to find someone worthy of me, and *she* was perfection.

"No, of course that's not the only thing I'm upset about! But it's kind of false pretenses, don't you think? I mean we … And I don't …"

I wrapped my fingers around hers and lowered our hands. Taking another step forward so we stood chest to chest. She tilted her head up to meet my gaze. To her credit, she didn't shrink away. No, she *glared* at me.

"And you don't typically have one-night stands with murderers."

"I don't."

"Nor do you often sleep with demons?"

Her head shook back and forth, mouth parting in a delightful, small *o*.

"Well, now you've done both. And does that change your opinion on the events?"

A bright crimson colored her cheeks.

"There it is." I leaned forward, pressing my tongue along the base of her jaw and tracing upward. "What I promised you. Shame. But you don't *need* to feel it. You can feel nothing, or you could feel something much better." Reaching down, I toyed with the button on her jeans. "Relief. Ecstasy. Letting go of those pesky societal norms everyone claims you *should* feel at a time like this."

Just as my fingers unhooked her button, she wrenched backward, shoving me off her. "I have to find my friends. If I have any hope of surviving the night, I need them by my side."

A sinful smile stretched up my lips. "You don't need anyone, but if it makes you feel better to have more fodder around you, by all means. I won't stop you." I took a step backward, giving her space to decide.

She eyed me warily. Perhaps in the past, no one gave her the opportunity to choose for herself. That was something I would change—as soon as I convinced her to dedicate her soul to me. After a deep inhale, Zoe turned and scurried down the hall, brown hair wild behind her. My feet ached to trail after her, but Thomas's lukewarm soul flared to life in my vision. Someone was trying to kill the bastard already, and I needed to witness whatever happened next. If I was going to be stuck with a person's soul, I needed information.

Hopping onto the handrail, I slid down to the bottom of the stairs. I dismounted and vaulted over the second body. I couldn't have planned it better myself—a catastrophe to convince everyone of how real and dire their situation had become. Truly, I adored the chaos humans created for themselves. They barely needed a demon's interference.

I drifted into the room with the pool table. Vaulted ceilings and low-emitting yellow lights gave this space a cozy feel. Made cozier still when my eyes landed on Thomas, who cowered like a cornered rabbit with a pool cue wielded in front of him. He held it like a bat, but one large impact, and that thing would snap in two.

I sighed.

Mercedes joined the crowd, but Ridley latched onto her hand, yanking her backward. She yelped, and I sidestepped the couple, eying the way Ridley's soul spasmed with several sparks. He pulled her away from the unruly group forming in front of Thomas. Honestly, I wanted them to stay out of it for now, as Zoe was convinced she needed them.

But the way Ridley's fingers dug into Mercedes's skin was harsher than I thought necessary.

I stepped up to the couple, ready to tear him away from her if required, but Mercedes beat me to it. With a flare of her nostrils, she ripped her arm out of his. "What the fuck, Ridley? That hurt."

"Sorry, but we need to get out of here before it gets worse." He dropped his voice into a low whisper.

I let out a breath. The apology was a reflex, not something truly felt, but at least she was going to stick up for herself.

Despite how uncomfortable her friends had made Zoe earlier, she felt a sense of fierce, unyielding loyalty to them. Unfortunately, that wouldn't disappear overnight, but I hoped to earn her loyalty once she embraced the fire within her soul.

Ridley reached for Mercedes again, but she stepped back and opened the space between them. "He needs to die," she said. "Babe, he's the whole reason this is happening. Who summons a fucking demon, anyway? Fucking Thomas! That dude's creepy AF, you know? He's *stared* at me. Don't you want to go all possessive guy on him and show him how you're in charge?"

Ridley's eyes rolled back in his head. "Too manly, not manly enough. I don't think you know what you want. But what we need to do is find Sasha and Tate." He stepped up to her. He ran his free hand over the back of his neck. "We don't have much time before shit hits the whole fucking fan. We need to arm up and get defensive. That's the only way out of this. Come on." He turned.

Mercedes let out a huff but tripped after him as he marched toward the kitchen.

"Haden!" Thomas screamed as one of the pool balls pelted him in the shoulder.

One of the guys in the crowd laughed. "Nice shot, Brett."

"Easy target."

"Haden! Come here! Please! I'll do whatever you want!" Thomas backed up against the fireplace. He reached behind him, finding a fire poker. As he brought it in front of him, his knuckles curled white around the steel.

The pool cue laid discarded in two pieces. Called it, but at least one guy had a nosebleed.

"Crying for your demon like a baby won't get you out of this," someone mocked.

"Whatever I want?" I asked. I approached from the side, giving the crowd a wide berth. "Including ending your own life to free me from my bond?"

He gaped at me.

"Didn't think so."

"No, I mean … Okay, I can end it! I can stop it! I can free you."

I laughed. "I've read your books, Thomas. You made me unable to descend, unable to use my magic, unable to become my true self. Do you know how that feels?"

Another person hurled a ball, and it grazed Thomas's face. A horrific crack sounded. The pool ball splintered down the middle as a piece of stone mantle chipped off.

"Do you understand what it feels like to be trapped in your own skin? Feel your true form itching to get out? Feel a hollowness so deep it threatens to eat you from the inside out, because being self-consumed would be better than living one more moment in a lie?"

"Please! I can figure it out! Get your demon form back at least!" He ducked underneath another ball. It bounced off the wall, dangerously close to his ear. Several guys laughed. "I can speak the words to give you ultimate freedom."

"Releasing me completely?" Oh, that'd be interesting.

"You need to end this first. Let them go. End your curse." He leaped to the side and brandished the poker in front of him as another ball was lobbed toward his abdomen. It grazed his side, and he grunted, but kept his eyes on those in front of him.

I glanced at the people who had formed around him as I contemplated the offer. They were all burly guys, thick and daunting. I imagined Zoe fighting one of them and frowned. That's not what I wanted for her either—though I doubted anyone could stop her once she embraced her spark. Still, having Thomas die right now at their hands wasn't the best thing for my long-term plans. I sure as shit wasn't going to save him tonight or stop the curse I started. Especially when the curse would give me what I wanted—being endlessly tied to *her*.

No, if he wanted to survive the night, he'd have to save himself.

But I'd help him get out of this one situation.

"No deal, but if you want to survive this room, listen to me and do exactly as I say."

"Just this room?" he squeaked.

"Thomas."

"Fine! Whatever! Maybe you'll trust me afterward."

"Duck."

He flattened himself to the ground the second a pool cue ripped through the air like a javelin. It missed him by a hair. His brown eyes widened as they took me in.

"Roll left."

Without hesitation, he maneuvered out of the way as a boot slammed against the ground.

"Thrust the crowbar forward in three … two … now."

He lodged the metal straight into one of the guy's knees. The man screamed, pinwheeling his arms. The man took two of the guys with him as they fell backward in a heap. Shouts rose from the group.

"Run to the kitchen."

Thomas scrambled upright and tore off in that direction. While Mercedes and Ridley might be in there, I would have an easier time distracting them. Besides, there were plenty of other people who were equally pissed at my stupid jailer. Someone would kill Thomas tonight, and then Zoe would kill them. After that, she'd be mine.

Maybe I wouldn't have to wait that long.

As soon as Thomas was tucked away somewhere relatively safe, I'd find her. I'd convince her to gaze into the darkest depths of her soul. Her eyes didn't hold disgust when she looked at me, which gave me hope. It would take convincing, but she'd get there. My girl wouldn't let anything stop her from getting what she wanted—not even the eternal damnation of her soul.

When I entered the kitchen, I sized up the competition.

Thankfully, most people were more interested in raiding the booze and paid little attention to the demon-raising fiend who had joined them. Someone yelled for another round of shots, and another replied, "To the end of the fucking world!" They laughed as they tossed back the alcohol.

I wrapped my arm around Thomas's shoulder. Sweat beaded along his brow, and his t-shirt clung to his skin. I wrinkled my nose, but said, "You can be taught. Proud of you."

He sneered and shook off my arm. "This is your fault." Shaking his head, he walked over to the locked liquor cabinet. He pulled out a lanyard from inside his shirt—of course he had a fucking key chain around his neck—and unlocked the door. "And if I'm going to die tonight, then I'm going to taste all this shit my parents got." Thomas yanked out a bottle of whiskey and uncorked it. His fist wrapped around the neck as he brought the bottle to his lips and took a large swig. He sputtered, coughed, and made a face as he shoved the cork back in. "Maybe the next one."

He played this game a few times before he settled on a bottle of vanilla bean infused vodka. Of course it was vanilla bean, and of course it was vodka. Of all the things. Snatching the whiskey myself, I joined him at the kitchen bar. Several people perked up when they noticed the expensive cabinet was open, grabbing whatever they could.

"To going to the fires!" some girl yelled.

"Cheers!"

"Can someone take my virginity tonight?" a guy asked.

"If you're a virgin, then I'll eat my own asshole."

Laughter broke out.

I took a long pull on the whiskey, licking my lips. Smooth caramel with a rounded hint of a bite. "We don't have long before the mob finds you again."

Thomas sighed and shrugged. "What's the point? You said I was doomed. You said you didn't want to walk out of here attached to me. So don't try to pretend otherwise now."

"Okay, I won't. But I also don't want to sit by while you pout. Do you want to fuck that girl from earlier?"

If his glare could cut, it'd drill straight through me. "Are you saying that if I walked up to her and said, 'Babe, I know you were crying earlier, but shit changed. Want to fuck now?' She'd just be … what? Down for it?"

"The prospect of death changes things for people. Provides perspective, if you will. Wouldn't you rather die … sated than this?" I gestured to him, taking another swig. It wasn't as smooth as the distilled embers we had in the fires, but the best I had since coming here.

"I don't want to be that kind of guy."

"Well, you wouldn't have to live with the guilt of being *that kind of guy* for long." We stared at each other for a beat. I let out a breath. "Why did you summon me?"

"To get ahead. To give myself an easier time in life. To be able to—"

I pressed my finger to his lips. "These are the lies you tell yourself. I'm asking why you *really* summoned me. Think about it. What made you desperate enough to bring evil incarnate to the planet?"

He shoved my finger away and took a long drink. Wiping his mouth with the back of his hand, he nodded to himself. "Because I wanted to feel something more. I've never been that guy, you know? The one people *notice*. I'm no Ridley. I'm no Mercedes. No, people who are like me … we just disappear. Even in high school. I hoped college would change that, but when I got there? It was the same crap. The same bullshit. People looked through me. I might as well have not existed." He tipped the bottle toward me. "That is why I summoned you."

"So, make yourself visible. Not to everyone. Fuck everyone. Make yourself visible to one person. One girl."

He perked up.

"No, not Mercedes. Dude, she has Ridley all over her ass right now. Like I said, facing death does things to people. Find the girl from earlier. Get something for yourself. Be selfish. You'll both enjoy it."

He let out a long breath. "What happens if I don't?"

"One of those jocks will find you, and the end result won't be pretty. I'm not saving you twice." I tapped him on the cheek, slid off the chair, and dragged the bottle of whiskey with me. "Now, I have a date with a girl who is viciously upset with me."

Thomas's brows lowered. "Did you fuck Zoe Francone?" After letting out a grunt, he swigged another gulp back. "Of course you got laid before I did."

"And of course you are arguing with me instead of finding that girl."

"Any idea where she is?"

"She's getting high with a few people downstairs."

Thomas stood from his chair, wobbling, but got his feet underneath him and headed toward the basement entrance. It was off the kitchen, so he didn't have far to go. A plume of smoke greeted him as he opened the door and slipped inside. The door latched behind him. No one seemed to notice where he had gone. Good. That would give him more time, and maybe one of the brutes wouldn't be the one to end him.

Of course, if they united—which they might—they would be a problem later. I'd deal with them if it came down to it. For now, I needed to find the only woman who mattered in this place. As I walked into the hallway toward the stairs, I overheard several bits of conversation.

"If we steal the kitchen knives—"

"Naw, the pool chemicals will—"

"We need to get high ground."

"That only applies in video games."

"Naw, dude. Here too. Easier to throw shit with gravity on your side."

"Do you think the broken cues will be sharp enough to gut someone?"

Old teammates fell back into the habit of relying on each other. But unfortunately for them, something would split them down the middle. No group could stay together when lives were on the line. Watching those endless reality television shows with Thomas proved one thing: people would betray each other if they felt like they were next on the chopping block.

Unfortunately for them, that was a literal possibility tonight. And I was excited to see what happened next.

12 Zoe

Five rooms later, I found the one they were in as soon as the handle wouldn't budge. It was the only locked door on the floor, so they had to be behind it. After the screaming from downstairs, it wouldn't have surprised me if they had barricaded themselves in and refused to come out.

Unfortunately for whatever defense they had concocted, our group needed to be together. Without all of us, we wouldn't survive the night. And even with the seven of us … only one would walk out alive. I shivered at the thought. But if the fires and the skies were real, then there was an afterlife, right?

Small victories, at least.

After banging my fist on the wood a few times, I yelled, "Corbin? Everett? It's Zoe. Listen, Merce and Ridley are trying to find Sasha and Tate." And probably trying to kill Thomas. "I need to tell you what happened, and we need to plan for the—" My voice cut off as the door opened.

Everett latched onto my arm and yanked me into the room, slamming the door shut behind us. His brown eyes were wide, darting behind me as if someone would burst through the threshold at any second. "Did anyone see you come here?" He tightened his grip on my bicep, but when I winced, he dropped his hold. "Shit, sorry. We just—we heard screaming. I heard …" Shaking his head, his eyes stared right at me. "I heard we couldn't leave? What in the fires is happening out there, Zoe?"

After rubbing my arm, I helped Everett push the dresser back into place. While we needed to open it again once the others got here, there was no point risking fate in the meantime. As we worked together, I explained, "If we lock down a room and defend it, we might be able to survive the night. And then we can figure out what happens next. We need weapons. Does this bedroom have an attached bath?" I let out a breath as the dresser settled into place.

Corbin nodded, swallowing as he watched me. He looked slightly less overwhelmed than Everett. "I still don't understand. What happened?"

"Okay, a bathroom is good. We might be here for a bit." I paced, both sets of eyes trailing after me. "You didn't hear any of it?"

They shook their heads. "We were a little busy." A blush crept across Corbin's cheeks.

Where did I start? "So … that guy I was in the hot tub with?"

"What guy?" Everett asked, brow furrowing.

I pressed my eyes shut, pinching the bridge of my nose. Explaining this was going to make it seem like I had lost my mind. If either of them came to me with the story like this, I wouldn't have believed them. If I were in their shoes, I would think everything was a fantasy. "Maybe I should wait for Ridley and Merce to come back."

"Zoe," Corbin's voice dipped low, dangerous. He took a step toward me. His eyes searched me over. "Tell us what's going on."

I let out a breath. "A demon cursed the party, and only one person can leave here alive. We need to stick together until we're the last group left, and then … draw straws or something." Shit, would we fall apart as quickly as the decorum in the party below? "I'm pretty sure it's all Thomas's fault or the demon's fault? But Thomas summoned the demon, so I think that makes everything Thomas's fault and distinctly not the demon's fault. Because the demon is just being a demon, right? I mean … isn't that what demons do?" That and give incredible oral sex and mind-bending orgasms. Fuck, I was doomed for the fires, wasn't I? Was there a point in trying to stay alive if my soul was already cursed by the flames?

"There's a demon," Corbin said, eyebrow arching.

"And it's in the house," Everett added.

"With us?"

"And everyone except one person is … what? Dying tonight?" Everett blinked, running a hand over his black, short-cropped hair. "What the fuck, Zoe?"

"You're saying my name like I knew something about it."

"But what does this have to do with the hot tub guy?" Corbin asked.

"Do you remember him?"

They exchanged a glance.

"Of course you don't. Anyway, hot tub guy is the demon. Thomas did some kind of curse or something so no one could see him since he was summoned. Until me. Which I can't even begin to sort through right now and I—"

"Zoe," Everett said. He put his hands on my shoulders. Unlike the aggression from earlier, his touch was simple, gentle, grounding. "Breathe. Okay? First things first, we need defenses, right?"

"And snacks," Corbin said. "If we're stuck in here, we need snacks."

"But weapons as a priority. Do you know if there are—"

"Juniper raided the gun safe."

Everett let out a breath, dropping his arms. "Of course they did. Maybe I could talk to them, get them to team up with us?"

Corbin shook his head, crossing his arms over his chest. Brown hair swept over his forehead. "Too risky. Juniper's still pissed about how you took that role from them in the final musical."

"Still? Wait, how do you know?" Everett cut his boyfriend a glare.

"People talk at the state school … It's like a second high school, but we're slightly more mature. Slightly."

"We're revisiting that later." Everett turned to me. "Okay, what about the kitchen? Pool hall?"

I shrugged. "Don't know. I'm sure there's some stuff, but I saw the old football team heading into the pool area. The kitchen might work—there was so much alcohol in there, people might take their sweet ass time to realize they need to gather supplies."

Everett nodded, putting his fingers up to his lips in thought. "Okay, one of us should go to the kitchen and get as much stuff as we can and bring it back here."

"Maybe two of us? Or all three?" I asked. Ridley had been right earlier—the more we split up, the more we invited death in.

Bangs came from the other side of the door. The three of us jumped. I sucked in a breath, not wanting to signal that the room was occupied. I held up my hands as we waited. It could be anyone in the hallway. My heart leaped into my throat, and I could feel my pulse throughout my entire body.

"Zoe?" Mercedes voice clipped out in a stern whisper. "Look, if you're in there, we need to—"

"Get the dresser." I nodded to the guys. "Yeah, we're opening it," I whispered back through the seam in the wood. "Did you find Sasha and Tate? Or … Thomas?" I hated asking the last part, because if they had killed him then …

A hushed argument welled from the other side. I couldn't hear what they were saying as the dresser scraped against the wooden floor. The sound burrowed into my skull. I wrenched the door open, and similar to what he did to me earlier, Everett wrapped his hands around both of them and brought them inside.

I slammed the door shut, and Corbin and I moved the furniture back into place. My breath came heavy from the effort.

"What happened to Sasha and Tate?" I said as it settled back into position.

Mercedes shook her head, blond locks cascading down her shoulders. A flush crossed her pale skin. "I don't know. I mean, we looked for them, but there was so much going on. Like *so* much. I couldn't corner Thomas either, and I *really* want to kick him in the teeth."

"I think I saw him in the kitchen, but when I looked again, it was like he had disappeared." Ridley flopped onto the bed after a few quick strides. "We passed a few people who were talking about how to use pool chemicals to win this."

"Win?" Everett asked.

"Yeah, like it's some kind of fucked up game."

"What are they winning?" Corbin asked.

Ridley propped himself up on his elbows. "I don't know. The demon's powers or whatever? I don't really want to be tied to that *thing* for the rest of my life, but I sure as shit don't want to die." He sighed and collapsed backward again, folding his hands behind his head while staring at the ceiling.

I bristled at how Ridley spoke about Haden.

"We need to regroup. If we have any hope of surviving this—" I started.

"Zoe, no offense, but didn't you hear the dude? Only one of us gets to walk out of here. So, you want us to … what, beat everyone else so we can turn against each other? Nah." Ridley shook his head. "Nope. I'm not putting in that much effort just to die later. We can hang out here and—"

"And what, Ridley?" Mercedes put her hands on her hips and shook her head. "I'm not going to sit here and wait to die with absolutely no defense. We need weapons. We need Sasha and Tate." She whirled toward me. "Do you think we could get supplies in time? I don't know. Maybe you'll have better luck with finding Sasha and Tate than we did."

"Why me?"

"Because you've always been the more thorough one, meticulous to a fault."

Not exactly a compliment.

Merce waved her hand. "You know me. I'm like a tornado. Whenever I look for things, I ultimately leave a path of destruction in my wake—just to find a pair of socks." She shrugged. "We could take Corbin with us."

Corbin held up his hands. "No way in the fires am I going out there. It sounded horrible, the shrieking and mayhem. I don't want any part of it."

"Even if it means being one of the last ones left alive?" Merce challenged with her dark blond eyebrow raised.

"I mean …" Corbin slid a glance at Everett. They locked gazes. "I'm good."

"So, what? Everyone is giving up?" My teeth clacked together as I clenched my jaw shut. I couldn't believe them.

Merce pressed her eyes closed and walked over to the desk chair. She pulled it out and plopped down. "If they don't think we can—"

"Really?" Since when did we depend on a bunch of guys to determine our future? I ran my hand through my hair, catching a few snarled edges. Ever since I got out of the shower, it had been slowly air drying, which always did outrageous things. It was going to be a wild, chaotic mess by the end of the night, but that seemed like such a minor problem in the scheme of things. "Just like that, you give up? It's barely started. I haven't heard a single scream since we locked ourselves in here."

My best friend let out a long breath. "Maybe they are right. Maybe it's not worth the panic and hassle. Maybe—"

I marched up to her and punched her hard in the shoulder.

"Ouch!"

"Mercedes Morgan Montgomery."

"Ooh, full name, babe," Ridley said, chuckling.

"Snap the fuck out of it right now. We're going to the kitchen. We'll get knives and snacks, then you and Corbin—"

"Hey, I never said I was coming."

I shot him a death glare.

"Besides, it should be the single one out of us who goes," Corbin muttered.

"I'm sorry, what?" Spine straightened as my nostrils flared. I couldn't believe this.

Ridley sat up. "Yeah, Zoe, it's not like you have someone waiting on you. If anyone's going to take a chance out there, it should be the person with no significant other."

"Do you hear yourself right now?" Everett asked. He crossed his thick arms over his chest. "But by all means, Ridley, if you want to keep digging that hole."

Rolling his shoulders, Ridley continued with narrowed eyes, "Think about it. We need to try to survive the night, right? If one of us goes and dies, the other would be destroyed. It'd be harder for us to endure. So, I think Zoe should go alone."

"I need to make sure I'm hearing you correctly, Ridley. Because

I don't have a significant other, my worth isn't as valuable as theirs?" I hooked my thumb at Corbin and Everett. "Or yours?"

Ridley sat up, running his hand through his black hair. "That's not what I said. Don't twist my words around. It will be harder for us to survive if one of us is in mourning. That's all I meant. And if we're trying to win, then this is about strategy moving forward. It's nothing personal."

"But you are saying if I die, no one is going to feel bad about it? No one will mourn if I get killed?"

"Ridley, that's pretty fucked up," Mercedes said. Her green eyes were watching her boyfriend with wariness. "I'd care if Zoe died."

"Thanks," I grumbled. Small solace, but at least I could count on her to be on my side.

Everett let out a long breath. "While I understand where Corbin and Ridley are coming from—because I would personally be useless if Corbin died—perhaps venturing into the rest of the house should be voluntary at this point. And—"

"No one is going to volunteer for that, Ev." Ridley scoffed. "Nah, we need to make someone go. And sorry, babe, I would vote in Zoe for this. She hasn't really done much for the group lately, and she missed my birthday party last year."

"What the fuck, Ridley. I was in college hundreds of miles away! You didn't come to my birthday either."

"Because you didn't invite me."

"Because it would have been impractical and stupid of me to invite you when you were hundreds of miles away. Be so for real right now," I seethed.

Mercedes sighed. "We won't get anywhere if we keep arguing like this. I'd really like to move on. Maybe we pick straws?"

"Sure. Just find us some straws in a cabin bedroom." Corbin's attitude was really pissing me off. I would happily kick both him and

Ridley out of the room.

My jaw ached as I clenched my teeth together. We needed to band together to form a stronger alliance, but he and Ridley seemed determined to tear us apart. This argument was making it worse—and with Sasha and Tate still being outside these walls, we might already be down two people. We had no idea how things were progressing, and that alone set me on edge. Was it a bloody mess outside, or were people still in shock? I hoped for the latter, as that bought us more time.

Emotions ran high, but that didn't excuse being a dick. But because the women were always supposed to be the practical ones in a group and not get too *emotional*, I tried to find my center. My center looked a lot like kicking Ridley in the balls.

"Here's the game plan. And I don't want to hear any arguments until you listen to the whole thing," I spat the words through gritted teeth.

Ridley and Corbin snapped their mouths shut as I glared at them.

"As I was saying, the three of us can find some supplies—food and weapons. Then Merce and Corbin can come back here and barricade the doors until the roof falls down on you for all I care. We need supplies if we have any hope of survival. But since everyone is worried about their own lives, once you two are safely headed back here, I'll search for Sasha and Tate alone. Heard?"

"I'll go instead of Corbin," Everett piped up.

Corbin cut his gaze to him. "Ever—"

He held up his hand. "I work out a lot more than you do. And Ridley—" Everett doesn't finish the thought, but his eyes roam over our useless mutual friend. "Let's find something that can make me look more intimidating. I'm betting it will buy us the time we need to get down there and back."

Corbin sighed. "But if it came down to a battle, you know I'd be the better one in a fight, right?"

Everett's cheeks flushed. "Yeah, but no one else knows that. Most of the time, it's about appearances. We'll make it back without a fight." His confidence was infectious.

Corbin blew out a breath but nodded. He wrapped Everett up in a hug, murmuring something I couldn't hear into his boyfriend's chest.

Mercedes kept her green eyes on me, head tilting to the side as she looked me up and down. She flicked her fingernails toward me. "I like this side of you. She's feisty."

I didn't tell Mercedes *why* I was feeling particularly fired up. I had amazing sex with a man who had a godlike body, but it turned out he was a literal demon who tore out the spine of one of my high school bullies. If that wasn't a recipe for mixed feelings, I didn't know what would be. Top that off with how my pussy kept throbbing at the thought of his dark eyes raking over my skin again, like my body still wanted him despite how he murdered someone.

Sure, tonight had been completely *normal.* Totally *fine.* I wasn't on the verge of panicking, which was exactly why I needed to stay busy. If there was calm before the storm, then we needed to get whatever we could to ride this out. Maybe I wouldn't be able to keep all of them safe, but if one of us made it out, that was worth something, right?

Plus, I wasn't being brave by venturing out there. I needed to find Haden. I wanted to confront him again, give him a piece of my mind. He *should* have found a way to warn me. He could have told me *why* he was cursed. Instead, he had delivered versions of the truth. Sure, the demon had confessed I would experience shame later—and I had. Not because of the sex, but because of the dark desire for it to happen *again,* knowing the truth. Not telling me everything was a twisted dance around the facts, and I didn't want to allow that to stand.

Though, most of my anger was because of the shame. It annoyed me. He was *right*. Despite everything, I still wanted him. Even while watching blood drip from his fingertips. A part of me wondered what it would feel like to have him pumping into me again, with red spread between us. Smeared across our skin. Having his eyes on me with overwhelming curiosity, like he hoped to see into the very depths of my soul.

Witnessing the spine dangling from his fist made me want to climb him, wrap my legs around him, and have him pound me into the nearest wall.

"Everyone ready? Corbin and Ridley, you're in charge of holding down the room and moving the barricades to get us back inside quickly." The three of us lined up at the door. Corbin gave Everett another kiss goodbye.

When Ridley tried to kiss Merce, she waved him off, giving me a wink. Despite spending their time in college together, she was putting our friendship first. It made my heart warm to know she still had my back. Maybe she had no idea what had gone on in my life, but it wasn't like I had rolled out the red carpet and invited her in.

There was something to be said about sisterhood.

But I missed the brother I used to have in Ridley. Whatever the fuck had gotten into him, I didn't like it.

When we slid open the door, the hallway was eerily quiet. Music played in the distance, murmurs rose from downstairs, and hushed whispers drifted from the other rooms upstairs. But no screaming, no yelling, nothing that sounded like murder and mayhem. I'd have to ask Haden what would happen if no one took part in his game— if we all sat on our hands and survived the night, what then? Would the spell or curse or force field or whatever be lifted? Or would we slowly starve to death until only one of us could crawl across the threshold, weak and emaciated?

Skies, my thoughts were getting dark.

"I don't like it," Everett said the moment the door clicked shut behind us. He held a thick curtain rod—the only weapon the bedroom had to offer. Everett seemed determined to play the part of protector, and I didn't have the heart to tell him that his warm, inviting face did nothing to create a sense of menace. Honestly, I loved him for trying. He certainly was in my people-I-wanted-to-keep-alive book, whereas Corbin and Ridley had lost a space almost immediately upon opening their stupid mouths.

We *had* been friends, but skies, what was wrong with them?

"Neither do I, but the sooner we finish scouting, the sooner you can leave. Let's go." With steeled nerves and fake confidence, I stepped toward the stairs, leaving my two friends to trail in my wake.

# 13 Haden

I watched them leave the bedroom from the shadows of the hallway, tracking the group as they cautiously made their way to the stairs, then slowly slinking down the steps.

"Suck it up and tell her how you feel." Juniper slipped into the hallway next to me. Eyebrow arched as they looked me over.

I growled from the shadows. "What the fuck."

"Look, I saw you from the beginning, but that's only because I have him." They hitched their thumb toward the door. "Guardian angel. Failing, if you ask me, since I'm trapped here with the likes of you. We'll probably both be burning in the fires after this. Unless there are second chances for guardians?"

I snorted. "Not always. He'll probably lose his wings when he gets back to the skies, then get booted down to the fires with you. Too bad. You seem—" Looking them over, I determined their soul was destined for the fires, but only by the smallest amount of warmth. Maybe it was stealing the guns in the house earlier that pushed them over. They had chosen to fight instead of sacrifice, but cases could be made if her angel was any decent in the sky courts. They would have never been in this situation had it not been for me. "Not terrible."

They shrugged, a wry smile curling on their lips. "Anyway, as I was saying, demon, you should talk to her. Tell her how you feel. She's probably freaked the fuck out and needs to know your plan to get her to take over for Thomas."

Narrowing my gaze at them, I opened my mouth to deny it. No one was supposed to know what truly started this—how I found my first ounce of hope for freedom inside a human.

With one narrow finger, they silenced me. "Don't kid yourself. I wasn't honest about who I was until college, so I know what that's like. If you don't embrace who you truly are, is there any hope you'll find your place in this world? Or in the fires?"

I clicked my jaw shut. They were right; of course they were. It had been years since I embraced my full demonic self—shadow and ember skin. I longed to be back in my body, my true form. Mostly Thomas's curse kept me wrapped in this skin, but I hadn't fought my hardest against him.

Because I hadn't wanted to go back. Too many expectations. Too many obligations. Rules I hadn't cared for. Quotas to meet.

Sure, Earth had grown boring, but only because Thomas was so horribly plain to be around. Being with him was like adding yogurt to mashed potatoes instead of sour cream. It worked, but did it taste as good? No.

Which was exactly how his mother made mashed potatoes every Thanksgiving. Thank the flames I wouldn't have to sit through another agonizing family dinner. Or so I hoped.

But if I wasn't honest with Zoe about who I truly was, how could I hope for her to accept me? To accept what we would become together? And could I change my nature after all this time?

Lying came naturally.

To myself most of all.

Running my tongue over my teeth, I contemplated this as I watched Zoe and her friends slink downstairs. No one had died yet; no one turned against each other. This was the denial phase, but they would get over that soon, especially once the old football team got involved. They were menaces, most of them headed for the fires before tonight even began. Those selfish assholes wouldn't wait more than two hours tops before they started taking heads. And one of them had found the hedge shears.

"So, what does your angel want you to do to save your immortal soul tonight?" I crossed my arms and leaned against the wall.

Juniper's breath came out as a puff as their back hit the threshold. Their sandy blond hair had streaks of purple in it. It made their light eyes stand out more against their face. A cascade of freckles ran over their nose, adding to the overall Gothic pixie look. Their dark clothes accented their demeanor. "He wants me to save at least three people. Even though they will die eventually anyway, because the *intention* is the point. Oh, and not kill anyone. I have all the guns, but I can't kill anyone unless I want to be consumed by the fires." They rolled their eyes.

"It's not so bad."

They leveled me a look. "Excuse me while I don't believe that from a demon." They shook their head. "Besides, if I burn, he burns. And … I don't know how I feel about that."

I shrugged. "Look, angels will always be biased toward the skies, but we throw some amazing parties in the fires."

"And do any of your subjects get invited to them?"

"Nope."

"Then I'll take my chances by saving some people tonight.

Consequently, if your girl needs anything, let me know. I suspect it might be morally gray to save her, but what can I say? I like the chaos." Their wolfish grin stretched across their face and contained such confidence and certainty. I liked them immediately.

Their angel must have had a shit time trying to save them.

"I'll let you know."

Juniper winked and slipped back into the bedroom. Voices sounded from the other side, one of which had an ethereal, breathy way of talking, which immediately reminded me of the skies. Occasionally, the King of the Fires and the Queen of the Skies would discuss their plans for Earth. It was a delicate truce. The old adage—good couldn't exist without evil—made sense. Evil only existed when someone good bore witness.

In order for both kingdoms to gain an influx of souls, demons interfered less than angels on Earth. Turned out, humans didn't need much to become corrupt. They were perfectly fine doing it themselves. Therefore, demons only came when summoned. Angels, however, attempted to save as many souls as they could—but it was a lifelong process, until death do they part bullshit.

Kind of like Thomas and me, except I didn't care if he went to the skies, fires, or nowhere after this life. Angels tended to get attached. I bet Juniper's angel was shitting himself over this predicament. Last chance to save someone's soul while stuck in a demon's curse. Horrible timing.

Zoe and her friends finally left the entrance way, so I drifted down the stairs after them. In the pool room, the football team had begun amassing an arsenal. Thomas was their first target, so Zoe would be safe enough for now, but if she lingered—

I trailed after the three of them. Her face scanned every room she walked into, likely looking for me. If she checked behind her, she would have seen me right on their heels, but she didn't. I had to swallow back the primal part of me that wanted to hunt her.

Maybe someday. When I hadn't turned a house party into a deathtrap.

When the three reached the kitchen, she barked out orders, telling the other two what to grab. As Everett headed for the fridge, a few girls shrank out of his path.

"Oh, for fuck's sake, Melinda. We've known each other for twenty-two years."

"Yeah? Why the weapon, then?" The girl's nose wrinkled as she sized him up.

Everett shook his head, breezing past her to the fridge. He piled food into his hands, using his shirt to carry more. Which was awkward with the hold he kept on the rod. I could have told him it was a useless weapon. The aluminum would bend at first contact.

Mercedes pulled off and raided the pantry.

Zoe zipped through the drawers. The knife block was already empty—wasn't sure who snatched those, but I looked forward to figuring it out later. She grabbed a huge pot, a cast iron frying pan, as well as two baking sheets, likely as shields. Wouldn't do much against a bullet but would provide a defense against knives. My girl was smart. Her hands were bursting as she turned around.

Her eyes locked with mine, and her lids narrowed. "You want to help?"

Mercedes popped her head out of the pantry. "Sure. Happy to. Actually, give me the pot. I can put a bunch of stuff in it. The chips are all gone, but there's other food in here." She grabbed the pot from Zoe and began tossing items into it. Chocolate, cookies, crackers, and more dropped inside. Zoe used the kitchen island to rearrange everything, but her eyes finally slid to mine.

I stood at the threshold.

"You and I have to talk later."

"About Ridley?" Merce answered, not realizing her friend was directing the comment at me.

I smirked. Zoe scowled.

"He was *such* an ass. I'm so sorry. He joined this online podcast group a few months ago, been listening to it religiously and hanging out with the guys after. Been getting amped about some stuff lately. I've been ignoring it, but after seeing how he spoke to you, I don't know. I need to confront him. He's been a dick."

"Wait, what podcast?"

She gave a wave of her hand. "I don't know. Some macho bullshit alpha male type of thing. He's been more demanding than ever—not like physically—but he's not being nice either. Remember on prom night when he and I got together? How he spent all night just *listening* to me? This Ridley wouldn't do that. I don't see any of that guy inside him anymore." Mercedes let out a long breath as she plunked the pot onto the counter next to Zoe's supplies.

Everett joined them a few seconds later. "Toss me those baking sheets?"

Zoe passed them over, and he arranged his items on top.

"We can eat the cold food first. There are a few bottles of water, but I figure the tap in the bathroom will be available worst-case scenario. It's not like we have to worry about flesh-eating bacteria if we're going to die anyway, right?" His smile gleamed bright white, showing lots of teeth, but the expression didn't meet his dark brown eyes. "Sorry, that sounded more light-hearted in my head."

"Don't worry about it. There's nothing that could have *prepared* us for this."

Yeah, she was still pissed. Oh well. Couldn't do much about it now, but Juniper was right. If I had any hope of convincing Zoe to embrace the fire within herself, I needed to show her what I could offer—my true self. Somehow, I'd have to show her the demon that was bound by protections inside my human body. That's where the true power was.

"I needed to surprise you." I leaned back. "Because without it, how would I have gotten your genuine reaction? The one that told me exactly how you were feeling underneath your facade?" I pointedly looked at her pants.

She scowled and shrank backward.

I wanted to wrap my hands around her face and pull her into me. Crush her lips to mine. She needed to bloom, drag oxygen inside her chest, and ignite from the inside out. This second guessing wouldn't do.

"Embrace it, Zoe. Feel the power coursing through you with acceptance. It turns you on, and I personally *love* that."

Her eyes rolled, and she shook her head. She went back to ignoring me, which made me want to pin her against a wall. She wouldn't be able to avoid me if her back was arching underneath my touch.

"Okay, so the pots, sheets, and pans are all we have for weapons."

"And this!" Mercedes pulled out a steel meat tenderizer. "Doesn't hurt to have, right?"

"Not at all." Zoe flashed her a brief smile. "Okay, I don't think this is great, but it's not terrible. And—" Pulling open another drawer, she plucked out a thin cheese grater. "People probably overlooked this, but it's sharp. That's why it has the plastic barrier. Scrape this across someone's face, and maybe you'll be able to get away."

"I love the way you think." Mercedes nudged Zoe's hips with hers. "Remind me why we don't talk more?"

Color blossomed on Zoe's cheeks at her friend's compliment. "Because we have our own lives. Look, we're going to make it. Let's get back before shit hits the fan. I'll keep this thing with me, and you guys can hole up until I find Tate and Sasha."

"Sounds good!" Mercedes beamed.

As the three turned around, it was Everett who halted first. "Fuck." The single word escaping his mouth caused my blood to cool.

I looked to the living room—the open part of the concept kitchen. The football team was rounding up some of the other party goers into the living room. Each burly guy held some kind of makeshift weapon, and everyone else looked terrified.

That signaled it. Things were about to get ugly. They had run out of time.

Zoe shoved everything she had at Everett, including the cheese grater. "Go. Now." She pushed him toward the stairs. He protested, but the moment Mercedes took off, Everett was right behind her.

A selfless act, which scored her soul even more cold points with the skies. I let out a breath, annoyed with how she continued to put them first. I craved that kind of loyalty, and perhaps, someday, she would give it to me instead.

"Where are they?"

"Who?"

Zoe marched up to me, closing the distance between us. A sneer crossed her features as she poked me in the shoulder. "You know who. Tate and Sasha."

"Downstairs, getting high."

"Great. Perfect. Fucking unreal. Normally, I don't care, but tonight of all nights? We need to try to—forget this. I don't have time." She whirled on her feet and rushed toward the back door, the one that led outside. Pausing, Zoe let out a breath and turned toward me. She spoke through clenched teeth. "Which fucking door is it?"

I jolted my thumb toward the one in the kitchen that went down to the basement.

"I hate you."

"You don't, though."

"Time will tell."

"Yes, it will." A smile curved my lips.

She bolted through the door, causing another cascade of smoke to fill the kitchen. Instead of following her, I sauntered toward the chaos. Some people were on their knees, already begging for their lives. It seemed the football team had gathered everyone who had been hanging out in the living room. There was a group trying to keep everyone quiet while another team headed toward the real prey inside the bedrooms.

Zoe had a few minutes, but each one would be precious.

I would bide time for her if I could. Anything to allow her a chance to escape back to her temporary haven.

It wouldn't be safe forever, but I had plans on how to protect her moving forward. This was step one. Her friends might not be worth saving, but there was potential there. If they elected not to be selfish and put their group before themselves, they would be an asset for her surviving the night. If not, then she'd have to survive on her own.

It was amazing any of her friends were going to the skies at all.

14 Zoe

The air in the basement hung heavy with smoke so thick that I coughed as it filled my lungs. It was a mixture of stale cigarettes and cheap weed. If I made it out of this room without getting a second-hand high, I was going to be surprised. Moans and grunts rose from the underbelly of the basement, and the light was so dim as I made my way down the steep, rickety, wooden stairs. The haze added to the melancholy in the air.

When I reached the bottom of the steps, I sought out the noise. Tate and Sasha never seemed to back down from their desires, so the best place to look would be at the moaning of someone in the throes of an orgasm. No time like the end of the world to get laid.

Unfortunately, I saw Thomas's bleached white ass as he pounded into some woman who was sprawled on top of a tool chest. Thomas was tall. Holy shit. The dude had doomed us all to die, and here he was getting off.

Fuck him.

As much as I wanted to punch him in the face, now was not the time to get distracted. Shit was going to get bad soon, especially if the frantic energy down here was any indication. People did weird things as they prepared for the end. Some let go of inhibitions, which seemed to be what a lot of people in the basement were doing. Others got depressed. And others? Angry.

And the ones getting angry? They were upstairs, gathering weapons. They would try to survive no matter what the cost, and I needed to escape their wrath before they could turn it on me.

Giving Thomas and his partner a wide berth, I made a circuit around the basement. My heart picked up speed as I went by more and more people. Several passed joints between them. Drugs laid out on one of the storage tables. Beer bottles were half-empty or hanging between fingertips. None of these people were Tate and Sasha.

Had Haden been wrong? Had he told me incorrect information to get me down here? Had they already escaped to another part of the house? But no, there was only one way in and out of this room, and my friends hadn't been upstairs. They *were* here. An awful part of me felt like I could trust Haden's word.

Still, none of this quelled the fear rising in my heart. Sweat beaded along my brow. The smoke burrowed into my skin. My breath came faster as my pulse raced. Where the heck were they?

Halfway through my second circuit, I heard Sasha—her voice soft and low, as if lulling someone to sleep. Brow furrowed, I closed the distance between myself and the slated closet door. Wrapping my fingers around the handle, I slid it to the side.

Tate's head was buried in their knees as they rocked back and forth. Sasha had her arms around them, whispering to them. Her red-rimmed eyes leaped up to mine, widening as she took in the scene. Her blue irises flashed, taking in the basement, searching desperately over my shoulder. No one was coming for them—not yet anyway. With a sigh, she went back to rubbing circles against their back.

"Tate's pretty fucked up over this. I thought maybe we'd take something, you know? Have sex, have some fun, but I don't know what that asshole Perry gave us. The dude went back upstairs, and Tate's been freaking out. I'm in this like … super pleasant head space, you know? I must have gotten a benzo or something." Sasha shook her head. "Can you help me get them out of here?"

"We're going to defend a bedroom upstairs. We have supplies. The football team is … well, shit's about to hit the fan soon."

Tate whimpered, rocking faster. Their head shook wildly back and forth. "No, no, no. Not like this. I can't like this."

"Don't talk about anything that happened. Not now. They'll be fine, but … it's touch and go. If we get them upstairs, I think that will help. It's so dreary in here." Sasha waved around. "That's why I dragged them away from everyone else. Figured it'd be quieter."

"Dreary everywhere, Sasha." Tate unwrapped themselves suddenly and pulled on Sasha's shirt. They fisted the cotton in their hands, bleaching their skin. "We can't leave. We're going to die here. I can't. Sasha, I can't."

"Shh, Tate. Shh." She pulled on their face, wrapping them against her stomach. She ran her hands through their short, dark brown hair. The way she brushed it away from their face was so intimate, it made me glance away.

Tate wrapped their arms around Sasha's, crying silently into her forearm.

"Sasha," I said, waiting for her to look at me again. "We can come up with a plan, but we can't do it here. There's not enough protection."

Sasha nodded. Her eyes were liquid water, barely holding it together herself. I couldn't blame her. Shit got real, and Haden …

well, to everyone else, he was a nightmare incarnate. To me … I still hadn't decided.

"Tate. Get up." I made my voice harsh. Sasha needed to be the caregiver right now, but I could give them tough love. I knelt next to them and shook their shoulders. Lowering my voice in a warning, I said, "Pull your shit together."

Tate's eyes blinked at me but were completely unfocused. They were bright red, either from the drugs, tears, or smoke.

Well, I never thought I would do this in my entire life. It felt too dramatic, but we had to move. We were on a ticking clock, and without our feet underneath us, Tate might doom us. With a sigh, I slapped them across the face. No malice, just business.

Sasha gasped in a breath and scrambled to her feet. "Zoe!"

"Fuck," Tate muttered through gritted teeth. "Fuck, Zoe. Fuck! Fuck!" Their hand went up to cup their cheek, already reddening.

"That anger? Hold on to it, Tate. Remember everything we had to fight for before tonight? Remember all those meetings we went to in high school that made everyone feel good about their activism? You had to fight so hard to make them see you, who *you really are*. You did that. And you can hold it together for this, too."

Tate swallowed, throat moving as they did so. Their brown eyes came back into focus, and they nodded. Lips pressed into a flat line. "But after tonight, I'm done fighting. Someone else needs to do it for me."

"If I make it out alive, I will fight for whatever you want me to." I stood and held my hand out. "Now get up."

Tate looked at Sasha again. Her hand was outstretched too. They latched onto both of us, and together, we lifted Tate onto their feet. They dusted themselves off and let out a long breath. "This is a *really* bad trip. I thought I saw a guy pull out someone's spine."

Sasha and I exchanged a look.

Since Tate wasn't stupid, they noticed, and their face fell. "That wasn't a trip, was it?"

Sasha stepped up to them. "Look, what's important is you stay here with me now, okay?"

Tate nodded, pressing their forehead against hers. "Okay."

"Sorry, Tate. I'd give you more time, but we're running out. Here's the deal, we have a bedroom secured. Juniper has all the guns, so the football team will have to settle for less effective weapons. We have a chance that one of us will make it out of this."

"Juniper is joining us?" Tate straightened.

"No, but they sure as shit aren't going to pass their guns off to anyone who would try to kill us first."

Sasha squeezed Tate's hand. Her blue eyes searched theirs. "It's okay. We don't need to talk to them. We can do this on our own."

I arched my eyebrow, but apparently, I wasn't going to get whatever back story there was between the three of them. Every one of my friends, except Ridley and Mercedes, seemed to have some intertwined history with Juniper. Since Sasha and Tate separated for a brief period during freshman year of college, it wouldn't have surprised me if either of them ended up with Juniper at some point. Juniper was a cool person but had never fallen into our group. Wasn't sure why, but they had their own friends.

Whatever had happened between them lingered in the air, but now was not the time to unpack that.

"Are you going to be able to run with us?" I asked Tate. Because that's the crux of it now. We needed to go, and we needed to go fast. Every second we spent inside the basement might sign our death warrant.

"Yeah, yeah. Let's go. Safety in numbers, right?" Their eyes glistened as they forced a smile to their lips. Their forehead crinkled. "Fuck. I'm swimming."

Sasha ran her hands along Tate's forearms, pulling them into a hug. "Let's do this."

They nodded into her chest.

Together, the three of us circled back to the stairs. Thomas and his partner were already finished, both frantically pulling on their clothes like neither had particularly enjoyed the experience. What a way to live the last moments of your life.

"It's the third door on the left upstairs. Grab a few cupcake trays from underneath the oven in the kitchen as shields and get there fast," I urged them, pushing them toward the steps.

"Zoe, separating seems like a bad idea," Sasha said at the same time Tate asked, "What are you going to do?"

"I have something to say to our esteemed host. I'll catch up. Stay safe."

Or maybe I wouldn't, because this might be the last stupid decision I made in my life. If I died, I could die knowing I gave this asshole a piece of my mind. Because *fuck* this guy. "Go!" I barked as I shoved them again.

Sasha was the first to get her feet underneath her, tugging on Tate's arm. The floor above us shook, and someone somewhere shrieked, which made the feeling in the basement shift. It was like watching a clock jolt backward. Time stilled but then rippled forward as people in the basement doubled down on whatever they were already doing.

Well, my time had run out, but I could still do this one last thing.

I marched up to Thomas. Tapping him on the shoulder, he turned toward me. His cheeks were beet red, and he had this sated after-sex glow. I never wanted to see Thomas like this, but I also never thought I would see someone's spine ripped out of their back like deboning a fish.

"Oh, hey, Zo—"

Not letting him finish, I punched him right in the nose. An ache flared up my fist. *Fuck.* I had never hit anyone before, but I savored the pain. Red burst from his nostrils as he grunted and stumbled backward, straight into the woman he'd been fucking earlier. His fingers shook as he cupped his face.

My grin felt positively feral as the blood seeped through his fingers and flooded over his knuckles. "You raised a demon from the literal fires and thought maybe I should throw a party with him? What in the skies is wrong with you, Thomas?!"

"I didn't want to throw the party. It was Haden's idea! Ouch, Zoe. Come on. You know me—"

"Do I?" I took a step up to him and poked him in the chest. "Because I thought you were a *smart* guy, Thomas. Kind of toast, you know, not all that interesting until you use jam or butter or something, but I thought you'd find your person in college. Thought you'd become someone. Instead, you what? You summoned a demon, and what? What have you been doing this whole time to get ahead in life? Cheating? Breezing through it all? Taking the easy way out?"

"No! Until tonight, I had never taken his advice!" Thomas reached into the top drawer of the tool chest and pulled out a rag. Who knew how long they had been there. He shook out the cloth and pressed it to his nose.

"What?" I wanted to laugh, to cry. He had summoned a demon to make his life easier but then hadn't had the balls to actually do anything about it. Wow, this was rich. Anger roiled through me. He deserved whatever was going to happen to him tonight.

Thomas let out a helpless breath. "I never listened to him until tonight. He gave me advice, things I could do to make my life easier. I bound his magic to my soul, so he couldn't enact anything without my explicit permission. Until he found some way around my safeguards."

I blinked. "This party. You agreed to it."

"Sort of? Begrudgingly? He sent the invites out, and then I felt like I had to host it. Because Mercedes said she would come, I allowed him to plan whatever he wanted. Clearly a mistake. I let my guard down because he had been good—"

"He was a captive fucking demon, and you believed him when he said he would show you a good fucking time? Are you an idiot?" I wanted to slap him, because I also didn't miss the subtle dig that partially blamed Merce for this whole mess.

But I also realized how hypocritical my words were, because didn't a part of me still want to believe Haden when he said the things he did? There was something beguiling about him.

"Before tonight, I would have argued against you."

The blond woman who had been beside him inched away from our conversation, sheepishly rubbing her arm. The three of us collectively cringed as another scream sounded from upstairs. Didn't sound like Tate or Sasha, but I would check it out in a minute.

"You're the only one who could get us out of this, but you're down here getting laid instead of helping."

"What do you want me to do, Zoe?"

"Not act like a helpless wanker!"

"I am helpless! I'm as helpless as the rest of you. I always have been."

I shoved him back into the chest and grabbed his shirt, pulling him close. I snarled, "That's how we got into this mess. Because of men like you who were too afraid to be vulnerable but not afraid enough to sit the fuck down. You should have been nice and honest with some girl from the jump, and she would have been all over your dick."

"Honest how? Like admit how self-conscious I am?" He rolled

his eyes. "Because we all know women love that."

"Some do. Some die for that cinnamon roll bullshit. You just needed to find the right person." I pushed him away from me. He grunted as his back slammed into the metal. "Instead, you summoned a fucking demon and doomed everyone in your graduating class, so I hope you're happy with whatever the headlines are going to say tomorrow."

Thomas opened his mouth, anger and hatred coloring his features. "It wasn't my fault that no one—"

I narrowed my eyes, giving him the deepest, most loathing glare I could muster. "By all means, Thomas, double down now. Blame women for your decision to summon a demon."

He snapped his mouth shut, shoulders slumping as if I had snatched the wind from his sails. I *almost* felt bad.

With a brief blink, he said, "You're right. This is my fault. And yeah, I decided to have sex instead of trying to fix it, but it's only because I don't know how. I've never been strong like ... you."

"Here's another secret, Thomas, something I think someone should have told you a long time ago. If it looks like we have confidence, it's because we're faking it. We're just as sad and lonely as you, and we're waiting for someone to notice us and say ..."

What do I have to do to convince you of your own beauty?

"To tell us we're worth it. And Thomas, you would have been worth it to someone. Now you and that person will never get the chance." I grabbed the handrail.

"Zoe."

I paused on the first step and glanced at him.

"I don't blame you."

"Blame me for what?"

"Fucking him."

I gritted my teeth. "I don't feel bad about my actions because they came before I knew the truth. You, however, sought out evil and brought it here."

He hung his head. "For what it's worth, I'm sorry. I fucked up. I fucked up royally." Tears streaked down his face as he gazed at me again, as if I could bring him redemption.

"I don't forgive you. This was too big of a mistake. But maybe someday, you can heal from this. In whatever afterlife waits for you." I pressed my eyes shut, fighting back a shudder as another shriek echoed off the walls, reverberated into my sternum, and kicked up my heart. There was no more hiding from the reality of our situation. Without giving myself any more time to hesitate, I rushed upstairs.

Haden

Unfortunately, the football team had made quick work of the first room. Their delight disgusted me. Maybe I had been around Thomas for too long, because this much death shouldn't bother me. However, it wasn't the death itself. It was the way three of the men embraced being killers. Once they had killed, they posed the bodies, treating it more like a hunting trophy than anything else. Some fucked up social media stunt.

One of them tried to post a photo online with the hashtag "Early Halloween." He had made a peace sign with his fingers while his other hand held up the severed head. A single blood droplet had hit the guy's cheek, becoming a strange kind of tattoo. But after the signal failed numerous times, they settled for snapping photos instead.

I found the behavior gross. We saved the worst of the tar pits for men like this, and being around them threatened to give me hives.

"No, bro, you have to hold it higher. Yeah, but like smile more.

Look more … Yeah, like that. Perfect maniac smile." The other nameless one took the photo. I didn't care to learn who these people were. They would be dead by morning. Burning in the fires like they deserved.

"Let me see it." The other one crossed the room as they flipped through photos. "That's sick. I've always hated that bitch."

"That bitch sucked your cock freshman year."

"That bitch used her *teeth*."

"At least you got some."

"Whatever. She can't use her teeth now, can she?" They exchanged a glance.

I pinched the bridge of my nose. Some people thought demons were the evil ones. While I craved chaos, I would never respect anyone who bragged about killing a person physically weaker than them. Their souls burned brightly with their newfound heat and kept growing hotter. They were making eternity worse for themselves by bullying those they had already killed. They were treating tonight like some twisted high school superlative bullshit.

I hated it.

I hated them.

"Don't you think your time would be better spent hunting down the rest of the party?" I forced myself into existence, feeling my magic drain out of me. It was like a weight, an albatross, a void sucking me down.

Fucking Thomas.

They whirled around, jaws opening. The third one ceased in his sawing of the other guy's torso. Blood covered every surface.

"The fucking demon."

"Get him!"

Faster than they could track, I leaped to the opposite side of the room—landing on top of the dresser. My girl needed time, and I'd give it to her. While she might not be ready to kill yet, she would be. While violence turned her on, she was still warming up to the idea. For now, I could protect her. Give her space. And later tonight, she would kill. She would claim Thomas's magic.

And a part of her would like it.

For now, however, she needed time. Too soon, and I might lose her forever. Her soul was still slated for the skies. If she continued to put her doomed friends first, she might still be destined for that cold tundra.

Unless … I could convince her to bind herself to me. If she were bound to me, she'd be mine. The skies would likely have to give up any claim they had to her.

Maybe I could convince her to give me her soul, especially with these three murderous villains in the midst of those trying to survive the night. If it helped her make it until sunrise, she would. It would take convincing, but I was determined to get her soul by the end of the night.

While I hoped none of these brutes killed Thomas soon, I needed them to weed through the competition. It would be a test of my patience, something I wasn't in abundance of. But hey, I couldn't be good at everything.

"Right here," I mocked.

They tripped over themselves, trying to pivot at the same time. Two fell in a heap with flailing arms and pained grunts. The third whistled, and a fourth guy crashed into the room.

"What?" he yelled, eyes wide and frantic. He choked back puke as he took in the walls, the floor, the blood. "Oh, fuck, you guys—"

"Deal with your stupid feelings, Kyle. The demon's in here," the only one left standing growled. He was thicker than the other two, looked like he could be a bouncer at a club. Intimidating as fuck to the average person. I didn't need him killing Thomas. Would rather one of the slightly less coordinated assholes sprawled on the floor end him. They'd be easier for Zoe to kill.

"Fuck you, David." Kyle visibly paled. His soul was still tepid, not getting burned up by the other three around him. He had started the night ice cold, but now was room temperature because of his affiliations. He would still be destined for the skies after this, but probably with the task of being a guardian for someone else first.

People were such herd creatures, and it amused me greatly. Kyle was terrified, and because of his fear, he turned toward the familiar, the people he had spent his entire life around. Despite how they were actively becoming the worst versions of themselves, Kyle hadn't broken that loyalty. That allegiance strengthened with every vile act they performed together.

Kyle knew if he walked away now, they would turn that same horrific energy toward him. Dread coiled around him, keeping him complacent with every terrible thing they did.

The skies would see his potential. They'd let him prove his worthiness. He'd have a chance for retribution—become a guardian to someone else, save them from the fate that he had succumbed to. A suitable punishment if there ever was one. Because if the guardian failed enough times, well … we'd see them eventually in the fires. And tying someone's fate to another corruptible human while trying to make them stay on the *right* path? It was befitting. Neat and organized.

I still preferred chaos.

The other three, however, had caved to their depravity quickly. It hadn't been hard for them to fall into their own flames. Two of them had warm souls to begin with, already doomed for the fires. Now, not an ounce of coolness swept among them. They had lived a life worth condemning. As they dripped in blood with glee in their gazes, it was easy to see why.

Honestly, I might ascend to a saint since I was removing these three from the planet. By the end of the night, they would be dead because of my curse. That thought made me smile. Three more souls for the fires, and oddly, I'd have some notoriety in the skies. It would confuse the fuck out of the King of the Fires, that's for sure.

The thought made me downright giddy for the first time in a long time. Because what kind of demon came to Earth and received commendations for their actions from the *skies*?

"There's no demon." Kyle hiked up his grip on the bat as he scanned the interior. The throw rug squished underneath his feet, and he grimaced. "There's literally no one here with you." He looked straight through me at the mirror on the wall. I was almost insulted.

"He was just here."

"Doing that disappearing thing again."

"Fuck this." The two on the floor extricated themselves from each other and stood up, dusting off their shirts. It was no use, of course, because red splattered them all. It coated their hands, arms, and legs. They'd be better off jumping in the pool to get clean.

"Why the fuck are you sawing them?"

"Why not?" One of them arched an eyebrow at Kyle and crossed his arms over his chest.

Kyle's cheeks flushed red as he ran a hand through his brown hair. "I don't know? It's fucked up." Blinking, he made eye contact with each of the guys who he used to know. Bitter realization swept across his face—he had no idea who these people were anymore. His shoulders sank. "You know what, as long as you promise not to kill me before the end of the night, fuck it."

"We're not doing a showdown until everyone else is dead." The stocky guy slapped Kyle on the back, a shit-eating grin on his face. His teeth had flecks of red on them. "And there are a lot of people to kill. Hey, you think we'll figure out what's underneath—"

I reappeared on the dresser. "For all this talk about how many people you plan to murder, you certainly aren't killing very many."

"Fuck!" Kyle jumped back at the same time as one of them tried to hit me with a crowbar.

I snatched it out of the air and shoved him backward, twisting my grip on the metal until he was forced to drop it. I tossed it across the room, where the pointy end careened straight into the drywall. "Here's the deal. I need you to kill a lot more people tonight, because the four of you are a means to a fucking end. But all you're doing is getting a gleeful high off desecrating corpses. It's boring, frankly. There are four people in the next room, but they have the door barricaded. You're better off attacking them through the linked bathroom."

"Fuck you!" One of them was being smart and threw their packet of pool chemicals at me.

I sighed, rolled my eyes, and waved the whole mess away, back toward his face. He coughed and hacked on the material. "You can't kill me. So, stop trying." I jumped off the dresser and strolled from the room, not taking a second to look back. But as soon as the door closed behind me, I melted the knob in place. One pounded on the door, but the frame didn't budge. Too bad their crowbar was stuck inside the wall now.

With any luck, they'd focus on the other room, which gave Zoe more time. As soon as I had the thought, her two friends scuttled by, booking it toward the stairs.

But where was she? She was supposed to be with them, heading up toward safety. I had no idea how long the guys would be occupied. There were plenty of people left alive, but what had been Zoe's relationship with the football team? Would she be an early target, or someone they saved for later?

Prowling toward the kitchen, I scanned each room. More and

more people were in collective huddles. Those who had been drinking their feelings previously now held broken bottles and knives. Several people in the living room wielded logs and fire pokers—those who were left alive, that was. There were three additional bodies on the floor, but none were as gruesome as the bedroom. Self-defense, seemed like.

As for the rest of them, no one else fought. The football team had taken first offensive blood, but most seemed to be on the defensive. No problem. For some, it took more to embrace their flames. As people were backed into corners, their fires would come alive. Their anger would drive them, fueling their need for survival. This house would burst with heat soon—souls for the fires to consume. I looked forward to seeing what the king thought upon my return.

Disappointment, probably. As usual.

As soon as I reached the kitchen, a battle cry sounded from the living room. Something slammed hard with a thwack. Guttural screams erupted, as well as low, wailing moans. Cries and shouts as more people joined the scuffle. Those in the kitchen glanced at each other. Sweat beaded along brows. Throats bobbed as people nervously swallowed. But they nodded, grips tightening on their knives. They prowled toward the living room, holding their weapons in front of them like action movie heroes. Their stances were wrong, but they would either learn how to survive or die trying to figure it out.

With the room now empty, I wrapped my grip around the basement doorknob, but it twisted underneath my hand. I stepped back; the door swung open. Zoe paused as her eyes landed on me. A growl crawled out of her throat as a Wilhelm scream came from the other room. Her eyes grew wide.

We were out of time.

Fighting and shouting broke out. Footsteps sounded in the hallway. Others rushed up from the basement. The house erupted. Yells, screams, cries. Her mouth gaped open, as if she wanted to chew me out, but failed to find the words. More people were about to round the corner into the kitchen, but I dragged her into the pantry with me and slammed the door shut.

"Fu—"

I pressed my hand against her mouth. She bit my palm. I snarled and pushed her back against the pantry shelves. "I'm trying to save your life."

She muttered something into my aching hand, but I didn't let up. Her nostrils flared as her brows came down low over her eyes. Her vehemence toward me rolled off her in waves, but that didn't matter right now. The footsteps outside stopped moving.

"Thought I heard—"

"There!"

"Thomas, fuck you!"

"Yeah, what in the fires, man?"

I didn't recognize any of the voices, but one door slammed shut. More pounding and yelling broke out. Thomas had run back into the basement, hiding out like the scared human he was. Not that I blamed him in this instance; I'd probably be shitting myself too if an angry mob tried to kill me—and if I were human.

Zoe reared back and slammed her forehead into my nose.

"Fuck." Ignoring the blood dripping down my face, I used my free hand to wrap my fist through her hair and pulled. I zeroed in on her, ignoring everything happening outside of this pantry. "That wasn't very nice."

She muttered something into my palm as tears welled in her eyes. The sight was achingly beautiful.

"If they hear us, they are going to kill you. So be quiet." Slowly,

I released the pressure on her mouth and dropped my hand.

She sucked in a breath. "I can't—" Her voice raised into a shriek, and I slammed my palm back over her lips. I rested my forehead against hers. She used her hands to shove my chest. When that didn't work, she tried to kick me. I pushed her legs aside and stepped in between her thighs, thrusting her back against the shelves. Her breath escaped her lungs in a puff against my skin.

Hot. Warm. Perfect.

"I'm going to distract you. Since you seem to not be understanding the gravity of our situation. I need you alive, and those people out there? They've finally realized what it means to be trapped here until the bitter end. I will not have you die just because you couldn't keep your mouth shut."

Her teeth sank into my palm again.

She could bite me forever for all I cared.

I inhaled her scent. The fear, the lust, all of it coated her skin like a pheromone designed specifically for me. It was like opening a three-hundred-dollar bottle of whiskey. Her hazel eyes were narrowed slits, brow wrinkled as she watched me. As her teeth broke through a layer of skin, I growled and rolled my hips against hers. Her eyes widened as she felt how hard I was.

"Keep biting. See what happens."

Her nose worked as her breath came more rapidly. I pressed a light kiss to her brow, then her temple, then her cheek. Her hands, which had been clawing at my chest, relaxed, pressed into me. Not pushing away, but not bringing me closer, either.

My tongue ran over the shell of her ear. "I want to fuck you in here. I want you screaming so loudly, they think you're dying. No one will come to rescue you, because they'll think, 'One less person for me to kill later.'"

She whimpered.

Trailing my tongue down her skin, I tasted the haze of the basement and the salt of her panic. But right now, she was calm next to me, shifting her body against mine. Her hips sought my length, and I wasn't sure she was consciously doing it.

Removing my hand from her face, I didn't give her time to protest. My lips crushed against hers. A moan escaped her as her mouth parted for me. I licked into her, greeted by the most delicious warmth. I grabbed hold of her legs, lifting her up. She wrapped herself around me, gasping as I thrust into her. The pantry shelves rattled.

"Grab hold of the top shelf."

Her arms instantly lifted as she latched onto it. The leverage allowed her to press forward, arching her back as she rode me. Fuck, I was so hard for her. My cock strained in my jeans. Something I will never understand about Earth is why they bothered to be so restricted all the time. Pants—especially ones with zippers—were sometimes *painful* when it came to arousal.

I shifted, adjusting myself so I could hit her core with every roll of her hips. And she met my motions so beautifully. The gasping breath she took as I settled against her was enough to ignite my soul on fire. A heady rush went through me. I wanted to claim her as I edged her. Her thighs widened as she brought me closer still, clearly as eager as I was to fuck again.

My mouth moved with hers. Our kisses became frantic, frenzied. Teeth mashed together as she groaned. Her aggression stemmed from anger, and mine was because I loved watching her become unhinged. How wild would our fervor become? And the moment I had her soul … the things I would do to her. This was just a taste.

If I slowly fed her parts of me, gradually opened her to the possibilities of what we could become, she would grow to love it. A promise, a threat, a complete totality of our futures as they merged.

One of my hands latched onto her neck, the other found her hips, grinding her into me as I bit her lower lip and sucked. She moaned as I picked up the pace, dragging her along my length. There were entirely too many clothes between us, and still I felt her wetness seeping through.

I brought her shirt up and wrapped it around her wrists. I forced her hands back against the shelf, and she grasped on, now with the makeshift binding. Her eyes searched mine as I undid the button on her pants.

"Keep holding onto that."

"This doesn't mean I like you," she said, keeping her voice soft. It came out with an edge of breathlessness.

I smirked. "Sure doesn't."

"Or that I feel shame."

I arched a brow. "You're telling me there's no shame in this? Letting me back inside you, even though you know what I am? What I've done?"

Her lower lip disappeared in between her teeth as she contemplated this, dragging the pink skin out slowly. While she thought it over, I removed her pants, leaving her in her bikini. I eyed her hips, her thighs, the way her stomach was perfectly soft. She held such strength in her form, in her beauty.

"Are you really going to fuck me bare?"

The sound of my zipper was loud, despite the commotion outside this room. We were so in tune with each other, our focus never straying. "Why would I bother with a condom when demons can't impregnate humans?"

"Is there anything else I should be worried about?"

As soon as my cock was out, I drew her back into me. Her breath came out as a harsh pant as I guided myself along her slit. Wetness soaked through her bikini. She whimpered as the head of my cock grazed her nerves.

"Nope." I nipped her jaw. "When I said I wasn't wearing a condom, I meant it. So, if we're doing this, then—" The pantry door opened.

A guy stood on the other side with a log in hand. Blood smeared across the end of it. Zoe flinched back. He opened his mouth to yell something, but didn't get the chance. I grabbed the closest jar—pickles—and hurled it at the guy's face. It shattered across his skin, piercing into his flesh with hundreds of tiny shards. He screamed, reeled back, and stumbled into the kitchen island.

I whipped the door shut and melted the knob in place for privacy.

I turned my attention back to her. Displayed. Legs settled around my hips. Perfect. "Now, where was I?"

Her eyes were huge, sparkling, watching the door as if reliving the single moment of violence. I liked how she got lost in it. I liked how she wanted more of it. She might not admit it, but it was there. Simmering below the surface and begging for release.

I turned her jaw back toward me. "Eyes on me."

She swallowed, mouth parting on an inhale.

"Yes, I did that. Yes, I hurt him. He's not the first, nor will he be the last. No, I don't care. Mortal lives are short-lived. It's the afterlife I'm worried about—what happens to your souls when you leave this plane. No, it's not fair that there's a demon roaming the earth. Yes, I would have left long ago had Thomas's stupid summoning circle been a little less protective." I pushed aside her panties with my fingers and tested her entrance. She was *soaking*.

But her soul was still breezy.

I ran my dick along her slit, getting myself nice and wet for her. "Any other questions before I fuck you?"

"I didn't ask a single one." Her eyes stayed on me as she sucked her lower lip in between her teeth again.

"Good girl." I slammed into her. Fuck. She was so tight. Warm. Perfect. Her body clenched as soon as I bottomed out inside her. Her legs pulled me in close as she gasped.

"Holy—"

"Nothing holy here." I dragged out and thrust forward again, making something on the shelf fall off and shatter next to our feet.

She let out a gasp as she struggled to get a better grip, but I pounded into her relentlessly. I had held back earlier, but I couldn't find it in me to do so any longer, not when she had tried to fight me, not when she still argued against the inevitability of us. We were meant to be together, and if I had to fuck her until she couldn't stand upright, I would. I would drag out as many orgasms as needed until she understood the simple fact: she would be mine.

And she would love it.

My lips found hers, as we smashed into each other. Her moans escaped her throat, pouring into my mouth as I moved inside her. Impossibly, she tightened around me, as I sank my teeth into her lower lip.

I wanted this girl naked in the fires with me. I wanted to watch her walk around with no clothes until the shame of nudity wore off. Needed to watch my cum drip down her legs.

Wanted to watch someone else lick it off her.

She would never be anyone else's, always mine, but if she ever cared to explore, I had a few demons I wouldn't mind watching her with—Silas in particular.

"Haden ..." A small groan escaped her lips as she flung her t-shirt off her wrists. Her arms came around my neck. Fingernails raked through my hair as she leaned her head back on a shelf. Her breasts swayed so prettily as I thrust into her.

I pulled on her hair, forcing her head to the side. My lips trailed down her neck, pressing my teeth against her collarbone. Her hips ground against mine, desperate to have me farther.

"You need more?"

She whimpered.

I licked a line to her ear. "Wait until I can take you in my demon form. Tongue and all. You'd look so perfect split open on my cock, stretched to the point of almost breaking."

Her pussy clamped around me as I fucked into her. Hands on my shoulders, nails dug into me. Pretty sure she burst my skin open, and I let her. She could flay me alive if it meant five more seconds buried inside her. She pressed her face against my shoulder, a scream escaping her lips, muffled as her teeth sank into me. I wanted her to bite, to taste the bitterness of my blood on her tongue, to have me inside all parts of her. I wanted to consume her.

I wanted her soul.

Craved it.

Her muscles slowly eased around my length, but I kept my rhythm, now chasing my release. "Stay with me," I demanded as her head lolled. Her body was relaxed, but legs still held me firm as I pumped several more times.

She panted into my shoulder, fingers tightening into my skin. She could take it.

"Haden!" the cry rushed out of her lips, and it was so divine, it unraveled me. I thrust as deep into her as I could, spilling inside her. Pulsing until there was nothing left to give, and even then, I refused to set her down. I wanted to stay like that, feel my cum inside her, the heat of her mixed with me. Her body still tried to pull me in, despite her exhaustion.

"You're perfect," I told her, pressing a kiss to her cheek. "Absolutely fucking perfect."

Instead of arguing or questioning, she melted against me. Her breath was hot along my skin.

"How am I almost naked, and you're just …"

I wrapped my hands through her hair, holding her firm as I drew her face away from me. I wanted to get a good look at the aftermath of our fuck. "You want to see me naked again?"

"It's such a power move, isn't it? Staying fully clothed when I'm … only in my panties."

"Did it disappoint you?"

Her throat moved, lips parted, eyes searched mine. Blinking, she shook her head, but only as far as my grip would let her move. "No, absolutely not. But I do like you naked. You're … You think I'm perfect, but—"

"No *thinking* about it. You are."

She narrowed her gaze. "But you're literally like a chiseled fucking statue."

"I hope I'm not as cold as one."

She laughed and shook her head again. I loosened my grip on her hair.

"Good." I pushed forward one last time, enjoying her groan against my skin. I pulled out of her, tucking myself away. I helped her onto her feet, holding her steady as she searched for her discarded clothes. As much as I wanted her to spend the rest of the night naked, the wretched material would provide *some* protection against whoever else was out there. "Besides, I don't want you to get too attached to this … human suit."

She tilted her head, and this adorable little furrow appeared over her brow as she clutched her clothes to her chest. "What do you mean?"

"My demonic form doesn't look like this. And my dick's a lot bigger."

"Were you bound in this body?"

"Not exactly. We're able to transform in order to blend in. This is my human form, but it's not my true form. That has been bound to Thomas, and I can't shift without using significant power or without his permission. Which—"

"He hasn't given you." She nodded, lips pursing. "I understand why you hate him so much. I shoved him downstairs, told him he was a piece of shit." She pulled her pants up and scowled. As her fingers fumbled with the button, I stopped her, dipping my fingers into her bikini.

"Haden …" The whine escaping her lips was cute. Her hands grasped onto my wrist. We paused like that for a moment. My eyes searched hers, and a coy smile broke out across her lips. Her grip loosened, allowing me to continue.

I found our collective wetness. Swirling it around my fingers, I shoved the mess back inside her. "Can't have you losing it all right away, can we? No distractions for your journey back up to the room."

She moaned, pressing her lips to mine. I savored her warmth as I pumped my fingers a few times, taking pleasure in how she felt full of my cum. There'd be more days like this. Many more. She let out a mewl the moment I pulled out of her again. I brought the mixture of us up to her lips and painted them with it. Her mouth dropped open, but I didn't push myself inside. I loved how she glistened with me.

"When you leave this room, you need to run. I can guide you, but you must listen to everything I say."

Her eyes narrowed again as I zipped her pants. "Listen to you? You started this mess," she hissed.

"And because I started it, I have some knowledge of how to best survive it. Understood?"

She wrinkled her nose. "I'll do fine on my own." Her hands pressed firmly on my chest. "This changes nothing. You understand?" Shoving me off, she made the final adjustments to her clothes and shook her head. "I'm still angry with you. That was hate sex." Her lips tightened, brows lowering, as if she couldn't decide on the accuracy of that statement.

"And I will beg for your forgiveness after tonight is over. On my knees if I have to."

A shiver tore through her.

"Don't go straight upstairs. Shit's about to hit the fan up there, and you don't want to get caught in the crossfire."

"But that's where my friends are." Her nose wrinkled. "I'm going upstairs. It'll be fine." She glanced toward the door. "Are you going to make it easier for me to get out of here or will I have to bust through?"

"Are you going to disobey me and run upstairs instantly?"

She glared at me. "There's no reason for me to avoid upstairs. You can't predict the future."

"Predict? No. Understand humans enough to feel when they are at their breaking points? Sense the shift in their souls? Yes. And I'm telling you, upstairs is dangerous."

Her snarling lips told me everything I needed to know. If she escaped the pantry, she would make a run for the stairs. Which meant I was leaving her in here to bide time.

I shrugged, pressing a light kiss on her nose. She shoved my face away. I smirked. "Enjoy getting out of here. The extra time should save your life." I went incorporeal and stepped through the door, ignoring her curses on the other side. Using my limited powers only lasted a moment, but it felt like wading through tar. Once I took a steadying breath, I decided on my next move. I had to scope out the rest of the party, see what was happening, and how to keep her safe.

He left me in the pantry.

Locked inside.

I imagined the door being opened with an ax. A ruddy-faced man poking in and screaming at me before taking the weapon to my stomach. I was in the middle of a massive murder scene, and here I was trapped in a pantry.

Haden seemed convinced that keeping me here would save my life, but for what purpose? Being with my friends felt like the best way to survive the night. There was strength in numbers, and as of right now, my friends had our defensive items and any potential weapons. They had a cast iron frying pan—that could do some damage—and I had nothing.

I regretted giving up the cheese grater.

Instead, I had my incredibly soiled bikini bottoms, pickle juice dripping off my arm, and a few jars I could hurl at people. Though I wouldn't be able to cause as much damage as Haden had.

I couldn't believe the force he had put behind his pitch of the pickle jar. It had splintered apart on Monty's face as if it had been made of sugar instead of glass. I couldn't stop thinking about the way blood welled from his wounds before Haden slammed the door shut. Monty's scream cut short as I focused solely on Haden.

My core had dampened because of the act of violence.

There was something seriously wrong with me, because the shame I felt earlier was diminishing with every passing moment. I had seen Haden rip out Jet's spine, witnessing the violence first-hand. Saw the destruction he created by trapping us here. And yet … I had allowed him to fuck me again—*enjoyed* it. We had done it without a condom, and I wasn't sure if I believed him about not being able to get me pregnant. It was too late to think about that now, and besides, why the fuck was I worried when I might open the pantry door and immediately be split in half with a machete?

Did Thomas's folks own machetes? Maybe I should have asked before I punched him in the face.

Now that my adrenaline and hormones had calmed down, my ears finally pricked to the noises outside of my little bubble. Screams echoed off the walls. Curses and insults were hurled. Wet thwacks, distant squelching, and other sounds I couldn't place filled my synapses. The smell of vinegar and copper invaded the pantry. Grunts, moans, and the wails of those dead or dying.

I was too late.

It had begun.

Maybe the pantry was the safest place for the moment, but I needed to reach my friends. Sitting here would make me an easy target once there were fewer people left alive. It was better to escape into the chaos, get lost in the crowd, weave through it like guiding myself on a wave. Allowing the swell of murder to rush me toward the shore.

I hoped there wouldn't be a riptide on the other side to greet me.

With a sigh, I examined the melted knob. There was no way out except through. I stepped to the opposite end of the closet, and with my shoulder aimed outward, I charged the door. Crashing into the wood made me bite down on my tongue. I flew backward, landing hard on my ass, and stared at the exit. Not so much as a splinter out of place.

People made it look so easy in movies. They broke through these things like there was nothing to it. Hollywood effects or something, because shit, that wood? It was hard.

With a growl, I stood and rolled my shoulders. My left one throbbed from the impact. Maybe I'd have a better chance at kicking it down, but that would make a lot of noise. Was I ready for the consequences of creating a commotion?

I didn't want to stay here all night, not with the wails growing louder and more desperate. My friends needed me. If one of us were to survive the night, then I had to be there for them. We had to be a team.

I sucked in another breath, steeling my nerves. Grabbing hold of the shelves on either side of the walls, I did a few test kicks, focusing on where I needed to place my heel for the best forward momentum. This had to work, right? Tightening my grip, I put every ounce of frustration, rage, and annoyance into a kick, aiming straight toward the latch.

The wood splintered, but didn't open.

Okay, progress. I could make this work.

Fighting against my rapid-fire pulse in my ears, I waited a few moments, forcing my breath steady while I strained to listen. Everything remained in chaos and madness, so I didn't think anyone heard my attempt at escape. Regardless, I was terrified of what I would see outside. Watching Haden perform a violent act had been darkly gorgeous, tormented and twisted in a way that soothed the wild part of my soul. But seeing my old classmates turn against each other? There was something horrid about that. Too close to home. Too real. I knew darkness simmered underneath the surface of numerous people, and I didn't want to come face to face with a single one of them. Not by myself. Not now.

Plus, watching Haden had been like seeing it on the silver screen. Surreal. But it *had* been real. The blood, the gore, the way viscera dropped to the floor. How his fist had curled around the bones with crushing force. And I had …

"Ugh," I said with a grunt, shoving forward my leg again. More wood fractured. I hit one last time, and the pantry door flew open. Someone grunted on the other side, as the door rammed into them.

"Where the fuck did you—"

I didn't wait to figure out who was speaking or what weapons they had. I flew. The hallway was slick with blood. Three bodies lay in heaps. Mangled pulps left behind in the violence of a pent-up generation. I kept running, careful not to skid on the slippery wood. Charging up the stairs, I counted the doors to where my friends should still be and pounded on it. But as soon as my fist hit the wood, gunshots sounded. Loud, close. Too close.

I whirled around, watching with widening eyes as some of the band members and Juniper fired shots at each other.

"You were always such an asshole!"

"I know I am, but what's your excuse?!" Juniper's face was speckled with blood, but their grin was unmistakable. There was a guy hovering at Juniper's side, not participating, but his eyes were solely on them. He had long, glowing brown hair, but still looked younger. He picked at his nails casually with a frown on his lips.

Guardian angels. Huh. Who knew?

Juniper discharged another shot, and this one ended in a mist of red. There wasn't so much as a scream as the person dropped to their knees. Their body teetered, hovered as if they were a puppet on a string. Then, with the string cut, they fell face forward. Dead.

Shrapnel from the bullet hitting the wall sheered across my skin, interrupting my reverie. Fuck. I pounded on the door another time, but it was no use—even if I yelled, my friends wouldn't be able to hear me over the screaming and shots being fired in the hallway. More obscenities as crimson painted the hallway.

Ducking, I practically tumbled down the stairs in my haste to get away from the violence, but the main floor was no different. Everywhere I turned, people were locked in combat. Panting, drenched with blood, scowling, crying, screaming. Clenched teeth and set jaws. Growling, scratching, and kicking. This was what people became when you took away everything that made them human, when you brought them to the edge and destroyed their reason to live, when you made them nothing more than a number. This was what we were at the core—survivors, fighters, rebellious creatures. This was primal.

Why in the fires did my body *like* this so much?

When we created society, we invented other kinds of monsters— the kind that dressed in suits and ties, the kind that could smile one minute and steal your home out from under you the next. We bolstered those who weren't afraid to be cutthroat in business, so how was this any different?

They would claim it was, but it's all the same. You kill someone slowly by picking away at their soul or you kill someone fast by slicing their throat.

I inched around those engaged in fights. Two guys laughed maniacally as they took turns punching each other in the jaw. Others screamed in their old rival's face. Two women pulled each other's hair. All these battles and wars reflected their bullshit rising to the surface—shit we thought was buried in high school. The snippets of conversations I caught were petty at best.

"Can't believe you slept with him after—"

"How could you lie to me all this time?"

"We were supposed to be best friends!"

"Why am I just learning about this?!"

"He was my brother, you fucking piece of shit."

The cacophony of noise was too much. I needed a place to regroup, a place to think. I stumbled into the living room, which was now a thronging mass of combat and dead bodies. Carnage was everywhere. My brain couldn't process the amount of gore and entrails in the room. The rest of the screams faded into the background, because red had seeped into every part of my brain. My thoughts, red. The walls, red. The smell, red. My bones, red. My soul, red.

Ever since we arrived at this party, nothing had felt real. The moment I locked eyes with Haden—the moment my life shifted—it felt surreal. And this too. There was nothing real about this. Effects. Special effects and make-up. Fake blood that would taste sweet if I licked it. Corn syrup and gelatin. That wasn't brain matter, but custom-built and designed to create a sense of horror.

Had this truly happened today? Tonight? Had the party only started a few hours ago? It felt like a lifetime. But now my shoes squelched in blood. Sour bile rose in my throat. Another roar thundered out from the pool area. I shook myself, not wanting to venture farther off course.

Haden had told me to stay in the pantry.

He had said it would be safer.

I should have believed him, but I had been so angry.

Letting out a breath, I turned, sprinting toward the downstairs bedrooms. While my friends had barricaded themselves in, maybe one on this floor was open. Maybe I could buy a few minutes to think or find a weapon on one of the fallen bodies.

But of course, it wasn't as easy as opening a room, because the first one I opened had a washer and dryer in it. The washer was going. Front loading with a see-through door, and my jaw unhinged when I realized a severed human head tumbled around inside. With suds and all.

What. The. Fuck.

I slammed the closet door shut, swallowing hard to settle my stomach. Glancing down the hallway, I refused to scream. This hallway was huge—long and seemingly more dangerous with who might be behind door number one. Of course, Thomas would have a mansion as a *cabin* on the secluded side of the lake. Of course, it's a maze we were trapped in like rats. Of course, he had been stupid enough to link himself to a demon who invited us over to die.

A hysterical laugh bubbled out of my lips, so quickly I couldn't keep it down. I shoved my hands over my mouth, silencing it as fast as I could as my heart raced inside my chest. I forced myself to continue my march forward, staring at the ground to avoid slipping on a stray piece of intestine. Was that actually—

You know what? Nope, I would not start identifying body parts.

I was going to die. I should never have come. If Mercedes hadn't spent so much time convincing me … she thought it would be good for me. *Get out more, be more social. Make friends, get a boyfriend, declare a major you are passionate about. Come with me to New York. We could have so much fun together.*

Yeah, some fun.

I pulled up short, almost running into Haden. He leaned against one of the door frames at the beginning of the long hallway. The end of the corridor had an L-shaped corner, and there had to be a safe bedroom somewhere up ahead. Right?

But my heart galloped inside me. The demon had a habit of appearing as soon as my life was in danger, and the hair on my neck rose. I glanced behind me, but no one had followed me down here. Still, I couldn't shake the feeling of eyes on me.

"Not this way."

"Not this way, like how you stuffed me in a pantry?"

"That sentence makes no sense." His black eyes looked me up and down, impossibly hungry again. His blond hair hung heavy around his ears, and his jaw worked, cheekbones catching the light of the wall sconces. He looked delicious.

"Sorry. I ran out of intelligent quips as soon as my shoes filled with blood." Anger roiled through me, because now my shoulder hurt. My foot radiated with pain from kicking the door open. And he still hadn't warned me about the curse to begin with. Despite having tons of things to hold against him, my body still leaned toward him.

"If I recall, I brought us both into the pantry, and then I stuffed *you* while we were inside." He grabbed onto my wrist, tugging me close. His breath caressed my skin like lightning.

I wanted to feel it in between my thighs.

"And I would do it again in a heartbeat. Just say the word."

"Absolutely the fuck not." I ducked around him. I failed to make it more than two steps away from him.

He pulled me back into his chest. I grunted as his arms came around me, holding me close. "I don't understand. You want me to warn you, but when I do, you refuse to listen. So, what's it going to be? You going to do the opposite of what I say each and every time? What point will that prove?" His tongue traced the shell of my ear. "Soon, you'll learn to listen to me. Thomas never did and look what happened."

I scoffed, wanting to come up with a witty retort, but the words got stuck on my tongue as his teeth grazed my skin.

A secluded bedroom had to be safer than the rest of the house. I'd seen what it was like—it was chaos, war. Death and destruction literally bled into the carpets. Each second we stood here increased my risk of being out in the open. Someone had to be chasing me, right?

But … the way Haden held me told me he wouldn't risk my life like that. I hesitated. I didn't understand his end game, other than getting Thomas detached from him. Why was he taking such an interest?

I tore myself out of his arms and darted forward, determined to find safety in a room up ahead.

His sigh licked at my heels. I took the corner as he called out, "If you refuse to listen to me, you might as well duck."

"What?" I glanced over my shoulder in time to see a door open. A man stumbled out with an ax. The weapon swung at my head. I yelped, plummeting to the floor. The blade cut a few strands of my hair off before lodging itself in the wooden wall with a sickening smack.

That could have been me.

If Haden hadn't said anything … He *was* trying to protect me. For whatever reason, he wanted me to survive this.

Well, I wouldn't waste a second of the advantage. I punched the guy's balls. He wheezed and sank to the floor, dropping his hold on the ax handle. His hands desperately clutched at his privates.

I leaped up and latched onto the ax, but the blade was lodged into the wall like Excalibur. I cursed, lamenting every single entity I knew while I tried to pry the thing out of the wall.

"Want this instead? Might come in handy." Haden offered me a knife. Flecks of blood still hung on the edges. I wondered who it had belonged to before they lost their fight. It was one of the missing butcher block knives and not nearly big enough to take down the brute who just tried to murder me.

But so far, Haden *had* tried to keep me safe. It was a risk to trust him, but it was better than nothing, especially as the guy on the floor came out of his stupor.

I gazed at the demon for a beat, wondering what his goal was *after* tonight. He arched an eyebrow as the guy scrambled to get his feet underneath him. I grabbed the knife and slashed forward. The guy rolled out of the way. And that's when I got a good look at his face.

"Brett?!"

"Oh, hey, Zoe." He swallowed, blinked, and crab-walked backward a few feet away from me and the glint of metal. His blue eyes went wide. "I didn't realize it was you. Shit. I wouldn't have swung if I had known."

"We've known each other since we were six!"

"Yeah." He at least had the decency to look sheepish as he rose to his feet. "Look, I want to be the last one alive, okay? There's nothing wrong with trying to survive, but we could join forces for now. Whoever survives from the living room is going to be armed to the teeth. There were so many weapons in that storage closet. Who knew repair tools would make such good bludgeons?" His eye shifted to the ax.

I stalked forward, brandishing my weapon. I needed to put more space between him and the ax, and it worked. Brett backed away with his hands held in front of him. I didn't believe for a second that he meant to surrender.

He tried reasoning with me. "Look, we'd be better off together, right? And then we can do some kind of duel at the end?" An easy smile spread across the side of his lips, as if he were trying to look innocent.

I tampered down the anger welling inside me. Brett had never looked innocent a day in his life—not when he copied off my math test in third grade, then blamed me for it when he got caught having the same answers as me. And that teacher? He had believed Brett. I scored a zero, got lunch detention for a week, and Brett had *bragged* about it.

Heat flooded my body as I remembered everything those stupid kids put me through. Yeah, we were young, but Brett still knew better. Or he should have.

I hadn't realized I was still holding onto that. Well, this was as good of a time as any to confront my past. My lips ticked upward. "You said it yourself, Brett. You want to be the survivor. If I team up with you, which I won't, I wouldn't have a chance against you once everyone else is dead. You're taller than me and stronger. If it came down to us at the end, you'd win."

Brett shook his head. "Shit, Zoe, I didn't mean it like *that*. You're reading into it too much."

Gaslighting fucking bullshit.

"Am I?" I tightened my grip on the knife and cocked my head to the side, glaring at him. "Or is that your excuse because I called out your bad behavior?"

"I haven't even killed anyone yet." He gestured wildly to the ax behind me. "That was my first attempt, and clearly, it didn't go very well." His voice arched upward. Too harsh for this space. If he were any louder, others might come.

Everything he said was a lie. The ax blade had blood on it. It wasn't his. Either he killed to *steal* the weapon, or he killed *with* the weapon. Regardless, I wouldn't cave to his bullshit.

I snarled, "Say your goodbyes, Brett."

I lunged for him. He sprinted down the hallway. I took off in pursuit. I needed this, needed to prove to myself that I *could* survive the night. Brett would absolutely be one of the people left alive at the end. He would and could kill me and my friends. He was part of the football team, and he was stronger now than he had been three years ago. Probably still played on scholarship.

Not that it would matter soon, because I was going to kill him.

Third grade me would be so proud.

Every move I made was one of pure instinct as I loped after him. He reached the last door, pulled on the knob, but it didn't budge. He whirled to face me again.

It was me, him, and a decorative end table.

"Fine. Have it your way. We could have been great allies for a while, so don't say I didn't warn you." He was so desperate to intimidate me.

I prowled toward him. My fingers trembled around the knife. I had to do this. There was no turning back. Brett needed to die. He tried to kill me. He had blood flecked on his hands. Lie after lie had spewed from his mouth—anything to make him look a little better, try to bend my sympathy toward him. But no more.

As soon as I took another step forward, Brett grabbed the handle of the end table's drawer and ripped the whole thing out of the base. I swiped forward with the knife, aiming for his throat. He whipped the drawer up. My blade glanced off the side of the wood. With a scream, I stabbed again, but he shifted his grip. The weapon sank into the particle board.

He twisted his hands sideways. My grip loosened. He flung the whole thing—drawer and knife—at the wall. My blade disappeared as the drawer shattered into pieces.

I huffed out a breath. Just Brett and me at the end of the hallway, but he was a lot bigger than me.

"Like you said, Zoe, if it came down to you against me, it was always going to be me." A sickening smile appeared as he threw out his fist.

I leaped sideways, but his fist grazed my ear. At least it hadn't hit me full force in the face, but my pulse throbbed in my head. Adrenaline kicked into full gear. I searched for any weapon, but Brett closed the gap between us. He kicked out, his shoe connecting with my hips. I smashed into the wall. My head snapped back, slamming against the drywall. Stars burst across my vision.

In my daze, Brett wrapped his hands around my throat. I smelled copper and alcohol. He leaned forward. "It's a shame, really, because we could have had a good time together. I would have taken you for a ride, Zoe. Best one of your life before I ended you."

I struggled to breathe.

He squeezed harder.

His eyes homed in on me, dark and calloused. Cold. Calculated. The same way he had looked after he had won—told the lie of my cheating and he got away with it. Who would ever believe me when he had spun such a fantastic story about studying harder than ever before?

I raked my hands along his skin. My vision darkened. My nails came away with other people's blood. How many had Brett murdered tonight? What number would I be for him?

"This really isn't a fair fight." Haden appeared out of thin air behind Brett. Whatever magical powers he had, gratitude flooded my system. "Wouldn't it be more entertaining for you if she had an advantage?"

I wheezed in a shallow breath.

"Fuck off, demon. *You* started this game."

"You're right; it is *my* game. And I suppose that means we play how I wish."

My vision tunneled, dark splotches blotting out most of my sight. Haden gave me a wink. He latched onto Brett's wrists. I must have been imagining it, because his fingers weren't fingers at all, but long, sharp black claws. They sank into Brett's skin like his body was made of butter. Blood burst from the wounds as a wail reverberated off the walls. With no effort, Haden ripped Brett off me. He wrestled both arms behind Brett's back.

"What the fuck!" Brett screamed. Red dripped from his wrists.

My legs swayed under me. I grasped my neck. I was alive because Haden saved me. As I watched the two of them, I scowled. There was nothing worse than admitting I couldn't save myself, but sometimes even I needed help.

"Go get a weapon. We can wait. Can't we, Brett?"

"Fuck yo—"

Haden jerked on his arms, and another loud shriek curled out of the man's lips. "Careful what you say, Brett. We still have time to play before she sends you to the fires. That's where you're going, you know? Or did you think what happened with Kate wouldn't catch up to you?"

"I have no idea what you're—"

"Lies you've told yourself for so long, you've forgotten the truth, but your soul hasn't. The fires haven't. We'll welcome you, but not with open arms, Brett. You're doomed for the pits." Haden leveled his lips with Brett's ear. The sinister smirk stretched on his face and the look smoldered inside my core. "And frankly, I'm excited to watch you burn."

An eager shiver tore up my spine.

Haden's dark eyes leveled with me. "Find a weapon."

Brett thrashed against him, making desperate, nonsensical pleas for his life.

"You'll take his life like he was trying to take yours." The low tenor of his voice was full of promise and thick with hunger. The way he spoke was more in tune with life than some of the living. How was it possible for him to be a demon when he seemed more human than some of the monsters I had met?

The drawer had splintered in the hallway; debris scattered among the blood. No bodies on this side of the hall—yet. Brett's would be the first to grace it. After a moment of knocking aside the broken remnants, I found the knife. As soon as I crossed the space back to them, Brett kicked out at me as he bucked against Haden.

My old classmate's eyes were wild. Spittle flew out of his mouth. His shirt had risen, displaying a myriad of colorful red marks—from handprints to the outlines of fists—where a few people had landed strikes against him before Brett won those battles.

Haden's lips curled, and he twisted his hands. Brett howled again. With a roll of his eyes, Haden glanced at me. "As much as I love listening to someone scream, I am bored with this one. Care to end him for me?" His words were a caress against my skin compared to the harsh reality of the world outside of this hallway.

I blinked. The sound didn't seem to faze Haden, because he had likely heard endless amounts of cries in the fires. He was a demon, after all.

And holy shit, the fires were real.

The fires were *real*.

My gaze shifted to the blade in my hand. I was too steady for how heady I felt, because the fires were real, and Brett was headed there for something he had done to someone else. Something bad. Something he deserved death for. Something worse than cheating off a girl's test and getting her in trouble for it.

And I was about to send him there as his executioner.

What I felt was power. Flushed with it.

"His wrists are broken."

"What?" I glanced up, meeting Haden's dark eyes. They were rimmed with the lightest bit of brown—the only thing keeping them from looking like the abyss. I could get lost in those eyes, happily.

Fall into oblivion and ask him to hold my hand while doing so.

Brett continued to scream.

"He tried to kick you, so I broke his wrists." Haden's jaw worked, nostrils flared.

"Why are you helping me?" I shifted my grip on the knife.

"I don't like other people playing with my things." His lower lip ran in between his teeth. "Unless there's an agreement to share."

"I'm not a thing, and I'm not yours." The words escaped my mouth but held none of the certainty I was hoping for. I was hopelessly his, drawn to him with something otherworldly snapping between us.

Brett slammed his foot down on Haden's, but the demon didn't flinch.

"Get off me, you bastard." It was the first coherent thing he'd spoken since Haden had coiled his arms around him. Spit flew out of the guy's mouth. Some hit my arm.

Gross.

"Demons can't be bastards, actually. It's a very human concept."

Brett's eyes turned red as the next shriek tore out of him. His voice broke with it. Deep crimson fell in rivulets onto the floor behind his bowed back, likely because of whatever Haden was doing to his destroyed arms.

"End this, Zoe."

I let out a breath. "What if I don't want to kill anyone?"

His tongue flicked out over his bottom lip, eyes narrowing. "Are you sure that's what you want?"

My eyes focused on the knife's point, which could disappear under the skin Haden presented to me, right into sinew. But what would that make me? To kill someone in cold blood without giving them any chance of fighting back?

"Are you sure you don't want to end the man who thought about killing you, then lied about it? He's done this many times before, to others. You could seek justice for everyone he's screwed over."

"Fuck you!"

Haden shook Brett as he snarled. "Why are you so scared, Brett? Because it's true? I bet you feel bad now, don't you? Everyone has a moment right before death when it catches up to them. Your conscience has been chasing you for years, and now it's finally seized you. It's a shame it happened too late to save any part of your soul." Shifting his grip, Haden grasped Brett's hair in his hand and yanked his head to the side. Brett hissed from the pull on his scalp. "It's one quick slash, Zoe."

There was another pause. Another moment where I hesitated.

Haden leaned forward. "He killed three women. All women. No men. He didn't have the balls to go against a man, out of fear of losing. He knew he could beat a woman, so he happily did."

Brett was a dick. He'd screwed with me in grade school cheating off the test but killing him this way also felt a bit like cheating. My gaze snapped up. It was the perfect retribution, wasn't it? He had cheated on a test, and now I was cheating at a survival game.

My grip tightened on the knife. I needed courage.

Haden lifted his head, as if sensing exactly what I desired. Maybe he could. Who knew how far demonic powers stretched? "He cornered each of them and waited until they begged for him to spare them. One of them even promised to suck his dick if he let her run. He allowed her to unzip his fly but sank his ax into her head right after."

I brought the blade up. What would it feel like? To tear into his flesh? To feel it part underneath me? To breathe in the new power of taking someone's life? And why did it give me such a rush? I could do this—for all the women who came before me who were led astray by the empty promises of men.

"Zoe, you have to trust me. I didn't want to do any of those things. You're really going to believe a demon over me? We've known each other since we were kids. I didn't kill anyone. I certainly wouldn't have—"

"Shove it, Brett. I know you're lying, just like you did when we were kids. You have blood on your hands, and it's under my fingernails now—from when *you* tried to kill *me*. You're fucked."

"It was only out of defense!"

"I'm sorry. When you tried to lob off my head at the beginning of all of this, that was self-defense?"

"I didn't know who you were!"

"And you copied my test answers!"

"I didn't! You copied mine! Don't blame me for shit you did." Brett blinked, sucked in a breath like he finally realized he should have spent the last few minutes begging instead of manipulating me. "Zoe, I don't want to die."

I sauntered forward, savoring the weight of the knife in my hand. The heaviness felt good. "Let me tell you a little secret, Brett. No one wants to die. But that doesn't stop death from claiming them in the cruelest of ways imaginable—or the most poetically, as the case may be."

Haden's eyes caught the light, sending sparkles across his irises. His smile broadened as he ran his tongue over his incisors. Sharp points I hadn't noticed before. Or had I? When they had sunk into my skin, threatening to tear into me, I had felt them. Maybe I wanted that—for him to mark me.

"Come on, Zoe. I didn't mean it." Brett's voice was a pathetic whimper.

Was this how everyone went out? Not meeting the end with grace, but with terror? With groveling? We had a finite amount of time on this planet, and I swore I would never meet the end with anything more than the utmost confidence.

"Too little, too late, Brett." I leaned forward, getting so close to him I could bite. "You should have apologized for stealing from me. You should have admitted the truth. You should have been a better person." I thrust the knife into his stomach. There was a pop as his skin parted around the blade. As soon as the handle was flush with his belly, I twisted my hand. His wail was so loud I thought my eardrums might rupture. Still, I kept circling the blade inside him, spinning it while fighting the resistance his guts gave. Blood gushed from the wound, making my hands slick with it. It was vile, filthy, disgusting.

And completely thrilling.

"I hear stomach wounds are one of the worst ways to die. You going to leave him hanging, love?" The demon stared at me like he was hungry, like he would devour me in the hallway if I asked.

A part of me wanted him to. The other part of me wanted to claim my independence, let him know he would never own me without my permission. I was my own person with autonomy. While I might love being controlled in bed, he had *nothing* on me out here, and it would take something extreme for me to hand him such power.

"I am not your love." I glared at him.

His lips quirked. "I disagree."

I edged the knife upward with another jerk of my wrist. Brett flailed against me, but I kept going until the bloodied mess of his insides tumbled down his front. Crimson bubbled between his lips as he coughed meekly.

"After this shit, what makes you think I'll fall for you? A fuck is different than love." I pulled the blade from Brett's stomach and ran the knife along his neck. His screaming ceased almost immediately. Silence. Bitter and perfect. His mouth opened and closed like a fish gasping on a dying breath.

Haden let him go, and his dying body flopped to our feet.

"Because a part of you already has. You can fight it all you want, but that thing that's woken inside you? It wants me." He stepped over Brett's prone form, closing the gap between us. His fingers had shrunk back into their human facade. With blood still smearing them, he cupped my jaw, forcing me to look at him. "I'll give you as much time as you need to process, but the side of you that's calloused and is no longer thinking about how you murdered a man? That's your truth. It's what has haunted you for so long. You need to embrace it. I want to watch it blossom, become so much—"

Haden didn't seem to understand my point of view. Instead of letting him finish his diatribe, I interrupted, "I am not yours." And to prove it, I slashed forward with the knife.

Haden

I couldn't believe she would do something so reckless as to lash out at me. I understood her anger, her righteous sense of feeling betrayed. It was something I experienced plenty of times during my life in the fires, but these things made us stronger, more independent.

At least, that's what history told me.

Still, as the slash of steel whipped toward me, a part of me thought it was adorable. Cute. It was a pathetic attempt to quell her internalized aggression, but it was still cute. She convinced herself she wanted revenge, but her soul screamed for something else. The other part of me wanted to sink to my knees and beg her to try it again. Give her accolades for her brazenness. Press my lips to hers and suck her breath into my lungs until she begged me to let her breathe.

While the jocks had attempted to strike me, they were too fumbling to accomplish much earlier. But her? She wasn't afraid of her anger. Zoe wanted to embrace it, ignite herself. She was braver than she gave herself credit for.

Because not even Thomas had grown enough of a backbone to take a swing at me.

But honestly, tonight was becoming a bore. The blood, the gore, the dead bodies. Three years with Thomas had been repetitive, but so was this. People became terrified, their fear bubbled to the surface, and their primal urge to survive rose with it. I wanted the night to be over, because I wanted to fuck her again. Bind her to me.

I also hadn't thought this night would last so long. Thomas was *still* hidden in the basement, making himself as scarce as possible. People were looking for him, determined to be the new one linked to me, but so far, he had remained concealed, elusive.

Latching onto her wrist, I pulled her into me. I breathed in her scent. My nostrils flared. She hated to admit it; how much she *loved* this. And I loved how slick her wrist felt, covered in the blood of someone who deserved much worse than she had given him. The fires would sort him out, eventually.

"You don't want to do that," I growled.

"Of course I do," she spat through gritted teeth. Her breath was hot on my face, and her lips curled with frustration. Brows taut. "I want to watch you bleed."

With every snarl, I wanted to force her jaw open and give her something else to choke on instead of the pretty words spilling from her mouth.

"Try again, love, because you're holding onto the wrong end."

Her eyes widened, glancing down at the knife in horror. She dropped the weapon to the ground. The blade sank into Brett's cooling skin. Shaking, Zoe stared at her palm, but the terror on her face transformed into confusion. Her eyes narrowed, and the hazel irises snapped back to mine. Lightning bolts of color surrounded her pupils.

"What the fuck was that?"

"Demon stuff."

"It felt like I was—" She halted as she wrenched her hand back to stare at it. Zoe tried to take a step away from me, but I grasped the small of her back, bringing her against me.

"It felt like you were holding the blade while it sliced deep layers into your muscle. Piercing your soft skin like butter? Grasping onto something while it tore you apart? You felt the warmth of your own blood pooling across your palm? Yeah, that happens sometimes, especially when you piss a demon off." In truth, I was anything but angry. Still, I wanted to give her a taste of the things I could do to her. The beautiful manipulation of her mind, as long as she would allow me.

"It was torture." Her misty eyes searched mine. "You actually torture people, don't you?"

"I torture souls, but yes."

Her mouth opened, jaw working. "Do you ... *have* to torture them?"

I traced my fingers over her cheeks. She leaned into me, likely subconsciously, but it made my cock ache to be inside her for the third time tonight. The fact that she was walking around with my cum in her practically made me hard. Once, maybe twice more. That would be enough to quench my insatiable hunger for her. For tonight, at least. "You wouldn't ask a lion if it had to eat meat."

The pout on her lips was luscious. "That's not the same thing, and you know it."

"I could have broken your wrists, thrown you across the room, *hurt* you in order to prevent you from wounding me. Instead, I played with your mind. I showed you my powers." I brought my lips to her ear. "Imagine the possibilities if I were to use that for your pleasure."

Her skin prickled underneath my breath. "Plus, I had to teach you a lesson about how dangerous crossing me can be." I shrugged, leaning back enough to take in her expression.

"And you think this will make me fall for you?" She shook her head, ripping away from me. Zoe opened the space between us, breathing hard. "This isn't over."

"Of course it's not, because *we're* not."

She bent down and scooped up the knife. Huffing, she tried to turn away, but I grabbed the back of her hair. A soft yelp escaped her lips, but she stopped. I wrapped my other arm around her. She didn't protest, but I had no plans to take this any further. Not right now.

"There are seven people prowling around the living room. A dozen are hiding in the bedrooms. There are about ten still left in the basement, not really understanding how dire their situation is soon going to become. Juniper won the battle but is losing the war. Your path will be clear back to your friends in five minutes. And only if you circle through the pool room."

"But that's where almost all the bodies are."

I nodded, cradling her against me. She leaned back as I relinquished my grip on her hair. "There is one person left in the same room Brett was in. She pretended to be dead while he attacked everyone else. She will try to kill you if you hide in one of these rooms. She has pepper spray; best not to get that anywhere near you." I kissed the side of her neck. "Go now. Pool room, circle around it, then go upstairs. You have five minutes."

As soon as I released her, Zoe glanced back for only a second before nodding. She pressed herself into the shadows, sliding along the floor to stay quiet. And like I had asked, she headed toward the pool.

Already she was proving to be a better listener than Thomas ever was. I wanted to be attached to her—no, *coveted* it. I needed her soul more than I needed to breathe. Stumbling upon her had been an accident, but I knew nothing would ever be the same because of our meeting.

As I watched her hips move, her low prowl, and her wild brown hair drifting behind her, I whispered, "Good girl." She didn't hear me, but she didn't need to. I'd make her learn of her exquisiteness on my knees as worship.

18 Zoe

Was every moment with Haden going to be lined with rules? I wondered how I felt about that long-term, because while I had been a rule follower most of my life, tonight had opened my eyes to something different, something divine. Society had set forth a list of what women should and shouldn't be, how we should act, and what we should say. A play book for every occasion, and I was sick of it.

Cover your drink if you aren't looking at it.

Leave nothing unattended.

Go to the bathroom in groups.

Never let your friend leave if she's inebriated.

Don't ask the guy out on a date. Wait for him to come to you.

Don't burp.

Don't overeat.

Don't under eat.

Don't talk too much.

Tonight, I tasted freedom. I wasn't sure I could give it up. I was so fucking sick of normalcy. It wasn't like I achieved anything from being *normal*. Looking at my life now, it wasn't like trying to fit in as a kid had gotten me anywhere. Not with my fingers slick with blood and the blade handle slippery from it. The areas that had dried on my skin became itchy, flaking off like bad Halloween make-up.

Still, I wanted to listen to Haden's commands, despite not knowing if I should. He had kept me alive so far, and it seemed like he wanted me to survive tonight, like he *needed* it. I trusted that quiet determination. Maybe nothing else was trustworthy about him, but my physical safety? I could trust him with that.

Sticking to the shadows, I ignored my racing heart. It pounded against my ribcage, threatening to leave me behind the moment it figured out how to flee my body. I crossed the hallway, ducking low as loud shouts sounded from the kitchen. The floor was covered in bloodied footprints that trailed in different directions. They told a story, one of panic and the frailty of human existence. They spoke of something finite, something tangible we'd fight to keep—our lives.

A gasp sounded to my left. I froze, turning my head toward the noise.

A woman lay in a bloodied heap. "Plea—" The word choked inside her throat, barely passing her lips as she sucked in a breath that sounded too wet. Red filled the whites of her eyes, contrasting the yellow and blues of her face. "Nn—" But the word didn't make sense.

I swallowed back bile. I had no idea who this girl was because I didn't recognize her. With the blood coating her skin, contusions covering her face, and how bloated her body had become, there was no telling her identity underneath the mess. If I could call for an ambulance, maybe she'd have enough time to be saved. But with our phones not working and no hope in sight, I didn't know how to handle someone on death's door.

"Ple—" She tried again, but the word cut off with a gurgle in her throat.

"Do you want me to end it?"

She blinked.

"Twice for yes."

Two blinks.

I let out a sigh. "I'm sorry, and I'm not sure what to say to make this better." Somewhere, in the back of my mind, I was conscious of time slipping by. I had to get to my friends in five minutes, after circling through the pool. That had been specific. If I spent too much time here, I risked missing my window. "Just know that wherever you go, I hope it's more peaceful than tonight. I hope it's better than here. I hope it gives you the relief you want." Taking out my knife, I found the pulse in her neck, barely beating against her skin.

I sank the blade in and through.

A trickle of blood oozed out. The girl let out an exhale, then stilled.

I waited for guilt. I waited for an unsavory feeling to creep up my spine and burrow into my brain. Become a parasite and feast on me from the inside out. Guilt was a wretched and unruly thing, one that plagued my friends, weighed on their souls. I watched it tear apart their thoughts, make them second-guess everything. But never had it affected me in the same way.

And it didn't upset me now, either.

Heat rose to my cheeks, because there was some shame there. I had tried to be a certain way my whole life, to fit in, but now I realized I had been doomed from the start. I was never meant to be anything other than who I was, and I was still figuring out exactly who that was.

I wiped the blade along her clothes and began to stand but threw myself to the ground as another shot rang out from above me.

I had to get to the pool.

Staying in the crouch, I inched forward, clinging to one wall. I cut through the living room, curved past the pool table, and headed into the pool room. The water was tinged coral. Two bodies floated face down in the water, another lay at the bottom of the pool. All three of them drifted at the gentle lapping of the current the filter created. Hair splayed around them like seaweed. Someone was dead in the jacuzzi, and the smell was a toxic, musty iron.

Not wanting the blood on me anymore, I dipped my arms into the pool, watching the red run from my skin, staining the water even darker. I grabbed a towel off a bench and dried myself as fast as I could. My heart rammed inside my chest, as I was running out of time.

It took no longer than a few seconds before I rushed around the pool, just as I was told. When I reached the other side, I checked my watch. I was over by one minute. As soon as I looked up, a shadow appeared in the archway between me and the living room.

Well, shit.

"Zoe."

I couldn't place the voice, but it held a low, resonating growl.

"Hi?"

"You stupid bitch." They took a step forward, and the light in the pool room sliced across their face. Devon stood there, a slick smile spreading up his cheek. "I remember what you said at junior prom." He clenched his fist around the chains in his hands. They were long and looked heavy.

Suddenly, my knife felt inadequate. Too light in my fingers. "What did I say to you?" I narrowed my gaze, because nowhere in the history of my memory did I recall saying anything remotely unflattering toward Devon. We've known each other since kindergarten. Heck, even before that, when his mother ran a not-so-legal daycare out of her house. We hadn't been friends, but we had certainly grown up together. Small town and all that.

He laughed. It grated on my skin, low and menacing. "Of course you don't remember, because you're such a whore. Willing to shell it out and spread your legs for anyone who asks."

"What the fuck are you talking about?" I doubted my two partners equated to his accusations, and my grip tightened on my knife.

"I danced with you." He took a step forward, eyes ducking into dark shadows again as a ceiling beam cut through the overhead lights. "I asked you if you'd think about going on a date with me. If I could have a chance."

"And I politely declined." My mouth dropped open. "Is that what this is about? You're upset because I denied you a date?"

Devon shrugged. "Men have killed women for worse reasons." His tone was cavalier, as if his logic made sense.

"What the fuck, Devon! You cannot justify murder because of someone else's—"

"Why not?" He snarled, taking another prowling step forward. "Men before me have done it, and plenty of men after will too. And who cares what you say? You're a fucking wh—"

I scoffed. "That makes sense. Either way, I'm a whore, right? If I slept with you, then I'd be living up to your expectations, and if I didn't, then I still am because you didn't get with me. Grow the fuck up." I held the knife out in front of me. "Bring it, assface."

Devon's brown eyes darkened as he let out a roar, charging straight toward me.

Okay, maybe calling someone bigger than me "assface" had been a bad plan, but the rest of my speech had been spot on. Plus, if I won this battle, it would be a win for every woman who had ever been looked down on for their sexual desires—or lack thereof. With a long exhale, I readied my stance, prepared to stand up for every person who had ever been bullied or judged in their lifetime.

But as soon as Devon reared his hand back, poised to strike with the metal in his hands, claws wrapped around his arm. A scream tore through him as his arm bent backwards, so far that there was tearing, ripping, and suddenly, the limb was separated from his body. Devon's momentum kept him stumbling forward as he shrieked. I stepped to the side as he floundered. I kicked his thighs. His body sailed into the water. He thrashed, sputtering as his blood readily left him, seeping into the pool.

My eyes darted to Haden.

He tossed the arm into the water. "For the record, a lot of sex workers are in the skies. Along with a lot of customer service employees. Endless amounts of patience." His tongue ran over one of his incisors as he watched me. "I refuse to stand by and let someone talk about women like that."

Blood splattered Haden's shirt, but for some reason, he reminded me more of an angel than someone from the depths of the fires. I opened my mouth to say so, but snapped it shut. Would that be an insult? I couldn't imagine an angel ripping someone's arm off for insulting women. Fires, I couldn't imagine anyone *doing* that. Thousands of people had stood by in the past and let it happen, but instead, Haden was an avenging force, rising from the depths to punish those who deserved it. And boy, did they deserve it.

"I wanted to fight him," I said.

"I know. Trust me, you'll get your chance."

Devon's head went under water with a last gasp. His single arm flailed for purchase, but his body must have been too weak from the blood loss. He didn't come back up as bubbles rose to the surface. Good fucking riddance.

"Well, not with him, but with someone else," Haden amended.

"Did he talk about other women that way?"

"Probably. Plenty of men feel entitled."

"Do you?"

His eyes narrowed. "First, I'm not a man. Demon. Am I entitled? No. Willing to do whatever it takes for you to be mine? Yes. Devoted is the word I would use, but if you want to call it entitlement, you can. Whatever makes you feel better." He took a step closer to me. Heat radiated off his body as he searched my face. "You're late." He twirled a lock of my hair in between his thumb and forefinger.

"I know. I tried." I frowned and let out a long breath. "This house freaks me out. Everyone is … becoming the worst versions of themselves. What's going to happen to my friends? Who am I going back to in that room?"

"People who will guard you until the time is right for you to guard them. But … since you are late, there have been some changes."

"What kind of changes?"

"You'll see when you get there." Haden closed the gap and pressed his lips to my forehead. "When I tell you to run, you need to full out sprint. No delays, no stopping, nothing. Okay?"

"How do you know all of this if you don't know the future?"

"I can sense where souls are—like a temperature moving in the house. That, along with my magic and knowledge of human psychology …" He shrugged. "I can explain more later."

"Can't you just … kill everyone except Thomas?"

"I could, but if I do that, you won't win against him. He'll feel empowered for the first time in his life. He'll finally ask me to do something for him." Haden opened the space between us. His dark eyes flickered toward the kitchen, then back to me. They hardened as he said, "I can't lose you tonight."

It was a strange, desperate hope he held. Unfortunately for him, I had already decided I would risk my life for my friends. If it meant one of them got to live, I would die. It wasn't a selflessness that I felt, but … a lack of desire to carry on. I had no direction. I had no instinct, no drive, no passion. The only thing I had felt in a long time was staring me right in the face. He was a demon. We'd find each other in the afterlife, wouldn't we? I had killed someone tonight, so clearly, I was no longer bound for the skies. There was no reason for me to stay alive when I could fight for them instead.

I'd rather be with Haden in the fires.

Before tonight, I had no idea what came after this life. That, however, was no longer a question. My afterlife would be with him. Maybe I was still upset, but I also didn't believe sex with anyone else would be as satisfying. Plus, seeing his claws come out … it destroyed whatever part of me thought I could be normal once this was over.

Screw normalcy.

"You won't lose me," I said, because no matter what, Haden would be in my life. Whether it was my eternal, ever-lasting life or this one on earth. There was no turning away from this—at least, not while we were still figuring it out.

"Good." He stepped back, clearing my path. "Run. Now."

I took off at a full sprint. Once I reached the corner of the hallway, I skidded on a blood smear, but scrambled my feet underneath me, catching myself. I latched onto the staircase railing and pulled myself forward, then rushed up the soggy carpeted steps. Leaping over a body at the top, I cringed as another shot rang out, but then the air became desperately still.

My breath was louder than any other noise.

I slammed my fist on the bedroom door. "Everett!"

"On it!" he answered with no hesitation. Scrambling from the other side as a bunch of items were pushed out of the way. I scanned for any movement in the hallway, but it stayed quiet—too quiet. The kind that made the hair on my arms stand on end. It promised darkness, promised something unforgiving. The door swung inward, and I stumbled inside. They slammed the door shut. A second hung in the air where we were getting our bearings. Me, slathered in blood, and them … with a dead Ridley on the bed.

"What the fuck happened here?" I said at the same time as Tate asked, "What the fuck happened to you?"

Tears streaked down Mercedes's face, but she was the only one here with blood on her hands. Tate and Sasha leaned against one wall, arms crossed in front of them, gaze switching between me and her. Tate's pupils were blown wide, watery and red-rimmed along the edges, which made their brown irises stand out. Corbin and Everett moved the dresser back into place behind me with a grunt.

Ridley's chest was still. Blood had poured out of him, drenching the only bed in the room, which was a shame if we needed to sleep here. A knitting needle stuck out of his neck, still plugged in there for everyone to witness. His eyes stared vacantly at the ceiling. Based on how he had treated me earlier, a part of me was glad he wouldn't be the person making it out alive.

He had been such a good friend in high school, but that hadn't been the case since.

"Zoe, what happened?" Everett asked, keeping his voice calm and low, like he was worried about spooking an animal.

Never mind me. I was more concerned with Mercedes and what

happened to Ridley.

"Merce?"

Her green eyes shifted to me. "Hm?" The ends of her blond hair had speckles of red tinging them.

"What happened?" I took a step toward her.

Everett grabbed my shoulder, halting my advance. "I wouldn't."

"Merce?"

Her eyes were glassy, as if she were a hundred miles away. Her gaze slipped back to Ridley, staring at his neck. The intrusion point of the knitting needle threaded into his skin. She blinked. Once, twice. We collectively held a breath.

A sick part of my brain thought she had aimed well.

"She's been like this since it happened," Everett whispered, stepping up to me and dropping his hand. "What happened out there, Zoe?"

"A lot. Brett and Devon tried to kill me. Separately."

"And they lost?"

How did I convey everything that happened outside this room? How could they trust me if they knew the truth? Haden was looking out for me, but he hadn't killed Brett—I had. Haden had set me up for revenge, and I had taken it. I had ended a life. Technically, Devon might have drowned before dying of blood loss. So maybe I killed both of them.

But I couldn't tell them the story without mentioning Haden. Telling my friends that the demon who trapped us here also helped me win those battles seemed like a bad idea.

"Something like that. I got a knife." I offered him the handle of the weapon. He took one look at the blood coating it and grimaced. I added, "I'll wash it off."

Everett nodded. "You should wash off too. I don't think Mercedes is going anywhere."

"I could talk to her?"

He shook his head. "We've tried. I know you were her best friend for a long time, but … I think she's in shock."

"What happened?"

Corbin strode up to me. He kept his voice low, but explained, "She hated how Ridley spoke to you before you left—sorry about how I was, by the way. I was … freaked out. Not an excuse, but an explanation. I'm owning how much of a dick I was."

"I appreciate that."

"Anyway, Ridley didn't let up, and it got worse when Everett and Mercedes came in without you. Turns out some shit happened this last year that Merce didn't like. He kept referencing some shit podcast, talking about how Mercedes should listen to him, since he was a man. He insinuated he knew better than you."

I narrowed my gaze. "What?" This didn't sound like Ridley.

Everett snorted. "He said something like, 'Merce, you should listen to me as your boyfriend, not some cunt. No woman will ever do for you what I can.'"

My jaw dropped open. What the fuck. Had the world gone down the shit hole in the last few hours? What gave him the right to talk like that? Threaten people with the end and their true colors came out. What had happened to Ridley to make him turn so vile? What a disaster. At least all the wicked souls would burn in the afterlife they deserved.

"So, she stabbed him?" I prompted. Despite the foul language, I couldn't imagine Mercedes being driven to the edge based on that alone.

"No, she sat quietly for a bit. Actually, I've never seen her so still before," Corbin whispered. "Then she went to the closet and rummaged around. Said she wanted to find anything she could to use as a weapon. Turns out, she found those."

"He kept saying crass things," Sasha said, her voice coated in disgust.

"And after Sasha and I got cleaned up, he asked if we wanted in on *that* action," Tate added.

I arched an eyebrow. "What action?"

Tate let out a breath, but it was Sasha who took over. She stepped forward, her nose wrinkled with revulsion. "Look, I know Tate and I can be a little much for some people. I get it. We get off on that shit, you know? But like … Mercedes doesn't. Her body language was all fucking messed up. Ridley suggested some kind of fucked up foursome since we were going to die, anyway."

"But I don't sleep with men," Tate scowled. "And he knows that. We're supposed to be friends. But he said—"

"Don't fucking repeat it," Mercedes said, voice deadly calm and level from the other side of the room. She turned toward me. No one dared to move. "It was so fucking inappropriate, Zoe. He was a fucking piece of work. That stupid podcast … it changed him. Turned him into someone he never was before. He started feeling entitled a while ago. I ignored it, you know? Because I thought … we're still together. We can make it through this. It's just rocky bullshit, you know? Every couple has it at some point. We'd been friends for so long, but he was going to come back to me. He had to. He was such a *good* guy before he found those assholes. So, I waited for the day he was going to wake up and realize they were the epitome of toxicity." She sniffed, eyes turning back to the body.

She continued, "We did a great job of raising feminists, but did a terrible job of teaching men how to handle their emotions. I was empowered to say no. Ridley didn't like that. He couldn't put his emotions into words. Just kept getting angry, trying again. This wasn't the first time this kind of thing happened, either. But I told him I didn't want to sleep with Tate and Sasha, and he kept pushing.

And pushing. He got loud, angry. He always got loud. Yelled all the time, became our second fucked up love language. And I snapped. I couldn't handle it anymore."

I crossed the room and wrapped my arms around her shoulders. She shook as tears fell from her eyes. "Shh. No one blames you for this."

"We're going to die anyway, right? I mean, I couldn't *listen* to that anymore."

I smoothed her hair down, which left little flakes of blood behind. Considering her hair had its own, I hoped she wouldn't mind. She buried her face in my stomach as I held on. I made eye contact with my friends.

"Right? We don't care that he's dead?" I prompted them.

Everett and Corbin shook their heads.

"If Mercedes hadn't killed him, I would have," Tate said. "The man who died on that bed wasn't Ridley. It was a twisted version of him; one I never care to see again."

"Agreed," Sasha added. Her fingers wrapped through Tate's. The smile Sasha gave them was the shiest I had ever seen.

"See, Merce? It's okay. No one blames you for this."

"It's not okay," she whispered. "I killed someone."

"I did too."

She sucked in a breath and pulled away from me. "Who?"

"Brett." And since I didn't want anyone finding out that I only semi-killed him, I added, "Devon too."

"Brett deserved it, but I always thought Devon was nice."

I snorted. "He called me a whore."

"Well, fuck him."

"Yeah, fuck him," Sasha added.

"Don't actually fuck him, though, because he's dead."

"So helpful, Tate," Everett laughed.

Hesitant chuckles filled the dead space Ridley's body left behind. The sound coiled around us. We couldn't stop once we started, tears filling our eyes as we keeled over. It wasn't *that* funny. In fact, it wasn't funny at all. That was the problem with tension; who knew when it was going to break?

"Fuck, you are *covered* in blood." Mercedes looked down, as if remembering her own hands. "Well, shit. Ugh. I'm going to wash this off in the sink, but like, you need to shower."

I shrugged. "What's the point if we're going to be dead in the morning?"

"The point is—" She let out a breath, stood up, and crossed to the bathroom. "—we're alive right now. And we don't know how long that will last, but we have to treat every moment like it's worth living. And right now? Blood under my fingernails is not it. You with me?"

Yeah, I was with her because having flecks of other people on my skin was absolutely not the way I wanted to spend the last moments of my life. Who knew when someone would burst through those doors, but being clean? That sounded like one small thing I could control.

"Sure, a shower sounds good."

Mercedes washed her hands as I cranked on the water. I turned to her, watching her scrub away the essence of Ridley from her skin. I wanted to say something comforting, something to soothe her soul, but what could I say? Having experienced murder myself, I knew what I should say—*sorry you had to do that, hope you didn't awaken some inner beast like I did*—but none of the words felt right. Whenever I was overwhelmed by the wrong things to say, I shut down, waiting in silence instead of putting my foot in my mouth.

"I'll be okay, Zoe," she said as she turned the sink off. Steam steadily filled the room as she looked at me. Her eyes were tired as she pursed her lips together. "We were doomed to fail. Might as well happen now, right? I was lying to myself when I thought I could make it work."

"But we've been—"

"It doesn't matter. Whatever once was doesn't matter when faced with the reality of now. Who we were back then plays no part in today. We are composed of histories, but we are who we decide to be. Ridley decided to be—" She flicked her hand in his direction. "—that. It's okay. I'll be fine."

I swallowed, hoping she was right. Would she be doomed to the fires as well for what happened today? Would her experience differ from mine?

"Look, I'll be out there, but don't worry about it. Okay? I can see your mind racing, and well, we don't have time to worry. We need action." A sad smile traced her lips as she turned.

"Wait!" I stepped forward. She hesitated in the threshold, whirling back to me. "Take the knife?" I offered it to her. "Look, I'm going to be ... in the shower and naked, so I kind of need someone watching out for me." I plastered on my best grin.

She plucked it from my fingers. "We'll be ready for whatever comes our way because of you. You gave us the best chance of success tonight." Merce winked and sauntered out the door.

As soon as she crossed the threshold, the bathroom door swung shut. Haden stood against the wall, behind where the door had been. He reached over and locked my only exit. I took a step toward him, wanting to say everything that was on my mind, but no words escaped me. The silence hung between us, interrupted by pounding fists from the hallway outside the bedroom door, where someone was now trying to break through.

My eyes went wide, stepping up to him. I stared into his dark eyes. "Don't stop me right now. They need me."

"I am stopping you, but only because they won't break through."
I narrowed my gaze.

"Trust me. Give it another minute." His lips parted as he started to count softly to himself.

My hands fell to my hips as I waited. Shadows formed on his hand as the doorknob went red hot, just like in the pantry. The lock melted into place. I rolled my eyes, but figured I might as well get clean, seeing as how I was stuck with him for the foreseeable future.

Turning back to the shower, I didn't miss the moment the pounding ceased, and a distant shout echoed in the hall. Someone barked out, "Get back here!" in an authoritative voice.

Putting my hand underneath the stream, I chanced a glance at Haden. "So, who was that?"

He ran his hand through his hair. Some of the blond stuck up at odd angles. His black eyes looked me over, hunger curling his features. "The jocks found some people who had been elusive. Thomas was one of them."

"But don't I need to kill Thomas to get access to your powers?"

"Not necessarily. You can kill whoever murders Thomas. But if anyone had opened that door, it would have been a bloodbath with most of your friends getting killed. Besides, I'm protecting you the best way I can right now." He took a step toward me.

"By keeping me out of it?" I hedged.

He nodded.

I let out a breath and scooped my hands underneath the hem of my shirt. Bringing it up and over my head, I dropped the fabric to the ground. My clothes were as good as ruined, anyway. "If you want to protect me, then find me something clean to wear." As I drew the curtain back, I couldn't help but meet his eyes again.

The darkness of his irises engulfed his whites for a second. Maybe I was imagining things. Amusement passed over his features. "Why bother?"

I arched a brow.

"You look better without them."

"Would you show me off?" I hooked my thumbs underneath my jeans, watching his eyes trail over me. Whenever other guys watched me like this, I felt vulnerable, exposed. But with Haden's gaze on me, I felt powerful, like I could suggest anything, and he'd fall on his knees and give me whatever I asked, but then he'd take what he wanted later. The push and pull lured me to him, more intense than anything else I had felt before.

"Would you want me to?"

I wiggled the hem over my hips, lingering as I pulled my jeans down past my bikini, over my thighs, and finally stepped out of the material, kicking it toward him. A beat passed. "I don't know. I've never … been looked at like that."

Haden prowled another step forward, the single advance that made me want to lean toward him instead of shrinking away. "If you'd allow it, I'd show you off to whoever was willing to look. I'd make them take in your beauty, until everyone in the fires understands exactly what I see. If you'd allow it, I'd share you with my best friend and tell him exactly how to make you come, because I'd love to see you fall apart on his fingers." He stood toe to toe with me now. His looming presence created a fire cascading along my skin. His fingers brushed a lock of hair behind my shoulder, revealing a clean patch of skin below my collarbone. "Get in the shower, love."

I shivered at his command. He reached behind me, pulled the curtain farther open, and gestured for me to get inside. I stepped backward into the tub. Haden stripped off his shirt as the water hit my shoulders, my neck. He unbuttoned his pants, rolled them down his hips, and exposed the deep v his muscles created.

My brain had forgotten the purpose of this shower. Distantly, I remembered how I needed to clean myself, but everything was at a standstill as he revealed his body to me.

He's a *demon*, a part of me argued, but I didn't care. He might be from the fires, but as far as I was concerned, the man standing in front of me was a god. His shoulders rolled back as he straightened. He was built, not with bulging muscles but with defined tone that captured light and shadow. A scar traced down his torso, slashing diagonally across his ribs. Black veins stretched out from his heart. His skin held a light sun-kissed hue but was still white. Maybe it was having a part of the fires with him that gave him an ethereal glow, but whatever it was, human guys were missing it.

He was in his boxer briefs, and the only thing left on my body was my bikini. He stepped into the tub, placed a hand on the wall next to my head, and pinned me in place underneath him. His blond hair instantly got caught in the spray, darkening as it swept over his forehead.

"Would you like that?"

"Like what?"

He chuckled. "Did I distract you?"

"Absolutely."

"Honesty goes a long way with me." His hand grabbed the back of my neck, holding me there. He moved us, adjusting my head so my hair was under the water. I let him. There was something so freeing about being under someone else's control. "Would you like it if I paraded you around?"

"I think so," I whispered the words, because the admission felt sinful to me. Wasn't that the whole point of the fires? "I haven't put a lot of thought into it before now."

"Tilt your head back." As soon as he asked, my body complied, and he moved me farther under the stream of hot water. Haden reached for a bottle and popped it open.

Was he really going to wash my hair?

"I would like to show you off, but I also enjoy having you to myself. I can be flexible." His fingers ran over my hair, along my skull, pressing down in a light massage. He worked the lather through blood, viscera, and the chaos the night had left behind. "As for sharing you specifically, I enjoy watching my lovers fall apart, whether it is by my hands or someone else's."

"Have you had many?"

He laughed. "Yes, as have most in the fires. We're fairly open. But you are the first human." His fingers soothed something inside me, releasing tension with each circular motion. "If you don't want to, we can arrange something else. Something perhaps more comforting."

"Like what?" I breathed.

"Like toys. You don't need another person to get the same effect. And if you're embarrassed, we can work on that too. It'll take as long as it will take for you to become comfortable with yourself, who you are, and what you want." He combed through my hair, and the luxury of it made me want to sleep in his arms.

At this rate, I would let him take me wherever he needed me to go.

"We go at your pace, or we don't go at all."

"What if I want to go at your pace?" I asked, voice raspier than I intended.

"Careful. If you give me the green light, I won't stop."

"Then let's play a game," I said as he angled my head back. The water cascaded over my locks, washing out the suds. It felt so nice to be pampered like this. But I was feeling bold. I had killed one person and participated in another's death—I could be a little playful sexually, couldn't I? "I give you the green light, but if I say red light, you stop."

"You expect to be able to speak." His fingers twisted in my hair, yanking at the roots. The bite was delicious, traveling straight to my core. "If I get my way with you, you'll be breathless, unable to say anything except to beg me for more. So, think carefully, Zoe. Is this what you want to begin?"

I kept my eyes steady on his as I whispered, "Green light."

Haden

Two glorious words tumbled from her lips, and I wanted her to regret them. She had no idea who she was toying with, but she'd learn, and I happened to be the perfect teacher. If she thought she was prepared, I would try my hardest to knock her off balance.

I slipped my fingers underneath the strap on her shoulder. It fell down her arm, catching on her muscle. "Take it off." I pulled the other strap down as I nodded to the lower part of her bikini.

She swallowed, maintaining eye contact as she moved it over her hips, revealing herself to me slowly. As I pulled the straps away from her breasts, she dropped the other part of her suit and kicked it aside. "You too," she said.

"You don't make the rules in here." I unwound the back of her bikini, watching as it loosened and fell away. Her nipples were taut. I took in all of her, gloriously naked before me. Vulnerable, yet standing strong. I brushed my thumb over the smooth swell of her breast, enjoying how she sucked in a breath the moment I contacted her sensitive skin.

I was going to thoroughly enjoy this. It hadn't been enough, despite watching her come apart as much as I had already. I would never get used to it.

"Use the conditioner," I said.

"Why aren't—" she stammered, words catching in her throat as I sank to my knees in front of her.

"Conditioner," I ordered.

She huffed out a breath, but snatched the bottle off the shelf, squirting some into her palm.

I pushed her legs apart. "Do not close these. Grab the shelf if you need help standing up."

As she ran her fingers through her hair, she gave me this knowing smirk, like I would never be able to fulfill my promise of making her forget how to speak. Showed what she knew. We had already fucked—multiple times, in fact—but that had nothing on the wretched things I wanted to do to her once we were in the fires, once her soul was mine. Right now, I couldn't risk destroying her, because she was only human. If I accidentally killed her without her soul being tied to me, she'd ascend straight up to the skies, where she'd be unreachable for the rest of eternity.

Talk about pressure.

Humans were rather delicate creatures. And while she had proved to be a formidable force against her enemies, she still had nothing on my powers—once they were unwrapped from the loathsome bindings, that was.

I curled my fingers along her thighs, savoring her warmth as the water cascaded down our skin. Coconut filled the air as she combed the conditioner through her hair. I leaned forward and inhaled her scent—the one beyond the perfume and soaps, which consisted of vanilla casks and a smoky caramel. Fuck, she smelled good enough to devour. Someday I would.

Today, I held myself back.

Leaning in, I gave her a long, languid lick across her nerves. Her hips rolled forward, but I growled and pushed back on her thighs.

"Conditioner," I rumbled.

She scrunched her nose but immediately went back to combing it through her hair. Though she looked incredibly distracted by what I was doing.

Settling back in between her thighs, I brushed the tip of my tongue against her most sensitive part. Her hips sought me out again, but this time, I was ready for her. I buried my fingertips in her skin, holding her steady. She sucked in a gasp. Her fingers attempted to soothe her hair, but her eyes had drifted shut. With every sweep of my tongue, her breathing became shallower and more heated. I tested different motions, observing her reactions to see what made her beg for the ledge. I watched patiently for the moments where pure ecstasy crossed her face. Finally, I pressed my tongue flat against her, undulating my muscle along her skin. She quivered, eyes rolling back. She'd forgotten about the conditioner in her hair.

"Rinse," I barked.

She whimpered, reaching for my hair.

"If you can't obey me, you're about to lose the privilege of using your hands."

That glorious pout crossed her face again, but she forced her head back underneath the stream, scrubbing furiously at her scalp, as if the process offended her.

I chuckled, nudging her thighs open. She complied, widening her stance and allowing me better access. My tongue roamed over her, not just her nerves, but down to her entrance, finding it slick for me.

She wouldn't leave this bathroom with her soul intact. No. Now that I'd tasted her sweetness for a second time, I needed it for eternity. There would be no more waiting, no more toying, especially as the survivors dwindled. She needed to give me her soul on the off chance I was wrong, and she didn't survive the night.

Of course, it had been a long time since I had sensed the outcomes of human souls incorrectly. But still … losing her to the skies would be unacceptable. Tying her to me would be a precaution, something a lot of demons had in droves when they accepted a human lure. That was why being stuck on Earth would get me a lot of shit when I finally arrived back in the fires. What demon would walk into a snare without a back-up plan?

A desperate one. One who needed change.

But I wouldn't waste this opportunity. It might be one of the last ones I received before the end of the night.

Wrapping my hands around to the back of her legs, I pulled her against my face, finally letting her ride me as my tongue played with her. Her cunt was soaked, and not just from the water cascading over her body. I groaned as she shamelessly sought the next touch of my tongue. I longed for my demon form, so I could push into her farther than she thought possible.

Sure, I could burst through some of the magic holding me back, but I couldn't risk her life. If my tongue came out, my fangs might too. The last thing I needed was to shred her underneath me while her thighs clenched around my face.

Grabbing one of her legs, I lifted it onto my shoulder, pressing the rest of her body against the shower wall. The air pushed out of her lungs in a soft moan as I did the same with the other leg. With her on my shoulders, I could get a better angle, deeper. My fingers stretched her open as my tongue rolled against her clit.

"Haden—" Perfectly breathless and gloriously close to falling to pieces. "Haden … I—"

"Come on my face."

The instant the command came out of my mouth, her thighs clenched around my ears, bearing down on me. I slid my tongue inside her along with my fingers, forcing her open despite how desperately her hips shook. She covered her mouth with her hand and screamed into it, blocking most of the sound from my ears.

That wouldn't fucking do.

I let her ride out her orgasm, waited until the shaking in her body subsided. I placed her back on the ground and stood up. Her arousal glistened on my face. The water was slow to wash it off. Her hazel eyes searched mine as she pulled her palm away from her mouth.

Capturing her wrists in my hands, I gave her a look of disappointment.

"What?"

"I never gave you permission to hold back."

Her eyes darted to the door. "My friends are in the other room."

"And?"

"And they might think I'm masturbating or something."

"So?" I arched an eyebrow. "Only one person in this scenario survives the night. Why do you care so much about what they think? They have much bigger problems on their hands—they wouldn't judge you for taking some pleasure for yourself in the last moments of your life."

"I don't know. I never thought I was an exhibitionist or anything, because that was more Tate and Sasha's thing." She shrugged, but color flushed her cheeks.

"Tell me what you're really thinking."

She swallowed, eyes turning away from me.

I cupped her jaw, brought her back to face me. "Tell me."

"But maybe the thought of you watching your friend fuck me might … uhm, turn me on."

"And?"

"And I feel less embarrassment when I'm with you—like sex could be so much more than it was before. I feel … safe. I know that sounds asinine, because you're the epitome of unsafe, but I—" She let out a long breath. "My emotions feel safe with you. The respect you have for me … it makes me feel seen. And that must say some fucked up shit about me, because you're the first one to have ever seen me in this way. I don't know. I really—"

I kissed her. Pressing our mouths together. She moved against me, unfurling her soul toward me. The coolness brushed my skin. Her mouth opened, and I accepted the invitation. Her tongue flicked mine, and her taste transferred with it. I peeled off my underwear, wanting to feel her skin against mine. She groaned as her hands wrapped around my waist, pulling me into her. My erection hit her core, and fuck, I wanted to be inside her as I claimed her soul for my own. I needed more time to plan. Zoe had been cautious to trust me. She might not hand over her soul if I didn't play this right.

I suspended us in the kiss, kept my jaw moving as her lips crushed mine. Ferocity built between us. I nipped her lower lip. Our teeth gnashed. I threaded my fingers through her hair and pulled. Her fingernails buried in my sides. She gasped into my mouth. I sucked in her breath, taking the air right from her lungs.

It was a push and pull, and I adored how she thought she could still have a fraction of her semblance of self. If she trusted me, if I made her feel safe, then I could push her farther. I could demand more.

I wondered how far she'd let me go.

And would I stop if she said red light?

I pulled away from her, stepping back.

"Where—"

Yanking the towel rack off the wall, I brought the metal in front of me. It was a cylindrical rod, so hopefully it wouldn't hurt with what I planned next. Her eyes widened, but I chuckled. "Relax, it's not a toy. It could be, but I have much more fun ones back at my place."

"In the fires."

"Yes, in the fires." Using a bit of my power, I heated the metal, bending it into a U-shape. She watched me, eyes curious and absorbing my movements. She was giving me some trust, and while I likely didn't deserve it, I would be worthy of her someday. Right now, I was driven by my impulses—my desire for her, to be rid of Thomas forevermore, and to go back to the fires accomplished. My plans were more than a little selfish, but she'd benefit from them long term. And I would make her feel good.

Regardless of anything else, I would never be a self-centered partner. "Hands above your head."

She lifted them, watching me as I maneuvered her wrists over one another on the wall. I guided her arms above the upper portion of the acrylic shower. Her wrists were next to the drywall now. Perfect.

Her eyes tracked me as I placed the metal rod above her wrists. My gaze locked on hers as I slammed it back. She gasped. Metal drove through the wall, raining dust down on us that the shower washed away. Her hands were pinned in place.

"What the fuck," she gasped. Her fingers wiggled. Her wrists had enough space to move, but not enough to escape.

"You covered your mouth without permission." I nipped her jaw. "If anyone will silence you, it will be me. But now? I want to hear you scream. No more hiding who you are."

She dragged her teeth along her lower lip. "Okay. No hiding." She arched her back, pressing herself against me. "What am I supposed to do if anyone bad walks into this room?"

"Skies help them, because the fires certainly won't. Lift." I cupped underneath her thighs. She obeyed, wrapping her legs around me, so I lined up perfectly with her center. I kissed the side of her neck, running my tongue along her skin and catching the water. Sucking, I felt myself twitch at the moan that escaped her lips.

Fuck, the thirst I felt for her was unquenchable. Running my length along her, but not caving to the carnal desire to thrust into her, was nearly impossible. Her wetness coated me. I grazed my teeth against her skin, nibbling her collar bone. My hands traced her sides, cupping her breasts between us. I pulled back to watch her as she writhed against me. She used her legs to get traction, thrusting herself against me shamelessly.

I pinched her nipples between my fingers and almost came right fucking then as she keened. The way she begged for me with her body language, the way she was so ready for me, everything about her was a wick. I was ready to explode. But no, I would be inside her for that. I wanted to push my cum back into her.

Needed to fill her.

My hand wrapped around her neck, and I crushed my lips to hers. Licking inside her mouth wasn't enough as my dick strained between us. Every time I rolled my hips into her, she moaned. Her hands scrambled to grab hold of anything, but she was stuck in place, constrained underneath me. Having her at my fucking mercy was worth everything that would happen once I got back to the fires. This was perfection, and anyone who argued otherwise hadn't experienced the beauty of watching a human become so overcome with yearning.

The passion with which humans felt things blew everything in the fires away. Sure, we fucked. We fed our kinks and desires. We were lustful. But this? This felt like her life depended on her next orgasm. Her body begged to be opened, to be claimed, to be remade.

The spark in her heart grew hotter, ready to explode into an inferno. And I wasn't nearly done with her yet.

I sank my teeth into her lower lip and sucked it into my mouth.

"Haden," she gasped. Her breathy whisper sent signals straight to my dick. My head toyed with her entrance. "Please, I need—"

I gave her nipple one last twist. She bucked into my hand as I trailed down her stomach, placing my thumb on her nerves. A scream tore from her lips, so quick and fast that one of her friends pounded on the door.

"Zoe! Are you okay?"

Her head hit the shower wall. "Fuck!"

"Zoe!"

"Fine! I'm fucking fine!"

I bit her jaw as a smirk formed on my lips, because she could barely get the words out. Her voice had arched with a crack. Pieces of her fell apart around me, and I still hadn't entered her. I needed to hear her scream my name; I was desperate for it.

"Better than fine, I hope," I murmured, burying my teeth into the soft flesh of her neck as I moved my hand to her nape. Giving my mouth better access to sink into her.

"Haden, I need you." She stretched her neck back. I lavished the exposed skin, kissing and sucking, doing everything I could to leave a long-lasting mark.

I wanted her to always remember tonight.

Thrusting up, she sucked in a breath as I entered her, invading her. Fuck, she was so wet. Her pussy fluttered, needy and wanting. I could watch her orgasm for the rest of my days. Would happily drown in her if it meant getting to experience this one last time.

"Haden, please!" She gasped my name so prettily.

I latched my hand onto the back of her neck, burrowed my teeth into her shoulder, and I fucked into her with one full thrust.

She screamed. The noise filled the bathroom as she clenched along my cock, practically strangling me with her orgasm. I kept my rhythm steady, pulling back and pounding into her. Her screams kept coming, made worse when I focused once again on her clit. Her legs crushed me into her.

"Haden!" It was a pathetic little whimper; one made by someone who was becoming overstimulated. I *loved* it. The begging, the pleading, the demand for it to be over. This was torture, pure and glorious, the kind I would give her again and again. "I—" But she was breathless and couldn't finish her sentence. Every muscle inside her coiled tight as she fell into pieces. It was in the last throes of her orgasm that I felt the magic shift, the change in the air. Everything outside this room had transformed. And to have her come at the same moment that my captor died?

Perfection.

Her walls finally unclenched, but I continued to ride her. I stopped moving my thumb as her body shuddered against me involuntarily. Her legs went lax as her breath came in small, wicked pants.

I held her with one hand underneath her ass, the other still on her neck. Pressing my forehead into hers, I said, "Fuck, I love watching you come."

A small squeak escaped her. "Haden."

"And hearing my name." I kissed her lightly, slowing down my pace to savor the feel of her along my length. The pull of her muscles against me and the way she wound so tightly around my cock. The primal urge to take her as a demon surged through me. I wondered if I could get her wet enough to bear it.

Fuck, she was tight already, but that would be glorious.

"I would stay like this all night until the water ran cold. I would fuck you forever, but unfortunately, our time is up."

"What?" Her eyes opened wide, staring at me with a dazed look. "What do you mean?"

"I mean—" Pounding started on the door. Shouts rose from the other room. "Thomas is dead, and I have a new master. You still need to survive the night."

She breathed out, rolled her hips along with mine. "Can I make you a deal? Do people make deals with demons?"

"It's generally not recommended," I said, thrusting into her deeply. The words pooled out of my mouth without permission. I should have jumped at the opportunity, but instead, I told her the truth. She shouldn't trust me—or *any* demons, for that matter.

A groan escaped her lips, and I captured the sweet sound with my mouth. Inhaling every part of her.

As soon as I released her, she said, "I could give you my soul."

I paused. Everything came to a halt. She murmured the one set of words I couldn't deny, and she had offered it without my suggestion. She had no idea what she proposed, did she? I wanted to tell her, send her screaming away from me.

But I would never let her go. Not now.

The spark inside her flickered to life, dancing at the idea of us being bound together, of her belonging to me and the fires.

"And what do you want in exchange?"

She blinked. "You can give me some kind of power, so I can help someone from my group of friends survive the night. You can have my soul as long as one of us survives."

"Do you realize what you are offering me? Do you understand an eternity in the fires means just that?" I needed to stop talking. I had planned for this, was going to convince her of it. Her soul was always going to be mine, but having her present it to me with such innocence was a shock. I wanted to accept, but I needed her to understand that her words held meaning. Humans never realized how much power their words contained.

Swallowing, her lips parted as she searched my face. Her eyes traced over me, and even though I had her pinned to the wall, it suddenly felt like she was the one in control. "It would mean that I'm yours forever, right?"

"Yes."

"And that no matter what happens after tonight, I'd belong to you?"

"Yes."

"Then I want that. I want to give you my soul so that one of my friends will live."

I hummed, licking my lips. "Your soul in exchange for someone from your friend group surviving tonight," I stated. "That's the offer."

Her eyes searched mine. "Yes. Take my soul. It was already yours anyway."

I growled, pulling back and burying myself deep inside her. My mouth smashed against hers with such violence it became all teeth. I fucked her, and I pressed my hand in between her breasts, nestled over where her heart was. Where the fire had already started.

My claws came out. I swallowed, breathing through the hold on my magic. I'd have to reel myself back in. Keep myself grounded. But I had to take what was now mine. My nails dug into her, bursting blood forth. It was a ritual, a way for me to call to the soul that lay underneath her skin. Her body writhed for me as I kept my pace. Between her shouting, her friends outside, and the men in the hallway, there was a cacophony of noise that made my body bliss out. My claws dug farther into her, piercing her skin.

Mine. Whispered the word so sweetly against her soul. The fire surged toward me, swirling around my fingers, like calling to like. It intertwined with me, danced with me, and melded into part of my being. A wave of coldness followed it, more unsure, not knowing if it was welcome. But it was mine too. I would take all of her, even the good inside her. I had imagined it being so much harder to convince her, but she had given it to me. Offered it willingly.

I came undone, spilling inside her as her soul brushed against mine. It was a gasp of air, a cool autumn breeze mingling under my skin. My claws dug into her chest as she gasped, clenching around me. I invaded her as much as she invaded me, and I wouldn't have our combining any other way.

She had given herself to me.

I breathed out, retracting my claws from her skin. My other thumb rolled over her clit through the final throes of her orgasm. My breath was unsteady as she gripped me tightly, but then she unfurled. Eyes popped open, staring straight into me. She blinked.

"Did you—"

"*Mine.*" Words would not come other than that one. Euphoria crossed all my senses, making me unable to process anything else than a need to prove to her how she would always belong to me.

Forever.

"Okay." Her head lolled forward, resting on my chest. She nodded against me, pressing her lips to my skin.

I reached over and turned the water off. I pulled out of her and visually took her in. Water drenching her perfect breasts as her legs shook underneath her. A blush crept over her cheeks as my eyes roamed over her. Her hands were still up above her head, unable to cover herself as I seared her to memory. The scar marks from my claws had already formed, a completion of her offer to me.

Cum dripped down her thigh, and she whimpered as I caught it. I reached for her core, and a breath hitched in her throat as I pumped my fingers inside her. "This is mine forever. *You* are mine forever." She writhed under my touch.

I had never claimed a human soul before, never had been so intrinsically tied to another living being. What Thomas had done was a spell, nothing with such permanence. The feeling of her swirled around me, coolness with a warm, liquid core. It felt right having her here with me. She shivered as I brushed my fingers over the mark I made. The puckered skin was warm to the touch, ignited from the small bit of fire I had left behind in her.

"So, how does this work? You give me powers so I can defeat the bad guys, or you send them to the fires with a snap of your fingers?"

I smirked. "You already have the most powerful weapon imaginable."

"You?"

I chuckled and snatched a towel. I wrapped it around her, bundling her up despite her hands still being above her head. Her fingers were turning purple. I'd let her down soon, but after I confessed to her how this was going to work. Because I needed her soul to be ignited, the spark in her to come to life, I needed *fire*.

"You see, you have something more powerful than anyone else in this house." I leaned close. "You have nothing left to lose."

She blinked. Anger washed over her features. Brows lowered, cheeks flushed, and a wave of furious energy crashed over me. "Haden." She pulled against her binding. "You better not be saying what I think you're saying."

I wrapped my fingers around the metal holding her in place as my lips brushed the shell of her ear. "I'm saying exactly what needs to be said. If your soul is already mine, what else do you have to lose? There's nothing more powerful than the fearlessness you're about to feel. Embrace it." I yanked the towel rod from the wall.

20 Zoe

The metal towel holder dropped away from my skin. I stumbled forward, shocked at the change in my circumstances, appalled by what he said, and peeved that I had the audacity to believe him. After I had given him *everything* I had to offer. The towel hung loosely around me, but instead of securing it, I shoved him. Hard. He leaped over the edge of the tub, landing on the tile outside of the shower. I prowled toward him.

"You said—"

"The offer was for someone in your group of friends to survive the night in exchange for your soul. I said nothing about giving you powers. Besides, my power is not mine to give. You must kill for it."

I scowled at him. "Then what was the point?!" Because what had been the point to any of this? Because he had been bored? Because he wanted me to be tied to him? But why?

"Now you have nothing left to lose. Trust me, that's as powerful of a feeling as you can get during your time on earth."

His words buzzed in my head. He was right, wasn't he? If he held my soul—because I had been stupid enough to trade my soul to a literal demon—then what more did I have to fear? I knew where I was going after this was over—straight to the fires, with him and whatever slow tortures he wanted to put me through. I'd spend my afterlife consumed by flames, but at least someone in my group would make it out alive.

That was the only thing I could hope for—for someone I once loved to be safe. Even if we had our differences now, even if it took a while for them to stand up to Ridley, even if it had taken them too long to see me, one of them deserved a chance to live—at least more than the people outside this room. One of my friends would do something great with their second chance. I was sure of it.

"I need clothes," I said.

"You can take mine." He gestured to the pile on the floor. New clothes spouted out of his skin, covering him from head to toe. It was the strangest thing to watch. "Part of being able to morph into a human vessel means having access to clothing, since most of you are opposed to nudity." His eyes raked over where the towel had parted. "Though I never understood why."

I opened my mouth to argue, but he was right. Most of my life had been spent ignoring my own pleasure—not watching porn, turning my nose up at romance novels, avoiding anything that would give me the slightest ounce of desire between my legs. Now, I wondered how much time I had wasted trying to fit myself into a box that was never meant for me. Besides, if my pleasure wasn't hurting anyone, why had I avoided it for so long?

I pulled on his pants and shirt. They smelled like him—a long burned-out campfire, lingering and cozy. The waist barely fit me, but he picked up my destroyed shirt and tore off a long strip of it.

Hammering fists rained against the exterior door, followed by shouting. Most of which I couldn't make out. So far, my friends seemed safe; no one could get inside the barricaded room. Even if they did, my friends had some weapons. Not many, but some. It had to be enough.

Haden stepped forward with the strip of material. His fingers worked it through my belt loops, slowly, methodically, lingering like he had all the time in the world. He tied it off in the front, and his gaze raked over me again, causing my cheeks to heat. His head tilted to the side, a coy smile stretching up his lips. I wanted to slap him, wipe the grin off his face, lick him, bite him, scream at him, rage. Everything all at once.

"You look good in my clothes."

"You're only saying that because you own my soul."

"And what a perfect creation it is." He pressed his lips to my forehead. "There are four of them outside. Jeremy is the one who killed Thomas."

"The football players?" I sighed, because of course it had to be a group of built men who had survived the night. And I was me—just me. "What weapons do they have?"

"A few knives and a gun, but there's not a single bullet left in this house, so don't let it intimidate you." Haden's hands went through my wet locks. "Mm." He picked up the towel and ran it over my hair.

How was I supposed to leave this pampering behind to go conquer more enemies? I wanted to fall into bed with him. He dried my hair until only dampness remained. As soon as his touch dropped away, I realized how much I had been leaning into him. The arrogant smile on his face increased my craving to bite him.

I nodded once, allowing the news to settle in. I was going to kill more people tonight, but at least after this, it would be done. My soul would go to the fires with Haden, and someone else would keep living. I had to hope my friends were built for survival, because they'd need it after a night like tonight.

My heart thudded against my chest as my mind raced through everything I could face out there. While there was a part of me that was furious with Haden, I also understood his true power was wrapped up in someone else's soul. It hadn't annoyed me when it had been Thomas, because he was innocuous, but someone like Jeremy didn't *deserve* that kind of power. Once I killed him, I could utilize whatever I needed in order to survive. Jeremy was the target. I didn't have to kill them all—just the one.

I had to hope that Jeremy didn't understand the gravity of what was at his disposal. Sure, Thomas hadn't either, because if he *had*, there was no way he would have died tonight. He was the one who summoned Haden in the first place, but I saw the grief all over his face. While Thomas had wanted more, he had regretted intertwining his fate to Haden's in the first place.

"Okay." I let out a breath. I would need something bigger than the knife in the other room and the frying pan we had stolen earlier. "Where the heck is the ax?" It was the perfect solution to make some heads roll.

Haden's grin made him look guiltless. His eyes were smug, satisfied. Network of veins showed through his skin, inky dark shadows webbing over his body. The sated, half-lidded look gave him a menacing appeal.

I poked him in the chest. "I'm still angry with you." The last thing I needed was an arrogant demon who thought he had won this argument.

He wrapped his hand around my finger and lowered it. "It's still in the wall where you left it. I'll give you a back exit. It'll be the easiest way to take them out. And remember, if you kill Jeremy first, you'll be able to command me." A fire entered his eyes with those words. "I'll have to do whatever you ask."

"Why wasn't offering my soul enough to get some of your powers?"

"You're bound to me, but I'm not bound to you." He dropped my hand and hooked a finger under my chin. His eyes felt endless. "But I want to be, so kill him fast. Then, whatever you order me to do, I'm yours. We can take the rest of them out together." His breath mingled with mine. Fuck, even through my frustration and just having terrific sex, my body still somehow wanted him again. His tongue flicked out, and he swiped it over my lips, tasting me.

"I wish I could ask you nicely to take care of them for me." I blinked up at him, feeling confidence I was unprepared for. Haden's energy made me want to be *more*.

"I would gladly tear out someone's heart for you. I've already torn off someone's arm." His lips brushed my nose. His breath warmed my skin. "With the way Thomas set up this binding spell, I can't be directly responsible for any attack against the one I'm bound to. I can help you get out of this room, and I can give you advice on how to take out the other three. I can *conspire*, but unfortunately, I cannot assist with Jeremy's demise." Haden wrapped his arms around me, squeezing me tightly. "That's up to you. I'm not used to putting my trust in someone else to get things done, but I am trying to believe you'll win this."

"You can sense how things could go wrong?"

"Yes, based on everything I know about the souls outside and yours, I can see how this could go very wrong."

"And you can't warn me?"

"Warning you would serve no purpose, because you'd be looking for that one outcome instead of others, which could put you at a disadvantage. So no, I will not tell you how I see things going. We have a good chance—*you* have a good chance." He pressed his lips to my temple, lingering against my damp locks.

I relaxed into him, taking a few moments before chaos broke out once more.

When I came to this party, the last thing on my mind had been meeting someone who I wanted to keep by my side. I thought I'd stand off to the side, be my awkward, introverted self. Maybe have a hook up if I had been lucky, and luckier still, a few orgasms. But meeting a demon? No way. Having the best sex of my life? Hadn't been on the bingo card. Before tonight, I barely believed in the paranormal or afterlife, but now a demon had a claim over my soul.

He held me like he never wanted to let me go.

There was strength here, in the way his arms folded around me. In the warmth flooding into my veins. In the way his power bloomed, bringing me into his orbit.

"No matter how bleak it gets, no matter how much you hurt, remember that no matter what, you're still mine."

I nodded into his chest. The smell of wood smoke curled into my nostrils, already familiar despite this being only one night of our lives together—one night at the beginning of an eternity. The thought almost made me giggle. Talk about a strange end to a one-night stand.

"So, no fear, no balking, no hesitation. At the end of the night, your soul belongs to me. It obeys me." He gently nudged me away, eyes searching mine. The black shadows running through his veins seeped away, drifting back under his clothes like they never were.

I wanted to see him without this suit he wore, what he looked like underneath. I wanted everything he had already promised and more. My body craved it, craved him, despite how I had just gotten fucked until I could barely breathe.

"Are you ready for this?" he asked, bringing me back down to earth.

"Ready to go against four asshats with nothing but an ax? Not really."

"Like I said—"

"Jeremy first. Yeah. I got it. If the opportunity arises to distract the rest of them, please feel free to do so."

He smirked. His fist shot straight out into the bathroom wall. I sucked in a breath as he tore through the drywall and wood all in one go.

The four were making so much noise trying to break into the bedroom, none of the shouting so much as stopped, let alone paused. I heard my group moving more furniture, and I had to hope that their barricade would hold.

Or at least hold long enough for me to kill Jeremy.

"Wish me luck."

"You don't need it. Not when you have something better on your side." He gave me a wink. "Nothing to lose. And avoid the third stair from the top."

I curled my fists at my sides. Nothing to lose, everything to gain. I could do this. I *would* do this. Without giving it much further thought, I stepped through the hole and scrambled into the hallway. Drywall dust coated my skin. The yelling and slamming against the door continued, which provided me with some hope of getting out of this unseen.

With soft footfalls, I inched down the hallway. It wasn't until I was above the stairs that the striking stopped.

"Did you hear that?" Lasher asked. Lance Lasher was one of those guys you wanted to punch in the face the moment he spoke. He said the "right" things, checked the "right" boxes, but something was inherently off about him. As soon as I heard how he hooked up with three different girls in one weekend—with each of them having the expectation of going exclusive based on their conversations with him—I realized what it was. Lasher was a salesman. A lying, cheating, and willing to do whatever it took to make himself look better kind of guy.

I stayed perfectly still, holding my breath. If the four of them turned on me now, I was absolutely screwed. My heart thudded in my ears, and I was convinced they could hear it.

"Man, we're almost through. Come on," Jeremy whined. Based on the groans from the other members of the group, it didn't sound like they were anywhere close.

"Stop for a second," Lasher hissed.

"I don't hear anything." This came from Kyle. Kyle had been one of the nicer football players, but right now, he was teamed up with the garbage. If I had to take out the trash, I would have to take out anyone associated with the refuse. I would try not to lose sleep over it.

Another thwack.

"Shut up!" Lasher insisted.

"You tripping." David's gruff voice reached my ears, making me shiver. David was the biggest of the group by far, and the one I was the most worried about. Thick shoulders, heavy arms, a body that could likely break me in two if he tried. He could fling me across the room with little effort. He looked like he started doing cross fit on the off season.

And I was supposed to fight four of them?

Nothing left to lose.

There was that.

My lungs burned in an effort to keep everything together. If I let out my breath now, I was at risk of delivering them a beacon straight to my location. Sweat built on my lower back. I strained to listen to their voices.

"Not tripping, bro. There was something." Lasher's voice curled with his complaint. "What if we missed someone?"

"Ain't no one left to miss," Kyle said. "You guys made sure of that." The last line was added with a docile resistance.

"Yeah, we even went through and double tapped a few people like you asked," Jeremy said. "Waste of bullets, if you ask me. Paranoid mother f—" Someone rammed something into the door.

Well, hopefully that meant Haden was right and they were out of bullets.

Jeremy Delroy had been the varsity football captain during our junior year, but when his father took a leave of absence, he lost the position to someone else. He used to be the star of everything he ever did, until things began to fall apart in senior year. No longer captain, and as far as I could tell from social media, Jeremy hadn't been successful in college either. He made the team but was nothing more than a bench warmer. Small fish in a bigger pond. His posts online grew mean, angry. While the others would be a challenge, I was excited to end Jeremy. That developing evil streak deserved to be snuffed out. Seeing the light drift from his eyes would be the saving grace of tonight.

The excitement about his demise felt wrong. But that's where I found myself now, longing for the promised destruction. The air held a promiscuity that I had never tasted before. I wanted it. The smell of copper, the way the blood would soak into the flooring. The far off look in their eyes—vacant, empty. Never to bully anyone ever again. Destroying the festering anger inside these men would be magnificent.

"Whatever. Let's get this door down."

Another round of thumping started. I breathed out a rush of air as soon as they made another noise. Slipping down the stairs, I avoided the third step from the top, as Haden requested. It had become so easy for me to fall into obeying him. I longed to see what that would bring about in the future, excited by the prospect of taking his orders in bed. I had to focus on the present, though, else I could lose whatever edge I had.

My feet reached the bottom landing. I glanced up at the balcony and waited. Nothing, other than the distant thudding impacts on the door.

Okay, get the ax and disembowel some more people. What could possibly go wrong?

Other than everything, but I pushed the doubt from my mind. Second-guessing would get me killed, and I had no reason to hesitate now.

Keeping my steps light, I rushed down the hallway, clambering over dead bodies. I kept my hand on the wall to avoid slipping on the slick puddles of blood. When did I become okay seeing this much death? Didn't matter. Not now. Not with my adrenaline making my heart thud in my ears.

The ax was at the end of the hallway.

Perfect.

Arms wrapped around me from behind, making my lungs explode as whoever it was clamped me to their chest.

"I thought I heard someone. You snake. How did you get out?" Lasher growled in my ear. He reeked of stale beer and metal— someone else's blood, I realized as wetness pressed against my back.

I had *just* showered.

"You'd love to know, wouldn't you?" I snarled.

"I would." His breath grazed my ear as his grip tightened. "I have nothing to kill you with. The guys took the weapons when I went off exploring—said I wouldn't need any with the last of you rats trapped away. Looks like they were wrong."

He squeezed.

I could barely suck in a breath to form my next words. "Am I a rat or a snake?"

"What?" His confusion caused him to loosen his grip.

I continued, "I can't be both. Rats and snakes aren't the same type of animal, not even in the same family." One of his hands curled around my neck as he braced me firmly against him with his other. He didn't tighten his hold, though. If I kept talking, then I'd figure out a way out of this. I knew where the ax was. I just needed to get to it. "So, which is it?"

"You always thought you were too good for us. Didn't you? Stuck up your fucking nose like the stupid bitch you are. You looked down on the entire team. But you know what?" His tongue licked the outside of my ear. Rage flooded me. If he kept this up, I might take his balls as a trophy. "It would have been your privilege to have me *look* at you. You would have been lucky to get with someone like me. But you're too much of a prude to understand how good you could have had it."

"Not a prude. Just don't date assholes like you. You probably don't even bother to get the girl off before you blow your load." I dropped my legs out from under me.

In the second of Lasher taking my weight, his hold shifted, and he couldn't tighten fast enough. I reared my elbow backward, landing straight in his crotch. As soon as he grunted, I knew it was now or never. Getting my feet underneath me, I shot up from the squat. We jetted backward from my momentum, and Lasher and I smashed against the wall. Too loud. Too much noise.

But finally, the asshole's grip loosened.

"Haden!" I got a breath in long enough to yell.

The demon appeared out of nowhere—there by my side in a blink. That was more than I could say about most humans. His hand wrapped around Lasher's throat. He thrust the man back against the wall. "Get the ax."

"Kill him for me?" I asked as I sauntered down the hallway. As much as I wanted to tear into Lasher for the way he treated women, I had to prepare for the other fights ahead. Men like Lasher didn't deserve the good fortune they received, as they used women like playthings. Maybe they forgot how we had emotions too, but he certainly wouldn't forget now, not with vengeance being wrapped around his throat.

Looking over my shoulder, Haden's black eyes shifted toward me. Inky darkness spread up his veins, consuming his forearms as his grip on Lasher tightened. Lasher's face turned from red to purple as his hands pried at Haden's, scraping his nails along his skin.

"Only because you asked so nicely. And because I'll enjoy it." As Haden's lips curled in a smile, I raced to the other end of the hallway. No point in being quiet now. The other three would be here before I knew it, and without a weapon, I'd be facing down three men and their demon—if Jeremy realized the power he had at his disposal. At least with Lasher out of the way, my odds of winning this fucked up game of hide and seek improved.

They sought.

I hid with an ax, ready to kill them.

As soon as I approached the weapon, I wrenched it out of the wall. Earlier, it had been stuck, but something told me Haden had loosened it for me. With the wooden handle in my grip—still tacky with blood—I took off to the nearest coat closet. I couldn't help but glance back the way I had come.

Haden was gone, but the evidence of him wasn't. Lasher's head faced the wrong direction, neck twisted around, and a silent scream stretched across his features. His body lay in a puddle of his own piss. Good riddance.

Footsteps pattered down the stairs. I was running out of time to get set up before they arrived. Slowly, I opened the closet door and slipped inside. My heart hammering in my ears was louder than the noise the door made as I shut it behind me. I strained to hear anything over my pulse. A wash of fear cascaded over me as I watched the gap underneath the door for any shadows in the quiet.

The absence of sound felt loud as I continued to listen for anything. In the darkness, I convinced myself that I had lost all sense of reality. Maybe I was alone in the house. Maybe all of this was some fucked up dream.

"What the fuck!" Kyle yelled. I practically jumped out of my skin from the suddenness of his voice as he ripped away the comfort of silence.

"Dude," Jeremy said.

David muttered something, but I couldn't hear him over the thudding in my ears.

"No. That's not normal, dude."

"We need to find that fucking demon." Jeremy's footsteps drew close. "Shouldn't he be staying out of this? I thought it was to figure out who would take over Thomas's stupid curse. Can't you summon him or something?"

"I don't know. I tried." Kyle's voice sounded meek compared to Jeremy's. Interesting. Haden had told me Jeremy had control, but whatever happened tonight led the group to believe it was Kyle who held the power.

Small victories, I supposed.

I choked up on the ax. In my mind, I ran through the movements, how it would feel the moment they opened the door. Swing. Hit. Swing. Hit. Swing. Hit. It didn't need to be a good hit. Arms, legs, anything to slow them down would be fine. The torso would be messy but would work all right. We were trapped here until one person was left alive, so they wouldn't survive a hit to the stomach. They'd have to bleed out eventually, right?

Still, I would love a neck shot—take off their head clean as a whistle. Exactly like what the old turn of phrase meant.

I almost giggled. Burying my mouth into my shoulder, I told myself to hold it together. Took little sips of air into my nose to fight back the laughter. Fuck, I was losing it. The old idiom meant nothing about a whistle, but the sound a sword made when it was swung perfectly to take someone's head off. Clean as a whistle. And skies, I *was* losing it.

My ears pricked.

Was it my imagination or had someone stopped outside the coat closet? It was like I could hear them breathing next to me. I swallowed.

"He should be answering to one of us now—because there's no way that stupid bitch killed anyone who had power," David growled.

Jeremy sighed. "What did you expect? Women are witches. She probably summoned it or something. Showed her fucking boobs or cast a spell. Who the fuck knows?"

Wow, were we going back to the sixteen hundreds?

"Jeremy, the demon literally said Thomas summoned him. And he's dead, so there's no one left to blame. We just need to—" Kyle stopped abruptly.

"The fuck you mean, there's no one left to blame." Something shifted, and a grunt sounded. "You can *always* blame women. You understand? They aren't good for anything. We've been taught that, told that; we *know* that. We're better. They need us more than we need them. They are good for one thing and one thing only—making the next generation of men."

Bile clawed up my throat. What the heck was *wrong* with these guys? If we were blaming anyone, then it should be Thomas. He was the one who summoned a demon in the first place.

And maybe we'd also have to blame Haden, since he had cast tonight's spell. I felt that was also unfair, because he hadn't forced anyone to take up weapons. He had only threatened the end. No, we were ready and willing to take up arms the moment someone else gave us permission to do so. We could toss the blame out all night, but it changed *nothing*. I wanted solutions, not more problems. Everything Jeremy said was another problem, not a solution. More and more problems with nothing practical to add to the conversation.

My solution? Kill Jeremy.

Nothing about him seemed worth saving, and rage roiled inside me. His words were despicable. Watching the red spill from his body, watching as his life flooded out of him, seeing how it splattered across the floor … that was something worth striving for. A small piece of perfected justice in the world.

A throaty laugh sounded as David chimed in. "Yeah, you can always blame women. They wear whatever they want and expect us not to fuck them. They flaunt it, but they don't put out. If they didn't want attention, they shouldn't try so hard. Besides, I am happy to give it to them." David's voice faded as a door opened to one bedroom.

"You better not be saying what I think you're saying," Kyle's voice. It dipped low into a growl.

"Come on, Kyle. You know *exactly* what I'm saying." A door shut somewhere in the hallway.

I pressed my hand to my mouth. Sucking in a few breaths, I forced my stomach to calm down. They would be dead. Both Jeremy and David would die tonight. Neither of them would walk out of here. This would be revenge for those women.

Tonight, vengeance had a name.

"They are both destined for the fires, the pits specifically." Haden's voice carried through from the other side of the door. "Kyle won't be. He hates them, but he hesitates to argue because I put him in an impossible situation. Had the party not been cursed, he wouldn't be so heavily involved in their shit. He might have even talked to Jennifer, heard the truth fall directly from her lips. But that's in a universe where I didn't cast a curse."

I sucked in a shaking breath.

"Talk softly. I can hear you," he murmured.

"None of what you said makes Kyle an upstanding citizen. He's still siding with them right now."

"You're right, but if the skies only accepted those who were truly good, everyone would end up in the fires. Unfortunately, there are a lot more tepid souls than they'd like to admit. He'll become a guardian, have to work to save someone else's soul."

A door opened, and I stopped breathing, not daring a whisper as I heard a single set of footsteps coming back. Haden likely made himself scarce, otherwise Jeremy could use him against me. Hitching up my grip on the handle, I braced myself against the wall, preparing my swing. As I rolled my shoulders, the knob on the closet moved.

My heart threatened to jump into my throat, but I forced myself to calm down. Haden owned my soul, no matter what. My friends had weapons and would survive the three of them. If I took out one more, that would increase their chances. I had this. There was nothing to fear. No matter what happened next, I would be dead by the morning. My soul would belong to Haden and the fires.

Absolution was a powerful emotion.

Venomous hatred a close second.

The closet door opened. I swung the ax.

David's scream burst from his throat as the blade buried in his chest. With shaking hands, he brought up his knife.

"Duck!" Haden's voice.

I listened immediately, dropping to the ground as the knife swung straight for where my neck had been. My brain throbbed from the ear-piercing screech erupting from David. As soon as he reached the tail end of his breath, a wet sound rattled with his inhale.

I aimed way too high for a gut shot, and now my stupid ax was buried in his ribcage. Footsteps sounded. A heady feeling ripped through me. I stood on the end of a cliff, staring at the ground hundreds of feet below.

"Grab the ax. Finish him. Find Jeremy." Haden's eyes widened as a growl emanated from his chest. "Fuck, he's finding you instead. Remember, the gun is empty, and—"

"Go!" I ordered as I grabbed a firm hold on the ax handle. Kicking forward, I thrust David's body backward as I wrenched the weapon out of his chest. Blood splattered across my face, and I winced from the hot stream of it.

David's wail turned into a wheeze. Air escaped his chest cavity as if from a balloon. "You ... fucking—"

"If you so much as think the word *bitch* right now, I will feed you your own balls." He deserved as much and so much more.

With shaking, bloody fingers, he reached for me, but his movements were slow, as if under water. I slashed out with the weapon again, making a cleaner swing this time. The blade cut across his arms, and a gasp escaped him as he stumbled backward. His back rammed into the wall just as Jeremy and Kyle appeared on opposite ends of the hallway—Jeremy near where I had faced off against Brett and Kyle toward the hallway's entrance.

Well, shit.

I had to make a split-second decision. Jeremy was the goal, but Kyle had the gun. I couldn't risk them trapping me between them, so I sprinted toward Kyle. He readied his weapon. If it had been any blades, I wouldn't stand a chance.

"Stop!" Jeremy yelled at me.

"I'll shoot!" Kyle's voice held less confidence than Jeremy's did.

I'd love to see him try. My lips peeled back, showing my teeth as my feet pounded against the floor. Kyle's hand shook around the gun. I continued to charge him.

Jeremy screamed something incoherent behind me.

The trigger clicked in Kyle's hand, not a single bullet coming out. My shoulder slammed into his. Fucking football player. I ricocheted off him. He bounced into the wall, and I hit the other side of the hallway. I had been ready for this. I used the momentum to rebound forward, out and away from him. My biggest concern was getting away from Jeremy, whose hatred spilled out of him like a volcanic force.

"Get her!"

"Why is this not loaded?" Kyle's voice sounded hurt.

"Because you fucking hesitated. Why would I ever give you—"

I flung around the corner, sprinting into the pool room. I hooked along the back of the room, letting their screams chase me as their arguing grew. With no time to think, I launched my body into the chemical closet, slamming the door shut behind me. The metal latch clicked into place. Thrumming drowned out any other noise as the filter and pump continued to flush the bloody contaminants from the system.

A body lay in the corner, covered in oozing chemical burns.

Bringing Haden's shirt over my nose, I clambered on top of what looked like a furnace. It was right by the door, and the top of it was hot. The metal groaned under my weight, but it held.

Ax to head. I had the leverage now, the space to do it. I could land it straight into their skull and split them in two.

The fumes in the room went straight to my head, giving me an ache behind my eyes. I tried not to think about what I was inhaling right now. Survive as long as I could. Take out as many as possible. Leave my friends to decide who will make it the rest of the way.

Maybe they will slowly starve instead of hurting each other. Or maybe Mercedes will turn against the rest of them. Maybe they would be doomed for the fires, and nothing I did tonight would save them.

Oh well. I had to try.

I tightened my grip as someone pushed the door inward. With a scream, I brought the blade down.

"Shit!" the guy danced to the side. The ax slammed into the side of their shoulder, taking off a piece of their flesh like carving a turkey. It slapped to the ground as crimson coated their arm.

"Fuck, Zoe!" Kyle grabbed his arm. "Look, fuck, stop!" He stumbled backward away from me, showing me his empty hands. "I don't want to fight you. Jeremy is a piece of shit. I'm trying to help you."

"And how am I supposed to believe that?"

"No weapon." He glowered as his good hand wrapped around the gushing wound. "They left me at this shit show of a party with no fucking weapon. You know what that means? They didn't care if I lived or died tonight. They would have been fine either way. Fuck that. Fuck them. I stopped talking to them after high school, and reconnecting tonight had been a mistake. Fuck my arm. Holy fuck. It's just like … sitting there." His eyes were glued to the slab of him on the ground.

"Use your shirt. Wrap it." I jumped down, glanced out the door, but didn't see Jeremy anywhere. Shutting it, I helped Kyle wrap his arm with a part of his shirt. He was bleeding like crazy, and red already burst through the material. I tightened it as best I could.

He pressed his eyes closed, swaying on his feet.

"Why do you hang out with those dip shits, anyway?"

Kyle sucked in a breath, opened his eyes, and leaned against the door. "Old habits, I guess. When I went to college, I didn't talk to them anymore. Didn't want to or need to, you know? Got my own friends and shit. Better than those. But I came back here, and I don't really know anyone else." His green irises settled on me. A blood vessel had burst open in his right eye, and red marred the side of his cheek. "And then when this happened, I figured no one else would beat them. If I stuck with them to the end, then maybe—"

"You could turn on them and win at the last minute?"

"Something like that." Kyle's blood trickled down his arm, dripping off his fingers. "But shit, Zoe, I'm probably going to die from this."

"I mean … maybe not."

"Nah. I'm a goner. But I can at least help you take out Jeremy. Got to be worth something up there, right?" He pointed toward the skies.

"Never took you for a believer, Kyle."

He leveled me with a look. "We saw a demon tonight, Zoe. I think we'd be stupid not to believe." A sad smile stretched on his lips. "Are there any other weapons in here?"

I shrugged. "I'm not giving you my ax."

"Wouldn't dream of asking, but Jeremy has knives. While I am feeling like a martyr, it has to be within reason." His eyes curled as the smile faded from his lips. There was something utterly charming about Kyle, and perhaps if he had chosen better friends, maybe he would have been surviving tonight. "There." He nodded past me, toward the giant pool cover. "Tear me off a large piece of it. I'll see what I can do."

"With a plastic tarp?" I snorted.

He shrugged. "He has short-range weapons, has to get in nice and personal. If I can throw the tarp over him, then you can—" Kyle sucked in a breath. His eyes fluttered.

I felt half-bad about what I had done. Of course, I had wanted it to be Jeremy, to be finished with this whole wretched night, but I hadn't gotten so lucky. I considered Kyle, wondering if he would betray me in the end, but Haden hadn't reappeared, so Kyle likely had good intentions.

"Okay," I said. "I'll cut you something. Watch the door and yell if he comes."

"Will do my best. But Zoe? Hurry." He rested his head against the wall. I glanced at the thickening rivulets of burgundy against his paling skin; it showed no sign of slowing.

"Will do my best," I echoed him.

Haden

Thomas's cabin was a ridiculous monstrosity, but I was now grateful for the height in the pool room. The arched ceilings had beams traveling across the top, which gave me the perfect perch to see how this played out. Kyle had followed Zoe into the utility closet. I had been ready to cause a distraction if needed but realized it would be unnecessary. She had this.

And with Kyle on her side—until he died of the inevitable blood loss—Jeremy was the only person remaining between me and my prize.

Sure, there would be her friends to deal with, but they were still hiding away in the bedroom. None of them had bothered to break into the bathroom. All of them were terrified that Zoe's screaming hadn't been in pleasure, but in pain, and none of them wanted to see what lay on the other side of that melted door.

Everything that happened next would serve them right. They didn't deserve her loyalty or love. She held an unwavering devotion to them, one I would break soon enough. If anyone commanded her obedience, it would be me. And I would prove it to her.

Jeremy prowled around the living room, looking underneath the couches. Honestly, he was dumber than the ones who tried to escape the fires. First, the furniture was too close to the ground to fit a child, let alone a fully grown adult. Maybe a cat could get under there, but that was it.

Second, he had yet to call on me. Thomas had tried when I was in the shower with Zoe. I had felt the vague tug on my tether, but it had been too little too late.

The magic transference had finished before he got the chance to summon me.

Jeremy hadn't realized it was *his* knife that committed the killing blow. He thought it was Kyle. That's why they had taken the weapons away from their friend, why they planned to turn against him last. They thought Kyle was too nice to turncoat.

Fortunately for me, Jeremy continued believing that Kyle's attack had been the last strike. Kyle hadn't broken the skin. He pretended, too scared to deny his friends, but too worried about his own afterlife to cave to depravity like the rest of them. It had been an act, a show, one Kyle had done well.

He had saved his soul, even while sticking by their side. But the life of a guardian was a tough one; one I didn't wish upon anyone.

Jeremy stood and dusted off his pants—a moot point, considering they were still stained and darkened with blood. He let out a long sigh.

"Demon!" he screamed.

My eyes widened as I latched onto the beam, refusing the call of magic. He didn't know that I *should* come when called, and he also didn't understand how to utilize any of the powers. Thomas had done a great job of keeping me caged, but a terrible job of making me compliant.

There was a huge difference between freedom and complacency.

Jeremy growled. "This is so stupid. Look, tell me where Kyle is. You don't want someone like that attached to you, right? That was the whole point—you hated being attached to Thomas. I saw it written all over your face. Well, Kyle is just as bad—"

I doubted that. Thomas was like plain yogurt. Good for you in theory, but it left you wanting *anything* better. Kyle seemed more like caramel ice cream. Pleasant. Simple. Delicious under the right circumstances.

Once the call passed, I eased up on my grip, still listening to the ranting man below me. He paced the length of the living room, now checking underneath dead bodies, which were clearly lying on the floor. How much had he drunk before my festivities started? Probably too much.

"—he'll be a buzz kill. He's always been that way, you know?" Jeremy sighed and pressed his eyes shut. "I never understood it." With a growl, he popped his eyes open and trudged toward the kitchen. No idea where he was going, but I was grateful for the break in his monotonous conversation with himself.

A few moments later, the door to the mechanical room swung open. Kyle walked out with a giant swatch of … pool covering? Interesting. Behind him was Zoe, carrying her ax with a casual grip and a sense of certainty. Her back was straight, holding a confidence she had gained throughout the night. I breathed out, grateful she appeared to be fine. If Kyle turned against her, I would kill him without a second thought.

They marched forward, keeping their feet light.

Jeremy, meanwhile, slammed drawers in the kitchen. His obscenities could be heard from here. Kyle and Zoe exchanged a glance.

Kyle didn't look well. His face was white as snow, and blood splattered the plastic covering he held.

"You got this?" Zoe asked in a hushed whisper.

He shrugged, wincing as the soaked fabric on his shoulder tightened with the gesture. "Now or never. Literally." A grimace passed over his features at the gravity of his words. He was right. It would be now or never for him.

Kyle surprised me. I hadn't expected him to turn against his friends, not so close to the end. But he seemed to want to make amends. Sometimes that happened to people—they were met with their inevitable demise, and they needed to fix things as quickly as possible.

And of course, the skies would take him with their facade of open arms. *Just do this one little favor for us first? Go be a guardian on Earth and relieve your soul of the guilt that stains you.* What a bunch of bullshit that was.

Unfortunately for me, Zoe's soul remained tepid, a moderate warmth in her body, but not enough to damn her to the fires. If she were to die, well … she *had* given me her soul, but by rights, she was still destined for the skies.

Would her soul be pulled apart by the magnitude of her promise? Would I weigh her down enough to keep her in the fires, or would she ascend?

I needed to corrupt her further in the short time we had left, but I didn't know how to do it. She had become a puzzle. Everything she did was for selfless reasons—even bonding with me. I scowled, wondering how to execute such a feat.

Perhaps I could convince her to destroy her friends? That would surely condemn her to the fires. But I had witnessed her determination. Her expression had been the same one I wore the day I left the fires by touching the obvious trap. She had a fierceness to prove everyone wrong—a stubbornness. It could be the reason we were bound forever or the reason she was torn away from me.

Time would tell. As much as I understood souls, I couldn't predict the future. I could make guesses, based on what I knew about human nature. No one was predestined for anything, but certain souls were easier to corrupt than others. Zoe's had proved difficult, a delicious challenge, but one I was losing patience for.

Even when she did bad things, she did them with good intentions. It's likely what drew me to her in the first place. The spark was the perchance for darkness, but the grace of her actions kept her soul breezy.

My claws extended, and I stared down at the black veins that pooled from them into my skin. I wished to show her my true form; become everything I was meant to be. Maybe if her soul understood how she was falling for a monster, it would be enough to make the flames grow hot.

But for now, I needed to bide time, to watch what happened next. Kyle reached the threshold of the kitchen.

I jumped down, keeping my footsteps soft as to not disturb either of them during their attack. Going to the opposite side of the pool, I circled around the house and entered the hallway outside the kitchen. Just in time for Kyle to stumble across the threshold. He was moving slowly from blood loss. His hands shook around the plastic.

"Kyle? What the fuck." Jeremy took a step toward him but paused. "What happened? Did you find that cu—"

Before Jeremy could finish, Kyle rushed him with a yell. He held the plastic tarp up in front of him. He had barely gotten it over Jeremy's head before the knife connected with his torso. Zoe came around the side while Jeremy was still wrapped up and took a swing with the ax.

I'm not sure how it happened—maybe Kyle's weight on Jeremy was too much, or maybe Jeremy heard the snap of the ax in the air, but they both stumbled forward. The swing went wide, and her stance was off, so the weight of the ax sent her off kilter. She missed.

Jeremy ripped the tarp off his head, whirling around with wild eyes. He caught sight of Zoe, who still was grappling with the weapon, trying to get in another attack. Their eyes met. Sparks ignited as Jeremy ripped the knife from Kyle's guts.

Kyle toppled over, gasping for breath as he clutched his stomach. But the blood was too great, too much too quickly. The light in his brown eyes dulled as his body stilled on the floor. There was a single moment of silence, where a slight smirk spread up Jeremy's features.

"Demon, come to me. Do what I need to end this." The command came out sure, because Jeremy knew he had possession of me now that Kyle was dead. With his demise, there was nothing that stood between us.

I gritted my teeth together. Regardless of his realization, I couldn't *fight* this anymore. I tried. Fuck, I tried so hard. Blood trickled from my nose. My eyes swelled, aching inside my skull. Everything in my brain pulsed. Energy slammed into me from every angle as I fought against the command. Every part that was bound to this asshole pulled me forward. I was helpless to stop it. I wondered if this was what people meant when they referenced out-of-body experiences. Because I *watched* myself get tugged along on a string, following through the orders I never wanted to obey.

I was somewhere else. Somewhere far away from the gruesome horror that was going to happen next.

My feet came to a halt by his side. I reached down to help him, and he grabbed onto my wrists. I hoisted him upright. My skin crawled from our brief contact as I took a single step backward, not going far enough.

Zoe watched me. Her hazel eyes searched for a solution that neither of us could create. Horror dawned across her features. We were too late.

She was too late.

I blinked at her, solemn and remorseful for the first time in my life. I wished there was something else I could do, but *she* had to kill Jeremy. That was it. She had to take the swing right now, otherwise everything would be lost. I opened my mouth to tell her, but it would be a direct violation of the protections that Thomas had created. The words died in my throat. I couldn't tell her to kill him.

She hesitated.

And Jeremy didn't.

22 Zoe

Jeremy summoned Haden to his side. The pinched brow and clenched jaw on my demon's face told me everything I needed to know—he wasn't happy about this situation; in fact, he was furious. Murder etched over his features, ready to tear Jeremy apart if he could. But he was at his mercy.

Seeing the rage coil across Haden's brow made me pause. My moment of weakness was exactly what Jeremy needed to get the upper hand. A slick smile spread up his lips, engulfing the lower portion of his face with a toothy, disgusting grin.

"Kill her," he commanded, keeping his voice low. His fingers twitched around the dripping blade in his hand.

But my eyes focused on Haden, because whatever Jeremy wanted to do to me wouldn't compare to the things a demon could do. Haden's lips curled as his jaw pulsed. A steady stream of crimson dripped from his nostrils. The blood rolled over his lips and gathered on the end of his chin. His eyes narrowed; brow creased with concentration. He held himself back, but at what cost?

Blackness spread up his limbs, charring away his skin like ash. His eyes darkened. Teeth seemed to elongate, or maybe I was seeing things because of my thumping heart.

Jeremy had the audacity to look smug, like he had already killed everyone else. He hadn't. My friends were still alive. There was no way he was going to walk out of here tonight.

Because *I* was still alive.

My gaze clashed with Haden's, and a million words went unspoken between us. Electricity crackled in the air, charged with the anger he felt toward this man. He wouldn't want me to hold back, but what the heck could I do against a demon from the fires?

Well, regardless, he was right—I had nothing left to lose. As soon as I tightened my grip on my weapon, he lunged. I ducked to the side, but Haden was faster. He tore the ax from my hand and tossed it across the room. I scrambled backward.

Jeremy laughed.

My back hit the kitchen island. If I recalled, there were a few butter knives left. Nothing but a distraction.

Haden prowled toward me. Blond hair toppled across his forehead, and dark blood smeared over his features, adding to the dangerous flare. The look on his face was dead, shut down, as if he wasn't inside himself any longer. That made it worse, because he should be trying to fight. Instead, I got this version of him—cold, detached, like a puppet being carried on strings.

I reached into the drawer, but he cut me off, slamming my fingers into it. I screamed. Something might have broken, because the nerves fired every warning to my brain.

His brow furrowed, a moment where everything paused. His breath rolled over my skin. Eyes turning as dark as the night right before dawn. He wrapped his fingers around my throat and squeezed.

"Wait!" Jeremy said.

Haden loosened his grip on me instantly.

Tears sprung to my eyes as I yanked my hand out of the drawer. I clutched my fingers with my other hand, trying to stem the stabbing signals flooding my brain.

Haden's irises resembled tar pits, bubbling and angry, ready to suck Jeremy into their depths and never let his pathetic soul go. I wondered what it would be like to be in control of Haden's power. I wondered what it would be like to be consumed by him.

His nostrils flared as his gaze swept over my body. His focus landed on my jeans for a second before flicking back to my eyes.

Jeremy took a step forward. "Hold her steady." He had his hands on the ax—*my* ax.

Haden's fingers pulsed along my throat, the slightest flutter. The heat of him seared into my skin, and despite everything, my body was an absolute betrayer. I knew Haden wasn't the one who hurt me—no, Jeremy had hurt me because of the magic. Despite the pain, every part of me flared to life as Haden toyed with my neck, grazing his extended claws against my skin, making me want to shudder despite the dire situation.

His nose twitched; his stare burrowing into mine.

Could he … sense my arousal?

Life breathed back into the endless nothing that had consumed him. The look he gave me screamed *more.*

"Here's the thing, Zoe. I never liked you, you know? You were kind of weird in school, quiet, hung out with those—" I tuned him out. His hateful speech and rhetoric. He would be dead soon if I had my way.

Instead, I focused on Haden—on the way his fingers shifted along my skin, almost like a caress. Imperceptible to our audience, I leaned into his grip, arching ever just so. I sucked in a breath, allowing the wood smoke scent to surround me. He wanted me. It was obvious in the way his eyes burned straight into me and how he held himself back. I was his. And he wouldn't let something as stupid as a binding spell separate us.

Somehow, I understood this without being inside his head. Was it from my soul belonging to him? Had passing myself over to him made me aware of his essence?

His grip quivered against my throat, tightening and loosening. A small gesture to reassure me how he was still in there, still fighting. I concentrated on that. The power running through his veins, how he held me so possessively, even when he had orders to keep me still for whatever monstrosity Jeremy was cooking up. Haden would go to war for me if needed. And as blood ran anew from his nose, I imagined myself licking it. I wondered what he would taste like.

His eyebrow arched, and the darkness faded from his eyes, becoming more curious once again, like I was an anomaly to him.

"Yours. Not his," I whispered.

A growl rumbled through his chest. Vibrated so deeply, I felt it in my toes. If he so much as dipped his fingers into my pants, he'd feel just how much I wanted him.

"So, I am *glad* to be the one to kill all of you," Jeremy ended his maniacal little villain speech with the final declaration.

As soon as he finished, Haden released me. Dark blood trickled from his nose, his eyes, his mouth. However, his gaze was steady, and his eyes flickered to Jeremy's crotch.

Jeremy swung the ax.

I kicked out, flinging myself backwards at the same time, crumpling to the ground. His swing went wide. Jeremy howled, grabbed his junk, and stumbled back a few feet. His other hand loosely held the ax in a two-fingered grip. I swept my leg underneath his ankles. He toppled backwards. The impact shook the kitchen.

I didn't wait. With a feral cry, I clambered on top of him, took his head in between my hands, and slammed it backward against the tiled floor. The first time, Jeremy's eyes grew distant, a fuzzy haze overtaking them as they stared past me toward the ceiling. Screaming again, I treated his head like a bludgeon and the floor as a castle wall I was desperate to breech.

Slam. Slam. Slam.

He deserved worse than this. Slower than this. I had lost all my patience.

"You. Mother. Fu—" Blood splattered my face. The taste of copper hit my tongue. I spat to the side but kept up the pace until I heard the crack of his skull opening like a coconut.

On the next hit, bits of brain matter oozed out, and I had to swallow back bile as I wrenched myself off him. My body trembled, but Haden was there, gathering me into his arms.

"You're okay. You're beautiful. You won." He kept repeating words that didn't settle anywhere in particular in my mind, because I couldn't tear myself away from the horror in front of me. The pieces of Jeremy that were left behind; the pieces of me I destroyed with him. My shoulders heaved. Haden's arms tightened. "I got you."

And that's when the dam broke inside me and the tears came. It was over.

His fingers tangled in my hair as he brought his lips to my forehead. Just a brush, but it centered me. "You did it."

I sighed into his shoulder, letting him take on my weight. One of his arms grasped onto my waist, bringing me firmly against him. The other had twined so far into my hair it made my scalp burn, but in the most beautiful way possible. It reminded me I was alive.

I had survived.

"Smart move earlier."

"What?" I breathed.

He tugged on my roots, pulling my face away from him so he could meet my eyes. His gaze was dark, intense, burning with passion and desire. Warmth pooled inside me. "Focusing on only me. Making yourself wet for me."

Blood had dried under his nose and along his eyes. His lips were tinged bright red as he flicked his tongue out. He licked some of it off.

"How much did it hurt you to do that? To fight him?"

"It took everything." His forehead pressed against mine, nostrils flaring. "And you? Are you okay?"

I leaned into him. Despite all the feelings welling inside me—regret, relief, satisfaction, dread, frustration, joy—one overpowered the rest. The lust I felt for him was surreal, like a whirlpool. It pulled my body down, threatening to trap me in an endless cycle of never feeling *enough* of this. My body clenched, drenched with *need*.

A growl escaped him, inhuman. "Tell me you release me."

"What?"

"From the bindings. Release me." His words brushed along my skin, dove into me, and wrapped around my heart.

"I'll still be yours, right?"

"Yes."

"And you're going to take me to the fires?"

"There's no way I will ever let you go." The darkness in his eyes ignited.

"What happens if I release you? What then?"

"I get my powers back—get myself back. I can bring you to the fires with me. There will no longer be magic holding me back from everything I am."

"And someone walks out of here alive?"

"Yes, of course. As promised."

My heart thudded against my chest. "What do you look like?"

A smirk split his face. "Release me and find out." He pressed his lips against mine, pulling me into an air-removing kiss. All thoughts left my head, as my focus became a pinpoint—only his lips, his teeth, and his wicked tongue dancing along mine. A heady feeling overtook me, like walking up to a cliff's edge.

"I release you," I whispered as his teeth sank into my lower lip.

Haden

My skin ignited. The lock released from my essence, my being, my power. Everything roared inside me, burning so brightly I had to suck in a breath around her lower lip. I sank my teeth farther into her skin, savoring her gasp as my canines came out, piercing her. Her blood was sweet and delicious. The kind of delicacy I had expected.

And she was *mine*.

My claws tore through my skin, elongating as they tangled into her hair. I curled my hand along her side, bringing her against my length. I hadn't transformed, not completely. This was a small stretch, a way to unfurl myself without terrifying her. Warm her up to the truth of who she was about to spend eternity with.

"Is … wait." Zoe pushed on my chest, staring at me with wide eyes. A bead of blood coated her lower lip, and I longed to lick it off. She blinked, hazel irises shining brilliantly. "Is that how big you are without …" She shook her head, unable to complete the thought.

"Not even close." I unwound my fingers from her brown hair and ran my claws against her soft cheek. Blood dotted in between her freckles. My middle finger caught her lower lip. She stuck her tongue out, and I pushed into her mouth, holding her jaw open for me. "But we'll work up to that."

The noise she made was primal, an animal caught with a life-or-death decision, and it was music to my ears. I would enjoy toying with her for the rest of her life and then eternity.

"I believe it's time for us to leave," I said as she closed her lips around my finger and sucked. Her eyes stayed steady on mine, as if in a challenge. "Or I can fuck you over Jeremy's dead body." A smirk curled on my lips, because I wouldn't mind that one bit.

She released my finger with a pop. "If you take me down to the fires, is there a shower?"

I chuckled. "You ask about the fires now? It's too late to change your mind, Zoe. Your soul belongs to me."

"It didn't seem important before." Red colored her cheeks.

"Well, you'll find the fires to be accommodating to your every need. We're not the skies, but we live quite well." My fingers trailed against her neck, and she hissed as my claws grazed against her sensitive skin. "As long as you aren't with us as a punishment, that is. And it's not often we get someone as unique as you."

"Unique how?"

"A soul with such … potential." The fire had engulfed the area around her heart but hadn't spread farther like I had expected it to. After her kills, I had hoped to see her engulfed in flames, heat exuding from every part of her. It seemed her reasons for killing were still for the greater good, not marring her soul to the true potential it could be.

But it would have to be enough, because she had given me her soul, and I was claiming it—now and for eternity.

"For corruption?"

"For passion, desire, beauty." I cupped my hand under her jaw and brought her once more to my mouth, tasting the inside of her as she opened for me.

My body ached, but she felt so good against me. I ignored my pain. I had told her the truth when I said it took everything to fight against Jeremy's control. My head still swam, but the power unfolding inside me was enough to piece me back together. My soul threatened to dissipate during my rebellion against his command. She had been my reason to keep fighting against the pull.

Perhaps the king had been right. He suggested Earth could be dangerous for us—for me. While I was confident I had corrupted enough souls during my stay here to avoid the ire of the king, my success wouldn't save me from everything. Likely there would be more disappointment. As if I were the problem. As if I needed to grow up.

As if I hadn't been bred to inspire rebellious acts and create chaos. Seeking my freedom had been an act of defiance, but that was the thing about the fires, wasn't it? None of us were there because we were particularly *good*.

Her tongue danced against mine, and I forced the thoughts from my head—removing the bitterness, anger, and dread about going home. Zoe would be by my side, and her presence alone had pulled me from the fail safes of Thomas's summoning spell. I had persevered and overcome the summoning magic because of her. If I had found her earlier, perhaps we could have avoided the house party curse all together. Though, the fires had more souls tonight because of us.

Flames licked at my heels as my powers burst from my skin. And damn, it was mesmerizing to feel my abilities encircling me again. Everything flaked away, becoming nothing but ash as the fires erupted around us.

She sucked in a breath and pulled back, but I held her firmly against me. "Haden, the fire—"

I pressed another kiss to her lips, enjoying how she melted into me despite the heat flooding the room. "Wrap your legs around my waist."

Zoe complied instantly, tucking her body against mine. Her hot core teased my erection. I ached to be inside her, and it would happen again soon enough. However, I had said only one person could walk out of here alive. I marched us toward the living room as the blaze spread out behind me with each step, scorching the cabin as we went. She buried her head in my shoulder, panting from the heat.

After we descended, the fires would burn brightly and be just as hot, but they'd never touch her. Living things couldn't be singed by the fires there, but up here, I had to be careful. Up here, she could burn.

"My friends," she said with a cough.

"Zoe," I said, crossing the threshold from the living room to the pool area. The smoke coiled up the stairs. Fire spread over the wooden surfaces, licking up the walls and igniting the kitchen ceiling. I could feel it as the flames chased every living thing left in the building. "I need you to look at me."

She lifted her head, her hazel eyes meeting mine. They brimmed with tears from the ash hanging in the air.

"When I said someone from your group of friends would survive, I meant you."

Her jaw loosened. "What?"

"You. You're going to survive tonight. You're part of your group of friends."

She struggled in my arms, but the harder she tried to get away from me, the more she thrust against me. "Fuck, Haden. Fuck!" Zoe slapped me across the face, and I longed for more aches like that, stings cutting across my body by her hand. The scowl on her lips made me want to worship her until she forgot her pain and frustration.

"If I allowed someone else to walk out of here, I would have become tied to them. You released me; they didn't. I don't want to be on this plane of existence for a moment longer. You've given me your soul, so I can bring you to the fires with me. Alive. You're the answer to everything. You always have been."

"You could have told me!" Her nails dug into my shoulders, but her breaths came quickly as she shamelessly rolled her hips against me. "Fuck, I'm so *mad* at you right now."

"And some other things."

"And some other very *confusing* things," she admitted as she bit my jaw, sucking on my skin.

I longed to transform. Push my full length inside her, feel how tight she'd be around me. I wanted to take her, pull her apart, mold her together into someone who belonged to me. I had already set part of her soul alight, but I needed more. Distantly, I wondered if I could satisfy the craving that hollowed out my very soul, because whenever I was around her, my instincts screamed for more.

"They are going to be fine, right? I mean, up in the skies?"

I chuckled. "I'm about to drag your living soul to the fires, and you're still worried about how your friends are going to fare in the afterlife?"

"Yes." She glared at me. The pout that crossed her lips was adorable. "Especially since I thought one of them would make it out of this alive."

I cradled the back of her head, pulling her lips to my neck. Her teeth sank into my skin, and I let out a breath. "Those who are going to the skies will be fine. Ridley is going to have a lot to make up for, likely years of being a guardian before he earns their forgiveness. Since he only said terrible things and never acted on them, he's going to get the chance to be in their good graces."

Her teeth threatened to cut into my skin. "He was a prick in the end, so he has a lot to fix."

"But Mercedes will be in the fires."

"What?!" She pounded a fist against my chest, rearing back. She didn't get very far, because my hold on her was firm.

I walked us to the edge of the pool room by the exit door, where we'd be able to escape into the open, fresh air once her friends were done with this life. It wouldn't be long now. Their distant screams rarely sounded over the roar of the fire, and I wondered if she heard anything above the hungry flames.

"What do you mean she's going to the fires?!"

"Exactly what I said." I rested her back against the window. She hissed at the sudden stroke of coolness against her skin. I ground my hips against her, and she let out a long, guttural moan.

"Stop distracting me."

"Stop being easily distracted." I kissed her neck, running my tongue along her skin. It pebbled underneath my touch. She stretched to allow me better access. My teeth grazed her neck as my hips kept a steady rhythm, dry humping her into the window. If it weren't for the barrier I erected, I might have thrust both of us through the fucking glass.

"Why is she going to the fires?"

"Because she killed Ridley with nothing more than verbal provocation. It wasn't in self-defense, but in hatred. Her soul was already on the cusp of burning, just needed one thing to push her over the edge."

"It's stupid that Ridley would be the reason for it." Zoe sucked in a breath as her legs tightened around me. Her head rolled back as we moved together. "He shouldn't have that kind of power over someone."

"He didn't."

"But he did." Zoe's hair clung to the window, splaying out behind her. She looked glorious like this. Sweat beading along her skin and brow, a spark flickering steadily in her soul. Pleasure breeched her features, mouth askew in an adorable gasp. I wanted to take a photo of her in this moment. Stunning. Perfect. *Mine.*

"If Mercedes had killed Ridley out of protection or for an injustice, she'd likely be in the same spot as him—needing to be a guardian before ascending. But she killed him with malice and hatred. While you were separated in college and Ridley became a darker version of himself, Mercedes became a more selfish version of herself. Her soul craved something to ruin her. Ridley was the accelerant. Nothing more."

"Promise?"

"Promise that her soul was doomed?" I ticked my mouth up in a smile. "Do you really believe anything I say after tonight?"

"Should I?" Her nostrils flared, brows lowered. "Probably not," she answered.

"Probably not," I agreed.

Her lower lip jutted out in a pout. Smoke filtered between us, and her nose wrinkled. "Will it be quick?"

"Burning alive? Absolutely not. But they deserve it. You *did* see the way they treated you tonight, right?"

Zoe let out a huff. "They were good to me in high school, but things have … changed. I guess I changed too." The way she looked at me with wide, hopeful eyes made my heart ice over. I brimmed with a happiness I hadn't felt in my lifetime.

"Yes, you certainly have."

"Fuck. I killed people tonight."

"You absolutely did."

"I didn't hate it, but I didn't like it either. Does that make sense?"

I nodded.

Her head pressed against the window as she let out a breath. She stared up at the starry sky outside. "I don't regret it, that's for sure. But I thought Mercedes or Everett would walk out of here. Fuck, I'm a terrible friend. She's about to burn for the rest of her existence, and here I am, dry humping you like my life depends on it."

"To be fair, you're also going to be in the fires for the rest of your existence." At least for as long as she was alive. I needed her soul to be hotter to truly combat whatever claim the skies might have over her. While she had given herself to me, I wasn't ready to admit that I had no idea what would happen if she died with a soul meant for the skies.

I needed her for eternity. I wouldn't settle for anything less.

"Will I get to see her?"

"Do you want to?"

She shrugged. "Maybe. I think I need time to process. A lot happened tonight." Her eyes went distant for a moment.

I brushed a stray lock of chestnut hair behind her ear. "Take all the time you need. With everything. There's no rush anymore." I pressed my lips to her forehead, and she leaned into me.

"But there was a rush, right? I hadn't been imagining that?"

"Not imagining, no. Tonight was a rush. A whirlwind. If Thomas had truly thought about the curse I cast on the house, then he might have found a way to break it."

"There was a way to break it?!" Zoe slapped my shoulder again.

I snarled and grabbed her hands, wrenching them above her head. "Yes. But it would have involved ritualistic sacrifices."

"For real?" She huffed out a breath.

"Yes. And plenty of people still would have died in the process."

"But not everyone."

"No, not everyone."

"You might as well tell me every other deep, dark secret you've been keeping from me. You already have my soul, so it's not like I can trade anything for the information."

I smirked. "Let me worship you and beg for your forgiveness, and I will tell you anything you want to know."

"Anything?" Her eyes sparkled.

"Yes."

"Then worship all you'd like."

A smile lit up my face. I grabbed her lower back and kicked the door open. The inferno raged at the other end of the house, but the screams were nonexistent. The barrier disappeared into nothing as we stepped into the backyard. I placed her down on the edge of a picnic table.

"Off."

She untied the makeshift belt I put around her and wiggled out of the pants. I tore them from her body and tossed them into the bushes. I pressed on her sternum, and she laid back, opening herself to me.

Fuck, she was perfect.

"Were you always going to cast the curse tonight, whether or not I was here?"

"Yes, because I needed to get rid of Thomas. He was making my life miserable." I ran my fingers along the inner part of her thighs. Her sex glistened and quivered, anticipating my touch, but not yet. "What else?"

"Who would have been the sacrifices?"

"You, Sasha, Tate, Everett—the people with souls destined for the skies."

Her head lifted. "And now, am I still destined for—"

I growled and shoved a finger inside her. She sucked in a breath, unable to finish the question. "You are destined for nothing but me, understand? I don't give a shit what your soul wants—it belongs to me."

Her back arched as she let out a wonderful whimper.

"What else?" I asked as I stroked inside her. Her body clung to my finger as I found her most sensitive spot. She clenched around me, and it took every ounce of control not to fuck her right now. I sank to my knees.

"Will anyone be angry about you dragging a living being down to the fires?"

"Counting on it." I leaned forward, breathing her in. The promise of mischief, the wealth of a soul worth fighting for, the gloriousness of a prosperous tomorrow. She gasped as my thumbs brushed over her clit. Flicking out my tongue, I ran it along her nerves. Her hips rose to meet my mouth. I sucked.

"Why do you sound satisfied by that fact?"

I pulled back enough to answer her, but my breath cascaded along her skin. "Because I'll be proving a point. Do you want to keep asking questions, or do you want me to fuck you with my tongue?" She was getting dangerously close to a few things I wanted to tell her, but later, after I had formally apologized for the bullshit of tonight.

"Will my friends be okay in their afterlives?"

I gave her one last lick before rising to meet her eyes. "Everyone gets the afterlife they deserve." We stared at each other for a long moment before she gave me a nod. I brushed my lips against her mound, kissing her.

"Then I'm fucked," she breathed.

I chuckled as my teeth found her nerves. Giving her a nip, I said,

"Not yet. But soon." My tongue traveled lower as I removed my finger. Sucking her juices into my mouth, I groaned at the taste of her. How could one person be so fucking *good?* It baffled me in the best way possible. I toyed with her entrance, enjoying how she fluttered while she waited for me.

"Haden, please—"

"Have I ever left you wanting?"

"No, but—"

"Then consider this the moment your torture begins." I ran a slow circle around her, continuing to play. She groaned and reached for my hair, but I slapped her hands away. "If you want to be treated like a good girl, then you stay still and let me have my way with you."

"And if I want to be treated like a bad girl?"

Oh, this was going to be fun. "Then you won't get the apology you deserve."

Her teeth sank into her lower lip. "What will I get instead?" She was goading me, playing with a demon as if I would ever be gentle with her. Obviously, I hadn't been rough enough inside the house— not having access to my powers had probably given her some ideas about me.

But now.

Now.

Fire spun around my skin as my claws came out. The flames danced around the sharpened points as I dragged them along her exposed thighs. She sucked in a breath and tried to flinch back, but I wrapped my hands around her and pulled her into my mouth. I pushed my tongue inside her at the same moment she let out a cry of pain. Despite my claws threatening to pierce her skin, Zoe rode my face, hips seeking the motion that would give her sweet relief, but I had no intention of letting her come—not yet. Not when I was so close to having everything I wanted.

"Focus on me," I said. I dragged my tongue up to her nerves, retracted my claws, and pushed two fingers inside her. "In order to open the portal, it's about to get even hotter." I curled my fingers, pressing against her sensitive spot. "I want to distract you, and this is the best way I know how. It also serves as my apology."

"Apology accepted. I want to touch you," she breathed.

"Give me your hand." I reached toward her. She wrapped her fingers through mine. Hers were so dainty in comparison to my true form, and while I still hadn't transformed yet, I was easing her into it. Fires help me, I wanted to see if she could take me. Her grip on my hand tightened as her hips sought me out.

I growled with warning as I pulsed my fingers against hers. "Patience."

She whimpered but stilled. She was going to be the perfect little submissive for me, and I was excited to show her off. The souls that ended up in the fires tended to be hardened. They ranged from sociopaths to controlling possessive assholes. But someone so gloriously soft? She would never be at the doors of the fires if she hadn't given me her soul. And even now, after everything she had been through, the skies still wanted to stake a claim on her with the cool breeze inside her. Someone like her never graced us with their presence. And she was *mine*.

I pumped my fingers into her, working against the bundle of nerves that made her clench around me. Her breathing quickened as she teetered toward the edge, but no. A climax now would still be too soon. The portal wasn't ready for us yet. With another lick, I pulled away from her. Her body sagged, still wound taut with need and wanton desire.

"Haden, please," she whined, and I loved hearing my name on her lips almost as much as I loved listening her come.

"Shh." I pressed my lips to the inside of her thigh. "The next part is the hardest." My claws came out again as I released more fire around us, feeding the portal that slowly bound the edges of our worlds. Heat grew around us as I teased her entrance with my tongue.

"Haden, the heat is too much."

"I got you." There was only one way to get to where we needed to go. "Can you take a little distraction?"

"A lot of distraction," she panted.

"Good." I thrust my tongue inside her. The flames spiraled together, spinning around until they formed a whirlwind of fire. The edges of the portal formed as the inferno threatened to swallow us whole.

Transforming my tongue, I pushed farther, thrusting deep within her. She let out a gasp with a small surprised, "Oh." If I could bottle that sound and replay it, I would. Her eyes darted to mine, shock widening them.

I licked her g-spot. Her hips bucked up, head slamming back against the table. The fires surrounded us, growing almost unbearably hot against her skin. I fucked her with my tongue until she squealed. She fell apart, wetness coating my lips. Her thighs clenched around my ears as her pussy pulsed against me. She screamed out my name, barely able to breathe as I coaxed her down from her release.

"Haden, I— That was—"

I pulled my tongue out, licking my lips. My eyes stayed locked on hers as the flames transformed from those on Earth to those of the fires, no longer adding any heat against her skin. Her breathing steadied, hazel eyes gazing at me with delight. I smiled as I latched my hands on her thighs. "Ready?" But I didn't give her time to respond.

I dragged her down to the fires below.

Don't miss the sequel:
To the Fires Below

Acknowledgments

For some reason, acknowledgments are the hardest part of the book to write. It's not a lack of gratitude, because I am so immensely grateful. This year, I reconnected with a community of people—from readers to authors—and I am so happy to be a part of this. Finding myself surrounded by people who I am growing to love every day is powerful and a little intimidating. I wouldn't have it any other way.

My fear is missing someone who has been a huge help to me. So, if I miss you, just know I feel incredibly guilty and terrible about it, okay? Okay. Now, let's begin.

Thank you to my alpha readers: Nika, Victoria, and Sarah. You are all incredible. The conversations I've had with you have kept me going, and I appreciate you so, so much.

Thank you to Amber D. Lewis, for listening to … well, everything. And for being a friend. I am so happy that we crashed into each other on the internet.

Thank you to my beta readers: Jacqueline, Samantha, Alexandra, and Laura. Thank you for letting me ask you all the questions. Thank you for letting me send you random eyeball emojis and general silliness. Thanks for allowing me to use all caps and understanding that it is excitement not … yelling. Or yelling excitement? You are my hype crew but also gave me amazing feedback.

A special shout out to Jacqueline for helping me with one plot hole in book two, and Samantha helping me with the plot hole that opened after I fixed the first plot hole. I know you haven't read book two yet, but that feedback has already changed this duet for the better.

Thank you to Brooke, Akita, Kim, and Mary Lou for signing up to be early ARC readers but also being there to chat and cheer me on. I appreciate all of you.

Thank you to my husband who had no idea how gory this book was until one day when he realized how gory this book was and looked at me with his jaw ajar and said, "This is a romance?" It's a romance. *sunglasses emoji, smugface emoji*

To my parents who are definitely NOT going to read this book (right?! RIGHT?!), thanks for your endless support.

To the Fantasy Author Legion, thank you for giving me a place to crash land and get to know other authors.

To my fellow indie authors: Liz Delton, Rian Adara, N. F. Schmitt, Anacostia Miller, Akita Sparks, Hazel Rockwood, Madison Nicole, David Decker, and Emilia Abraham, thank you!

To all the readers who picked up this book with the promise of a bloody good time, I hope you enjoyed it. I hope it was a fun, twisted romp for you, and I hope you'll continue the duet into book two. We're going to explore the fires, and I am excited for the world building that has gone into bringing the fires alive.

Thank you for taking a chance on an indie author. Thank you for reading.

Subscribe to the publisher's newsletter on https://www.spacefoxbooks.com for regular updates, apply to become an early reader, or apply to become a Cadet Fox and join the street team!

Follow the publisher on Instagram, TikTok, or Facebook @spacefoxbooks

Thank you for reading.

About the Author

Ariel Rae was raised in a small New Hampshire town but left it behind to attend Emerson College in Boston. After graduating with a degree in Writing, Literature, and Publishing, she moved to southern California.

Working as a barista, she somehow turned her life into a cliché and met her husband while serving him coffee. They fell in love, got married, adopted a bunch of cats, moved to the rainy side of Oregon, and eventually moved back to New England.

When she's not writing, she plays video games, drinks tea, reads way too much (though, she wonders if there is such a thing as too much reading), and snowboards.

She also writes YA literature under R. A. Desilets.

Find her online at:

@arielraeauthor

spacefoxbooks.com/ariel-rae-links

Other Work

Blood Hunted series by Ariel Rae

Spicy Dark Romantasy, completed series with bonus 2.5 novel

All the Fae she had been with were dead.

Scarlet earned her title of Fae Slayer, but despite the amount of bodies in her wake, she has no leads on where to find the Fae king. In the aftermath of the Fae invasion, she has three rules for her survival:

1. Never negotiate.
2. Never trust a pretty face.
3. Never tell anyone how she started the apocalypse.

After one of her hunts, she's cornered by an assassin hired by the Fae king himself. Voss is a Blood Hunter, and he knows Scarlet opened the Fae door, making her the only human capable of ending the king's rule. He has a proposition: an alliance to kill the king.

Carter Ortese is Trouble by R. A. Desilets
YA Contemporary Romance

Everyone knows Carter Ortese is trouble, so it's a shock when band geek Emma asks him out as a dare. When he says yes, she refuses to back down. But no one knows why she asks him on a second date. Or a third.

A contemporary young adult romance you don't want to miss.

Break Free by R. A. Desilets
YA Time Loop with Mental Health

What happens when your best friend is stuck in a time loop and you reset day after day?

On Tuesday, Leida skips school with her best friend, Ozzie. Today will be a perfect day at the local amusement park.

But as Ozzie repeats Tuesday over and over again, Leida has to cope with Ozzie's erratic behavior. Can Leida help Ozzie break free, or are they doomed to live the same day forever?

Start Small by R. A. Desilets
YA Contemporary with Found Family

My bucket list was meant to stay buried—a wish list from a dying girl. But when my best friend Harper finds it after our senior year, she wants a do-over with our friend group. It's our last summer to say goodbye. We've graduated, and there's nothing left to lose.

From holding our breaths to shooting off fireworks to climbing a mountain, we complete the items. Maybe before the end, I'll tell Owen how I feel. But since he's flirting with another girl and pretending I don't exist, it might already be too late.